Escape from Hy-Brasil

Written by Erik Lange

Cover art by Erik Frankhouse

First Printing, 2018
First edition

ISBN 978-1-7324326-1-1☐

This book is dedicated to the intrepid Charlotte Smith

Thomas Davies is a bachelor enjoying a comfortable life working from his flat in London. His chosen profession: researching and locating rare books.

A visit to the British Museum to view a recently discovered Sumerian artifact ends in bloodshed and a cover-up.

Just when Thomas thinks the events of the recent past are behind him, a strange man visits his flat unannounced. Not long after, the carnage from the museum is repeated within his own home.

Unsure whether he has been rescued or kidnapped and surrounded by military veterans in the service of the enigmatic Karl Lark, Thomas finds himself captive to what appears to be a diabolical criminal organization with supernatural capabilities.

After being given an invitation to join, being made fully aware there is no option B, he soon discovers his murder at the hands of the eccentric Mr. Lark is the least of his worries...

Chapter 1

"Higgebotham, I thought you were never going to call me again. Your exact words were that I was persona non grata." I said to the man on the other side of the phone line.

Keith Higgebotham was not a bad sort but he was still being an ass. A few months back one of my clients had made a private purchase of a rare text. Unfortunately for Keith he had been lobbying the same owner to donate it to the British Museum. Keith and the museum lost and I won. The commission had been quite handsome to boot.

A big pile of money beat out philanthropy. Go figure.

Higgebotham replied in a hostile tone, "Thomas, this is not how I like to start my Monday's either. Nothing has changed, I still don't want you here. But the curator wants your opinion. This is your area of expertise and the request comes from her."

"Why are you calling me then? Why doesn't she call me?" I asked the question already knowing the reply. Dr. Elizabeth Chatzas was an archeology purist. She disapproved of my commercial activities even more than Higgebotham.

"Because she's my boss and she told me too," snapped Keith.

Between Higgebotham and Dr. Chatzas I did not believe a visit would be pleasant, or even all that civil. Whatever they wanted me for, it was to look at something that was museum property. So there was no commercial opportunity to be had either. I was not seeing my motivation here.

After a long pause, Keith, speaking in a more persuasive tone, said, "Thomas, we found something unique. It is a book and it is very old and no one here has any idea what it is. For your own sake you should see this."

I was still not feeling convinced. I already had a significant workload to deal with for my paying clients. Spending a day or even a couple of days on museum business was not really part of my plan.

"Will I be getting paid for this?" I asked.

"Dr. Chatzas feels that when you see what we have you won't be worried about the money," replied Keith.

That was an odd thing to say. It took years of study, hard work, and travel to get me to where I was in my field and I am always keen on getting paid. Time is money as the Americans say.

Keith sensed my hesitation. His next words surprised me even more than being asked to do something for free.

"Dr. Chatzas told me to tell you 'please'," Keith said.

What had they found? Dr. Chatzas was a career archaeologist who had clawed her way to one of the most prestigious posts a person in her profession could achieve. Prior to this conversation I would not have thought 'please' was in her vocabulary.

What the hell. It would not hurt to take a look and maybe get some good will out of it.

"Okay Keith you sold me. I will come and take a look. But you need to give me some background before I visit. What will I be looking at?" He could not be expecting me to show up blind.

"Until the museum is sure this is not a hoax, nothing can be public. You will need to sign a confidentiality agreement when you get here. Nobody is going to risk their careers on this. Dr. Chatzas is not even allowing photographs at this point," replied Keith.

The plot thickens. So I would be going in blind. Normally I would prepare before I look at something. Keith was telling me that was not going to happen.

Since I had said I would participate, it was time to ask, "When should I visit?"

Keith replied,"Dr. Chatzas' invitation is immediate. We would like you to come as soon as possible. Today even, if you could."

That explains why this call is at 8am on a Monday morning. They were in a hurry. That is a red flag. Nobody in archaeology is in a hurry. Glacial appears in the dictionary right under archaeology.

"I have to tie up some urgent tasks. How about after lunch?" was my reply. This would give me more time to think about this phone call.

"Fine, right after lunch. Call me when you are close to arriving. Remember there are things to sign first when you get here. Goodbye Thomas," I could hear in Keith's voice, my agreeing to take a look at the find had made his day. I imagine his going back to Dr. Chatzas empty handed would have been unpleasant.

Hopefully whatever it was is as interesting as Keith implied and this was not going to be a waste of my time.

The rest of the morning until my appointment was spent on work for clients. As noon approached I made a light lunch, cleaned up, dressed semi-professionally, and took a taxi to the museum. I called Keith as the taxi pulled away from my flat, giving him at least a twenty minute warning.

Higgebotham was actually waiting for me by the information desk at the main entrance of the museum. Keith is a man of average height and slim build with the coloring of a Caucasian man who spends most of his time indoors and he dresses like a professor who does not own an iron. As we approached each other I noticed the manila folder in his hand.

I had made sure to be on time so as not to give him something else to complain about. Keith not only smiled at me, but he also shook my hand and thanked me for coming.

It was a surreal moment. The last time we had seen each other was also at the museum. Keith had been an angry, red faced Neanderthal, his words had been less than professional and spoken with such force I was sure his spit was on my shirt by the time I left.

The manila folder contained the confidentiality agreement which I quickly signed. With the formalities out of the way we headed straight to an elevator to take us into the bowels of the museum. Keith had to swipe a card and enter a code to start the elevator downwards. That meant the fourth sublevel, high security. I knew it existed but had never been there.

There was no small talk on the way to wherever we were going. Keith was happy I was doing his boss's bidding but I could still sense his dislike of me. On our way, he called Dr. Chatzas using his cell phone, to let her know we were in the museum and on our way down.

We arrived deeper under the museum than I had ever been before. Leaving the elevator we walked for some distance down a long hall passing rooms on our right and left. The air was dry, the humidity kept low to protect the artifacts. The décor was as bland and lifeless as any warehouse. As we walked our footfalls echoed down the hallways. There was apparently no one else around and most of the lights in the hall and in all the rooms we passed were extinguished. It was dark, with just enough lighting to make our way to our destination.

Deep in the museum, poorly lit, no people around, for a fleeting moment the ambiance had me wondering if there really was a book. If Keith wanted to do away with me this would be the place.

I looked at Keith and shook my head, clearing my mind of the paranoid thoughts. Keith was an archaeologist not a murderer. *Get a grip,* I thought to myself.

Finally, we entered through an open doorway into a small, brightly lit room.

The room was empty except for a heavy-duty steel table standing in its center. About the table were adjustable spotlights and a large magnifying lens on an arm that could be repositioned for viewing from different angles.

In the middle of the table was a black box, apparently made of black stone. On the surface facing up it had been painted at some point. The paint had mostly chipped away over the years with only small patches to show something had been there.

It was not a book however, it was a box.

I felt the need to point this out to Keith, "That does not look like a book."

"The book is inside. The box is made from andesite stone, super hard stuff. The paint on the top is how we dated the find," Keith replied with disdain. He continued, "Put on the gloves, you know the routine." Keith pulled a pair of linen gloves in a plastic bag from his pocket and handed them to me.

While I pulled on the gloves, Keith did likewise and approached the table and opened the box. It turned out the painted top cover hinged upwards and back.

"It appears the hinge is part of the stone box. All carved from one piece," I observed out loud.

"That is one of the mysteries. How could something this old have been built like this? Carving stone this hard, into a complex shape, would be almost impossible even today, There are similar examples that exist such as the Incan site at Pumapunku or the Schist Disk in Egypt," Keith replied.

"How old did it date to?"

"Close to three thousand BCE, give or take."

Inside the box was what looked to be a shiny copper tablet stamped with Sumerian cuneiform. No corrosion or green oxide, just shiny copper. I looked closer and told Keith what I was seeing. "This copper tablet is in Sumerian." I stated.

"Yes, the stamped cuneiform matches a known Sumerian form. And this is not a tablet," Keith said as he ran a finger into a grove on the inside of the box. He hooked the edge of the copper revealing it to be a page that could be flipped up, just like the cover. Underneath, another copper page could be seen.

On the backside of the thin copper sheet you could see the text stamped out the other side.

"I am not an expert on Sumerian but to my knowledge, everything discovered to date is only on clay tablets," I stated while looking on with elation. This find could be groundbreaking I thought, if it was real.

"How many pages?" I asked.

"Seven."

"So instead of pressing characters into wet clay with a stylus they used a punch on copper sheets? I have never heard of this."

A woman's voice came from behind me. "Yes, we have never heard of it before either and our hope is you will have more to contribute to our understanding."

I knew who it was before I turned to look. I had met Dr. Chatzas before and I turned completely around to face her. She is tall, almost six foot, brunette and pretty. If I had to guess she was in her early forties like me but she had classical good looks that made placing her age difficult.

She dressed professionally, skirt and blouse, tasteful jewelry. Her hair was down. Dr. Chatzas did not just look good, she looked almost perfect, clothes, makeup, hair.

To sum up her stance and gaze I would use the word imperious. She could look down on you even if you were taller than her.

Yes, beautiful, intelligent, successful, and arrogant. She was very difficult to like.

She also had a reason to dislike me. Not just the reason Keith hated me for. There was another reason. A few years back a politically connected sponsor donated a rare book, an original. I was paid to provide a third-party valuation for the insurance company.

I visited the museum to perform my due diligence. Except the book was a fake. I documented the forgery and turned my report over to Dr. Chatzas.

Because of the donor's political ties, nothing could be done. Publicly announcing the forgery would have caused a scandal. The museum buried the donation, never to speak of it again. It was a brilliant move on the part of the donor. He received a significant tax credit for his charitable donation and coincidentally disposed of a valueless forgery.

Even though I was not responsible for the forgery, I was still the messenger and Dr. Chatzas firmly believes in shooting the messenger and she has been barely civil to me since. The museum still employed my services but only begrudgingly.

"It is always a pleasure to be invited," I said deciding to err on the side of diplomacy. It was tough not bringing up the 'please' Keith had mentioned. It was a childish urge on my part but it would be fun to see if she would react.

Dr. Chatzas sniffed and shifted her gaze to the book. "The British empire spanned over three hundred years.

During that time archaeological finds from the four corners of the earth were brought here. Even though the empire is gone, there is a backlog of archaeological research to be done. This was found in one of the chambers below the museum. Unfortunately there were no records found with it. We have no history of the book, where or how it was found"

"It is very impressive," a male voice with an American accent came from behind Dr. Chatzas. Dr. Chatzas, Keith, and I turned to see a man in his sixties with all white hair, of average height and wearing a tailored grey suit walk through the doorway. The man carried a cane with a large polished brass sphere at the top.

The sphere was out of place. It was too large to fit in the man's hand while walking. Instead he held the cane by the shaft using his right hand, just under the sphere.

I thought to myself: Why have a walking stick you cannot hold properly?

"Who are you and how did you get in here? This area is for museum personnel only" demanded Dr. Chatzas in an icy tone. She glared at the man with open hostility while her hand went to her cell phone at her waist. I am guessing she intended to call security with it.

"My name is Karl Lark and I heard about this find in the announcement," he replied. He appeared unconcerned and smiled at Dr. Chatzas, seemingly immune to her hostility.

"What announcement?" deadpanned Dr. Chatzas.

"There was no announcement? For such an important find? Why not?" commented Mr. Lark. His face now showed a feigned attempt at innocence. I was unsure if his weird reply was genuine or a poor attempt at humor.

There was an awkward silence with the four of us staring at each other. During this brief pause, I became aware of two men silently emerging from the shadows behind Mr. Lark to stand one on each side and slightly behind him.

Both men wore grey suits that looked really good on them, probably tailored. One man stood over six feet tall and had short cropped blonde hair. The other man was just less than six foot tall. He had handsome features and short black hair. I am not into guys (not that there is anything wrong with that) but even I could tell the black haired guy would be considered a good looking man. Both men were of athletic build.

They looked relaxed, intense, competent, and vigilant all at the same time. I guessed they were Mr. Lark's personal security.

Dr. Chatzas was holding her phone in her hand with a finger hovering over the call icon. "And how did you get in here?"

"I have been a generous supporter of the museum for several years. As you know such support has its privileges, including limited access to my areas of interest and this book interests me," replied Mr. Lark.

"We have never met at any of the events our patrons attend."

"That explains the 'anonymous' part of my support."

Mr. Lark had her boxed in. She could pursue this with security but if he really was a generous anonymous donor then she would have a problem. In the end his presence won the discussion. How else could he have come to be here...

Another tense long pause ensued which I ended by extending my hand to Mr. Lark, "My name is Thomas Davies. I am here in a consulting capacity. This gentleman here," I pointed at Keith, "Is Keith Higgebotham, resident archaeologist. It is our pleasure to meet you."

Keith nodded while looking at Dr. Chatzas for a clue on what to do, if anything. Both of us were waiting to see how this man's sudden and unusual appearance would play out.

Mr. Lark shook my hand, looked me in the eyes and then nodded his head to me. "It is a pleasure Mr. Davies."

During our exchange, Dr. Chatzas had apparently decided to accept Mr. Lark's presence. She extended her right hand and said, "I am Dr. Chatzas, curator of the ancient Middle Eastern collection of the museum. I hope you understand my response was only in concern about the museum. How can I assist you?"

I saw the phone disappear from her hand. I had to give it to her. As soon as money was involved, she switched gears pretty fast. I also loved her non-apology apology.

I was also starting to feel claustrophobic. Six people in this small room made it crowded.

Both bodyguards remained within arm's length of Mr. Lark. They looked highly professional to me. I have other clients who have bodyguards. Most of them are either former law enforcement or really big, thuggish looking guys. Mr. Lark's bodyguards more reminded me of who you would see guarding foreign dignitaries.

Before Mr. Lark could reply to Dr. Chatzas' offer, four more men showed up at the door to the room. All four were big burly guys, around six feet tall and wearing full body coveralls. Once they saw a crowded room full of people, they stopped and looked at each other. I could tell they were genuinely surprised at finding this many people crowded into this little room.

A patch on their coveralls said 'Executive Transport'. All four men were of similar height and weight. Even their facial features and dark curly hair were similar. The impression I had was they were related. Their mannerisms also seemed oddly out of place. The way they stood and looked around.

The third long pause of the morning came next as we all stared at each other.

One of the four men nodded to the others and then two of the men rushed Mr. Lark's bodyguards. The other two men quickly unzipped their coveralls and began reaching inside.

The attack on the bodyguards did not go as the attackers would have liked. The dark haired bodyguard sidestepped and lunged forward while sweeping his arm upwards hooking the neck of his attacker. The man flipped over backwards going down hard on the concrete floor, flat on his back.

The blonde bodyguard grappled with his attacker and swung completely around him, building up momentum. He then flung his opponent onto the two others as they pulled pistols out from inside their coveralls.

One of their guns went off. In the small room it was deafening and I found my hearing gone. The sound of Keith and Dr. Chatzas' screaming was faint even though they were standing right next to me. I was frozen in place, silent, shocked by what I was witnessing.

In the middle of all this mayhem stood Karl Lark, next to the table, looking unconcerned while leaning on his walking stick.

A second gunshot went off, the flash strobing the room with orange light.

No sooner was one attacker flat on his back and the other in a pile on top of the other two, when Mr. Lark's bodyguards drew pistols from under their jackets with remarkable speed and dexterity.

The attacker flat on his back saw this and rolled over onto his feet and sprinted out the door. The second attacker actually pushed down on the two men with pistols underneath him to get to his feet, following on the heels of his compatriot running out the door.

The remaining two men were trying to recover from being bowled over by one of their own. Having been further pushed down did not help their recovery. Perhaps they realized getting to their feet would take too long because they stopped trying to get up and just shifted on the ground while trying to bring their guns to bear on the bodyguards.

It was too little too late. They never got a chance to fire. Each bodyguard had picked a target and fired a short burst of shots into the semi-prone men in coveralls. The sound of gunfire was more of a 'boom' compared to the 'crack' of the earlier shots.

I saw blood and looked away. Not even morbid curiosity could get me to look back.

This is when I noticed Keith slumped against a far wall. One of the shots from the men in coveralls had hit him in the chest by accident. He was pale and not moving.

I could not understand what was happening. I had always found Keith unpleasant but I would have never wished something like this on him. My hearing came back with a rushing noise.

"...Both of the armed men are dead," I turned to see the blond bodyguard talking.

"And the archaeologist, Mr. Held?" Karl Lark asked.

The blonde bodyguard, apparently his last name was Held, walked over to Keith and put his fingers to Keith's neck. "Dead."

My legs started to wobble and I found myself supporting my weight by leaning against the table. All I could think was: *What just happened?*

"Dr. Chatzas, this is all most unfortunate. However, I must avoid any legal entanglements. I will take my leave now." Mr. Lark said while nodding his head towards Dr. Chatzas. He then turned and started out of the room.

Mr. Lark spoke to me as he was leaving, "Mr. Davies, please accompany me to my car."

I realized the dark-haired bodyguard was next to me now.

"Mr. Daugherty, please assist Mr. Davies if necessary. It is time to go." I received the impression my leaving with Mr. Lark was not optional.

The blond man fell in next to Mr. Lark as they walked out of the room. I stumbled along behind them my ability to walk recovering quickly. Mr. Held strode ahead and half-way to the elevator I found myself alongside Mr. Lark. The hall to the elevator was just as dark and quiet as when I had arrived. I noticed the bodyguards still had their guns out.

"What just happened?" I asked.

"That is a good question to ask. Perhaps you should start by asking why it happened," was his reply.

The elevator car must have been close by, because the doors opened in less than a minute after pushing the button to summon it. The four of us crowded into the elevator and Mr. Held pushed a button. After the doors closed the bodyguards returned their pistols under their jackets. The ride up was quiet. I don't know for sure but I might have been in shock. My ability to put thoughts together was not working well.

After leaving the elevator we walked out a side door to exit the museum and followed a sidewalk taking us to the nearby VIP parking, Mr. Lark offered to give me a ride home. I nodded in acceptance and gave him my address.

Soon we were in a large grey Mercedes driving in the general direction of my flat.

My ability to process thoughts returned in the car. "Shouldn't we be waiting for the police to give our statements? Couldn't we be charged with fleeing the scene of a crime?"

"Dr. Chatzas will not be calling the police," replied Mr. Lark apparently unconcerned with the multiple felonies committed minutes ago.

Now that he mentioned it, I realized that the phone she had pulled out in a blink of an eye when Karl Lark showed up had stayed in her pocket after the shooting. What was that about?

I had another thought, "How did you know about the book?"

"I make regular donations to Mr. Higgebotham's vacation fund. He kept me apprised of things of interest. His death is unfortunate. I will now need to cultivate another source of information."

"He informed me today was the only day the book would be in a predictable location and relatively easy to get to, so I decided to visit. Apparently, I was not the only one with similar plans," Mr. Lark said, thinking out loud.

"Who were those other guys? Why were they there? And why did they have guns?" I asked.

"Slow down Mr. Davies. You are getting over-excited. I am fairly sure they were there to take the book." Mr. Lark was as unflappably calm now as he had been through this whole experience.

"Is that why you were there? To take the book?" My questions had come out harsh and demanding. My emotional state was showing in what I was saying.

"Taking the book was unnecessary, I just wanted to see the book and look at its pages. Once I have viewed it there is no need for the original," was Mr. Lark's reply.

"The interruption of your visit kept that from happening."

"Not at all, it only took a moment for me to flip through seven pages. I did that during the exchange of gunfire," Mr. Lark was smiling now.

"You see Thomas, I have an eidetic memory. All I need to do is view each page for a brief second and it is recorded forever."

"Why the violence? Archeology is a peaceful science. That book is thousands of years old. Whatever is in it will only be of interest to archeologists," I offered.

"Don't be so naïve. Modern archeology is a form of control. To join, one must spend years toiling away for little to no pay. Year after year proving oneself to the orthodoxy. Any brilliance or initiative is weeded out when unapproved questions are asked."

"Should you graduate to an upper level of the priesthood of archaeology you are almost entirely dependent on museums and universities for your livelihood. Even a minor deviation from the defined narrative will see you cast out. And what living can an archaeologist earn for themselves outside of archaeology?"

"The question you should be asking Thomas, is why such control has been instituted over the study of the past?"

I was stunned. What Mr. Lark had said was cynical.

It was also true.

"Here is your door. May I call on you in a few days? I may have more to discuss."

I just stared at him. He wanted to see me again?

"Certainly, please call ahead if possible. Here is my card," I mumbled, while digging in my pockets for one of my cards and then handing it to him."

"Thomas, you may be considering contacting the authorities. My suggestion is you wait to see if they contact you first."

This was followed by my exit from the car. While walking up the steps to my front door I could hear the Mercedes leaving behind me.

I entered my flat and closed my door. Two thoughts were in my head. What had just happened and why was this Karl Lark coming back?

Chapter 2

In the two days after the events at the museum I had a hard time concentrating or sleeping. The waiting to hear a knock at the door, expecting to find the police there, was like an itch between my shoulder blades I could not reach. I kept checking the internet, looking for something about a shooting at the museum.

There was nothing to see. Apparently what I witnessed was not brought to the attention of the authorities or the media.

It was lunchtime and I was finishing what passed for the lunch of a perpetual bachelor.

Not that it was a goal of mine to be single. I do date women, just less often than I would have liked. My work tended to get in the way of romantic attachments.

On more than one occasion I got caught up in a project and forgot about a lunch or dinner date. Sometimes I even forget to stay in touch regularly. Members of the opposite sex found that particularly offensive and it would become a black mark on the relationship. No amount of apologizing would make up for my becoming sidetracked.

The business I was in was actually great for meeting someone of the opposite sex. The libraries, universities, book stores, and book events I often frequent are a great way to meet women. My average looks and non-threatening nature make women feel comfortable approaching me and apparently I am easy to talk to, at least that is what I have been told. My work is endlessly fascinating to women who enjoy books and reading. This would lead to dating and a few times the relationships became serious. Then work would get in the way and it was all downhill from there.

My lunch was warm beer and a can of soup. No influence of the feminine there.

Then the doorbell rang.

I looked up from my desk to the door. No one was expected nor should I be receiving a delivery. I felt a moment of panic, wondering if the police were finally here, or worse, it could be Karl Lark.

The doorbell rang again. This time twice in short succession. Someone was impatient.

I was already on my feet and almost to the door when the bell was triple rung. I unbolted the door and opened it. Today was overcast and it was dim outside even though it was midday. It had rained in the morning and everything outside was still wet.

Standing not a foot past the door opening was a short man. He was barely five feet four inches tall if that and dark, very dark, a dark brown-black complexion with a little olive color mixed in, probably Middle Eastern in origin. He was dressed in an all-black suit with a bright red tie. Thick, jet black hair was pulled back into a pony tail.

I found myself staring into the stranger's eyes. They were too large, with the pigment of his eye color being a dark shade of amber. I found myself speechless. I had never seen anyone close to the appearance of the man standing in front of me.

After a short pause, with me staring at him, the man spoke, "I am Amal Halluk". No hand was extended. "May I enter your home and discuss business with you?" Amal's voice was low in timbre and accented. I have travelled Europe extensively and visited most regions of the world in service of my clients and I could not place Amal's accent.

I felt disturbed in a subconscious way, like an almost imperceptible itch. Like something was happening that should not be happening.

My reply sounded mechanical in my ears. "Please enter," I did not feel comfortable saying it, but to say anything else would have been rude.

I stepped back away from the doorway and Amal entered. My flat consists of a great room with doors on two walls leading to smaller rooms. Those doors lead to my bedroom, the loo, and a small kitchen. Amal walked to the center of the great room and started looking around.

I closed the door and bolted it and walked slowly towards the man. When he was within hand shaking distance I extended my right hand and said, "Thomas Davies at your service." Amal looked at me and then at my extended hand as if thinking about whether to shake it or not. His hand finally came up and clasped mine. His skin was uncomfortably hot and he shook my hand in one quick motion and withdrew.

My original feeling of being disturbed had grown to mild anxiety I could feel in the core of my being. This situation, Amal Halluk, it felt wrong.

I asked, "How may I help you Mr. Halluk?" This brought a brief small smile to Amal's face.

"I have recently learned of you and your successes in locating items of age and value. This interests me. I may make use of your services but I need to know more. Please tell me of your recent successes," was his reply.

Amal was blunt to say the least. This bluntness, showing up unannounced, demanding entry, and now asking about my business gave me pause.

"Please be seated and we can discuss your interests further", is what I said versus what I thought: *Please leave.* Amal reviewed the seating options in turn and picked an overstuffed leather chair.

"Before we begin may I extend the hospitality of tea or perhaps sparkling water?" I asked Amal. At least my manners were catching up with the situation.

The offer of hospitality seemed to have a positive impact on him. "Thank you for the consideration, Thomas, but I am pressed for time."

I sat down opposite the man in an equally overstuffed leather chair. Down to business then. "I provide a service to locate rare books and documents."

"What about other things?" Amal inquired.

I felt my mood lifting. If Amal is looking for art works I will be able to say this is not my area of expertise and he would leave. "Unfortunately I do not locate art works, that requires a skill set I do not have."

"I did not say art. I meant artifacts and trinkets from the ancient past," Amal's face was emotionless but his tone gave away mild irritation.

"I do occasionally take a commission to locate difficult to find objects of an archaeological nature." I was now feeling intrigue mixed with the anxiety from earlier.

"Can you tell me about any recent successes in finding an object?" Amal persisted.

"Client confidentiality prevents my sharing details about a specific search. I have had success recently in locating something very old and unique for a client. The search took nine months but will result in the client being able to acquire what he was looking for". That was as far as I could go regarding a past success without giving away too many details.

Amal was not satisfied with my limited response, "What was the nature of the object? I wish to know more. I cannot make a decision to hire your services with so little understanding of your abilities."

This conversation was not as professional as I would have preferred and I knew I had to be careful. "My most recent accomplishment was in locating the owner of an object that was several thousand years old. Only an old photograph from the 1920's showed that the object existed. It took significant effort to assemble its history from that photo to its current owner. I then facilitated communications between the current owner and my client. A delicate bit of work but it ended well". I tried to give my most reassuring smile. For me 'ending well' meant everyone got what they wanted, including a fat commission for myself.

Amal smiled back, this time a full smile showing his teeth. The teeth were bright white and more narrow than they should have been. When framed in his dark face, including his too large eyes, it was a scary predatory looking visage, "Perhaps you are competent. My decision in visiting you is proving productive. You will be contacted when your services are needed. I must leave now".

Amal stood and regarded me for a moment. I also stood and realized that he knew where I lived but I had not given him my contact information. I pulled one of my business cards from my pocket and extended it to him, "Mr. Halluk, my card should you wish to contact me." He looked at the card extended to him between two of my fingers. His left hand came up and took the card.

He walked to the door without speaking further and stood waiting for me to unbolt and open it. Amal Halluk then left without saying another word. He walked down the stairs leading up to my door, turned right and walked away.

I stood in the doorway feeling my anxiety decrease proportionally to the further away Amal was. Stepping back inside, I closed and bolted the door again. All I could think was how unpleasant the dark man's visit had been. This was one of the few times in my career I genuinely hoped someone would never become a client.

He seemed more interested in what I am working on currently. His brief visit was awkward, like he was in a hurry to get out.

I decided to move on and get back to work.

Chapter 3

It was Friday morning just two days after the unpleasant visit from Amal Halluk. I rose at my usual time and began working immediately. Feeling particularly invigorated at an early hour I dove into my projects. I had a lead on one of the original copies (not the original itself) from the 15th century of the *Liber Juratus*. This copy did not have a digital copy online and I was hoping to convince the owner to make and share one or digital photos of the book and its pages. Comparing this to online copies of the other versions I have already located, I was hoping to learn more about the contents of the original. All of this was an ongoing project for a repeat client.

As the morning progressed I noticed the flat felt chilly for a summer morning. Almost like something inside the flat was radiating cold. The air itself was not cold, it just felt like the walls and ceiling around the corner my desk sat in were cold.

When living in merry old England you get used to the cold and damp and I knew the best way to deal with it. I opened the windows to let the warm summer air in and returned to my desk. I could still feel the radiating cold but the warm air coming from the windows was making it reasonably comfortable. I settled in and returned to work.

I made a call to the contact number for the owner of the privately owned 15th century copy of the *Liber Juratus*. The call had a positive outcome. The owner would share a digital scan of his copy in exchange for my sharing any history found during the search. I explained to him there should be no problem with such an arrangement provided my client did not object. All in all it was a satisfying exchange.

No sooner had I ended the call and set my cell phone down on the desk and it started ringing. The number shown was unfamiliar. This was not unusual. I receive calls every day from numbers I do not recognize. Probably more than half of my contact with other human beings comes from phone calls. I picked up the phone and answered, "Thomas Davies speaking."

"Hello Thomas!" a cheery voice answered back. It took a moment and then I realized it was Karl Lark.

I was not sure what to say. Just a few days ago three men had died violently and it had apparently been covered up. Mr. Lark was a central part of that event. Why would he be calling me?

I finally went with, "Mr. Lark, how may I help you?"

"I found myself between tasks and thought of you. If you feel up to it I will stop by your flat. I feel we have some unfinished business," Mr. Lark replied.

What kind of unfinished business? I was feeling out of my depth with this. Was Mr. Lark some sort of organized crime figure? And Karl Lark was such an odd name, was that even his real name? Was this visit to snuff out a witness to a homicide?

All of these thoughts raced through my mind in an instant. My last thought was: if he had wanted me dead it would have happened at the museum.

One of the downsides of working on my own, were the long periods of time without social contact. I am an introvert and valued my time alone as much as any other introvert. But too much time alone makes me occasionally chatty, either in person or on the phone. I felt that despite my trepidation, I would probably enjoy talking to Mr. Lark. Perhaps he would explain what had happened at the museum?

"When today would you be stopping by?" I asked.

"In twenty minutes if it is not too inconvenient," Mr. Lark replied.

This week has been all about murder and mayhem and people dropping by unexpectedly I thought.

"Certainly, please ring the bell when you arrive," I replied and hung up. This gave me a few minutes to prepare. I rushed to the bathroom to run a comb through my hair. I cleared my desk of the evidence of my lunch and picked up and organized a few things. There was no time to address the three days of stubble on my face.

The doorbell rang.

I opened the door and there stood Mr. Lark in a grey suit just like I had seen him on Monday. He was flanked by the same two bodyguards. I recall him addressing them as Mr. Held and Mr. Daugherty.

Mr. Lark was smiling a broad friendly smile. He looked at me and said, "May I enter your home?"

I froze for a second. Isn't that what Amal Halluk had said just two days ago?

"Please come in," was my reply. I stood back while the three men entered, then I closed and bolted the door behind them.

Mr. Lark walked to the center of the great room and started looking around. Mr. Held went into a corner to one side of the door and Mr. Daugherty went to the other side. The way the three men had entered and positioned themselves was intimidating.

"Would you like to sit? May I get you some tea or sparkling water?" I asked. Talk about déjà vu.

"No thank you on the refreshments. And yes, let's sit and talk," replied Mr. Lark.

"To what do I owe the pleasure of your visit?"

"I am interested in the services you provide. I have a private library that needs organizing. I also have several acquisitions I would like to make. Can you help me?"

He made no mention of the carnage at the museum. I decided not to be the first to mention the shared experience.

"I provide search services to locate older, sometimes quite rare, texts and documents."

"How did you come to be in such a business?"

"It sort of just happened. Originally I went to university for cryptography but I could not keep up with the math. My love of old books then took me in a different direction. An Italian firm specializing in protecting and rejuvenating old books and documents hired me. I worked there for the better part of a decade finishing university along the way."

"Ah, I see. This is how you became involved with the older books."

"Yes, in addition to my restoration work I became involved with numerous university and private libraries. Soon I was spending as much time generating business as I was restoring."

"This place was a sort of nexus in the old books world?"

"Yes, it provided a common place for everyone in the book business to meet. This progressed into becoming a neutral third party communicating between the different book owners."

Mr. Lark was looking at me intently, obviously enjoying the story.

"This business of moving information between customers was not part of my employer's business model. They recognized the value of it though and encouraged me to pursue it on my own as a business. Of course they expect a discount from me on services rendered and to promote them to my clients when possible. In the end it worked out."

"Fascinating, how very entrepreneurial. So I could hire you to find books for me? I was not aware such a service existed before meeting you. What about cataloging and organizing my library?"

"Yes, you can hire me. I have done such work organizing private libraries. Private libraries sometimes need a third party evaluation. This is typically for insurance purposes." I really liked where this discussion was going. I was thinking Mr. Lark might hire me to organize his private library. The thought of what could be there almost made me giddy. Like the feeling you had as a child walking down the stairs on Christmas morning to see what was under the tree.

"How long have you been doing this?" asked Mr. Lark.

"Including my time with my previous employer, over fifteen years," I replied.

"I believe we will discuss terms on your organizing my collection. You would need to see it first?"

"That would not be necessary. My fees are based on the amount of time applied to the project. I would begin at your convenience."

Mr. Lark looked around the great room again and then back to me. "If the offer for sparkling water still stands I will have it."

"Certainly, and your companions?" I said while nodding to one of the bodyguards. Both of them had been standing in their respective corners quietly keeping a watchful eye.

"They are here for my security. Based on the events from a few days ago you can see why. They have no need for refreshment. Please ignore their presence," Mr. Lark replied dryly.

I nodded and headed for the kitchen for water and glasses.

"I see you opened your windows to let in the summer air," observed Mr. Lark, his voice carrying over from the other room.

"Not so much to let the summer in as to fight the cold inside. The flat had a colder than usual draft today," I made this comment and then regretted having done so.

It was more personal and did not contribute anything of value to the client. This is what happens when I do not get out enough I thought to myself. I get chatty.

He did not seem to mind and continued the discussion, "A cold draft in the middle of summer? Sometimes older buildings have those."

"Yes, the flat can be drafty, especially in the winter with the large fireplace. It is not usually an issue in the summer though. I had to open the windows to warm things up. It must have been unusually cold last night." Hopefully that ended the line of discussion. I did not want to bore Mr. Lark with domestic issues.

Mr. Lark was quiet while I gathered up a tray, water, and glasses. When I walked back out into the great room I stopped in the kitchen doorway. Mr. Lark was sitting up in his chair holding his cane vertically with his hand just below the brass sphere headpiece. His eyes were closed.

After a moment Mr. Lark's eyes snapped open and he exclaimed one word, "Ciorii!"

What the hell is Ciorii and why is my guest yelling?

In a blur of motion both bodyguards produced handguns from under their suit coats. Mr. Lark stood up and reached inside his suit coat. But instead of pulling out a pistol he pulled his hand out with something clenched in it.

I could hear a clicking noise to my left in the direction of my desk in the corner. I looked over and realized the clicking noise was coming from above my desk. I found my eyes looking up at the ceiling corner. Something was there now and the clicking was getting louder. It was an oval shaped, greyish blur. Like something from an out of focus photograph.

Out of the corner of my eye I could see Mr. Lark and the bodyguards moving towards my desk. The body guards had their pistols in two hands but instead of pointing them upwards they were pointed level into the corner.

Mr. Lark snapped at me, "Thomas, get behind us."

I did not move and instead focused back on the blur in the corner. A feeling of cold dread spread through me. My feet would not obey Mr. Lark's command. Something was wrong here, very, very wrong.

The grey blur was wrong, and the more focused whatever it was became, the more wrong it looked. The grey blur became *something*. It was folded up, its impossibly long and thin arms over similarly long thin legs pressed up against its body. Shades of grey, almost black, were its colors. There was a reflective slimy sheen to it. A head, too long and narrow to be human, with huge solid black eyes were staring right at me. The thing was making the clicking noises.

Right about the time I could clearly make out the features of whatever the monster was, Mr. Lark's right hand extended in an underhand toss of something small and white, like a stone or marble. Its flight path was horizontal from his hand to the desk. But instead of landing on the desk, the white stone changed course, accelerated upwards towards the thing in the corner. It struck the creature in what I could only guess was its abdomen. The instant the stone made contact the *thing* came completely into focus and fell from the ceiling corner straight onto the top of my desk.

The appearance of the creature had shocked me to the core. I was still standing in the kitchen doorway. I could feel my mouth hanging open. *What is happening?*

Then, for the second time this week my hearing went out as the gunfire started. Both body guards opened fire and the flash of their gunfire strobed the inside of the flat. I jumped in surprise dropping the tray with the glasses and water on it to the floor at my feet.

The thing on the desktop was convulsing and thrashing about. I was not more than ten feet away and I could clearly see the effect of the gunfire. Fluids sprayed across the walls behind the creature. The part of the monsters body where the white stone had impacted shown like a bright white light. The creature's whole body was moving around except for that one bright point of light. It appeared to be holding the thing in place.

Mr. Lark produced a large handgun looking like something out of a WWII movie from inside his suit coat. He then started shooting at the creature just like the other two men.

Their shooting was controlled, each shot carefully aimed. Even so, the rate of their fire was a manic staccato. Each man in turn had their pistol slides lock open indicating the need to reload. This was done so quickly and smoothly that if you blinked you would have missed it. Once a fresh magazine was inserted they released the weapons slide forward and continued blazing away at the creature. The smell of weapons fire filled the flat.

The effect on the monster started as sprays of ichor. As the shooting continued, chunks were blown free. The wall behind my desk was looking like something out of a slaughter house.

Each man must have reloaded three times when Mr. Lark did something I would never have expected. He dropped his handgun and pulled a foot long white spike from inside his suit coat and sprinted towards the creature still convulsing on top of the desk. He stabbed it with the white spike it at the point where the white light was shining.

The creature went stiff for a second and I could faintly hear a high pitched scream through my gunfire induced deafness. Then it flopped down on the desk going completely limp. Its impossibly long arms and legs dangled over the edges of the desk all the way down to the floor.

Every surface near the creature was a mess. Splatters of whatever passed for the things blood were everywhere. Chunks of its flesh, blown free by the concentrated gunfire lay about the desk. Mr. Lark withdrew the spike, pulled a handkerchief from a pocket, and wiped it clean. He then casually dropped the soiled handkerchief to the floor and the white spike disappeared back inside his suit coat.

The dead creature on the desk began to give off a vapor like it was being cooked.

The three men did not even pause to observe their handiwork. Instead they bent down and began retrieving spent magazines. Mr. Lark picked up the gun he had dropped, reloaded it, and holstered it under his suit coat.

I watched all this while looking around the warzone that was my flat. Spent brass casings were scattered about, lying on the floor, on the leather furniture, on the tables, everywhere.

My hearing then returned in a rush. At most a minute had passed since the gunfire had started and I did what any person exposed to sudden, close proximity violence against a hideous monster would do.

I vomited.

I retched and my body started to shake while my vision went grey. I was barely able to stay on my feet. While bent over I saw the dropped the tray at my feet and the glasses had shattered and shards of it were spread out around me. I covered the tray and broken glass with the contents of my stomach.

When I was finished being sick, my vision and control of my legs returning, I stood upright and found all three men standing in a semi-circle facing of me. The body guards had holstered their weapons and their neutral passive expressions had returned. Mr. Lark was smiling at me in a way eerily similar to the day of our first meeting.

"No time to explain, time to leave", he stated and turned to walk towards the front door. Mr. Held grabbed my right arm and coaxed me towards the door while Mr. Daugherty strode past everyone to unbolt and open it.

After we were all outside Mr. Daugherty closed and locked the door behind us. *Where did he get my keys?* I thought.

Chapter 4

The Mercedes that had taken me home earlier this week pulled up to the sidewalk decelerating quickly to a stop. Mr. Lark got into the front passenger seat and the two bodyguards crushed me between them in the back seat. The car then accelerated away quickly.

I wondered if I should be objecting to being taken? Was I being rescued or kidnapped? I was pretty sure my opinion did not count for much in the current situation and I would be going where they wanted to take me regardless.

The driver was a big man, burly, barrel chested and very muscular. He was also attired in the same grey suit as the others and spoke as soon as we were seated, "Is there pursuit?" Mr. Lark responded, "No, drive normally and conform to the local laws." From my center position I could see Mr. Lark's face. He was leaning back with his eyes closed like he had been while sitting in my flat just before that thing had appeared.

The Mercedes windows were heavily tinted and anyone standing next to the car would see vague outlines and nothing more. The modern world is a strange place. One moment you are in a war zone and the next you are quietly driving down the streets of London.

"Is the transfer point clear and ready," Mr. Lark said in a neutral tone.

The driver responded, "Yes, everything is ready. With current traffic our ETA is less than 15 minutes."

A few minutes of silent driving passed, and Mr. Lark spoke again, "Police are notified and responding to multiple calls of loud noises, possibly gunfire, in the area of Thomas' flat."

I did not see how he could know this. Mr. Lark was just sitting in the front seat.

After another several minutes of silence he spoke again from his closed eye reverie, "Nothing on police channels describing a vehicle or a specific address."

"The building had thick brick walls and there was no one immediately outside. If the police drive through they will not see anything and there are no witnesses."

We drove through London's back streets. I was sitting dazed, realizing my breath was really unpleasant and not really paying attention to where we were or how we got there. Our final destination was in an old industrial zone, one of many scattered around London.

How cliché, I thought. The Mercedes pulled into a large warehouse through an open truck door. As soon as we entered the building the door rolled down shut behind us. I did not need to look to know. The extinguishing of light coming through the back window of the car told me our entry point had been closed.

We drove perhaps 200 meters through the middle of the industrial building with dark, silent machines on both sides of us. There were no lights inside the building, only the Mercedes headlights illuminated the path ahead. A door loomed out of the darkness. Someone must have triggered it to open vertically with just enough room for the car to drive through.

We arrived in a well-lit square space perhaps a hundred feet across. It was a clean and bright white with no other windows or doors. Once the car was completely in the room it stopped. Everyone opened their respective car doors and got out.

Mr. Held encouraged me to exit the vehicle with a tug of my arm and started walking me towards the center of the room. I felt like I was on automatic pilot, cold and distant. *Where are we going?*

None of this made sense. They were not planning on killing me. They could have done that with one bullet back in my flat. Or for that matter back at the museum. Why bring me to this room in an old building? I looked around the room and there were no doors other than the one we had come in.

The center of the room had a circle perhaps 10 feet in diameter with a perimeter made up of evenly spaced black stones. Each cylindrical stone was maybe a foot in diameter and three feet tall. I counted nine in total.

Just inside the circle of stones was another circle made of copper bar lying on the floor and unbroken in its circumference. Was this some kind of ritual setup?

Mr. Lark walked past one of the stones, stepping over the copper bar and came to a stop in the approximate center of the circle. Mr. Held coaxed me into the circle to stand next to Mr. Lark. We were then joined by the other bodyguards. *Why are we standing here?* I thought.

Five men standing next to each other in the middle of the room all acting like this was perfectly normal. These thoughts bumped against each other in my confused mind.

Without warning everything went black. Not like when the lights are turned off and the light fades out quickly. The blackness was instant, no overhead lights providing a brief afterglow, just black. A moment of pitch back and silence that seemed to last forever.

The light came back, just as instantaneously, but it was much dimmer. And it was freezing cold. I could see my breath when I exhaled. We were standing in another, much larger, ring of stones. These stones were also black and cylindrical but taller and the circle was maybe fifty feet in diameter. The surface we stood on was smooth black rock. Mr. Lark and his body guards appeared unfazed by the instantaneous change in scenery.

I felt a wave of cold nausea roll over me and I would have fallen if Mr. Held did not have a hold of me.

Mr. Lark barked, "Put him in the cell and wrap him up to keep him warm before he goes into shock". He then walked away, heading out of the circle. Two of the bodyguards each grabbed an arm and half-dragged me in a different direction than where Mr. Lark was headed.

Just before crossing between the stone circle pillars I saw a copper or bronze metal circle recessed in the smooth stone floor.

On the other side of the pillars, outside the circle, was a building. It was six sided and the size of a small house. One of its six walls faced the circle and the walls and domed ceiling were solid black with a circular opening mounting a bank vault style plug door hanging next to it. Walking into the vault we had to step over a threshold that came up from the floor almost a foot. In stepping over it I could see the wall was also perhaps a foot thick. *Who makes a vault with foot thick walls?*

I tripped over the threshold and the bodyguards caught me and virtually carried me the rest of the way into the room.

The floor was the same black material as the walls and the domed ceiling overhead and differed in appearance from the polished smooth stone outside the room. Inside the room was a cot with a big cocoon sleeping bag in a military olive drab color laid out. Next to the cot appeared to be a drinks cooler. Atop the cooler was a small electric camping lantern. It was the only light in the room and the light it generated was sucked up by the black material of the floor, walls, and ceiling. Standing in the middle of the room next to the lamp felt like floating in an endless black sky.

The bodyguards left me standing on my own in the center of the room, while one of them unzipped and opened the sleeping bag. Mr. Held took the lamp and placed it on the on the floor. He then opened the cooler. Pulling out a bottle of water, he unscrewed its cap and handed it to me. "Drink", he said. The first words I had heard him say today other than 'reloading' back at the flat.

I took the bottle in unsteady hands and took a drink. I found I was very thirsty and drank half the bottle before pausing. Mr. Held took the bottle when I was done, capped it and put it back in the cooler. "Get in the sleeping bag" he said next pointing to the open bag. I did not object. I was starting to shiver, the cold taking the feeling from my hands.

I climbed into the sleeping bag and Mr. Daugherty zipped me in until only part of my face was exposed. Mr. Held pointed to the cooler, "There is more water and some crackers in the cooler. Don't turn out the light. If you do it will be completely black inside this room. There is no other light". "Over against the wall is a small chemical toilet," he said pointing towards a dim white object against the wall.

With that said both men turned back to the doorway and walked out. I could vaguely make out the vault door closing with a great booming sound followed by a metal against metal grinding noise. The excitement of the last 20 minutes caught up with me as I felt the comfortable spreading warmth of the sleeping bag and I remembered no more.

Chapter 5

I was awoken by the need to relieve myself and felt around inside the sleeping bag until I found the bag's zipper. Opening the sleeping bag confirmed what my face had been telling me. It was really cold. If I had to guess the temperature, it was well below freezing. My breath formed a cloud in front of me when I exhaled.

Lifting myself from the cot, I stumbled to the box against the wall in the direction Mr. Held had pointed to earlier, finding a compact camping toilet with a traditional lid on top.

Afterwards I walked around the inside of what I decided to call a vault. The six interior walls formed a hexagon. The lamp barely lit the room and the domed ceiling above was almost lost in the darkness. I touched the walls and they felt like metal and were burning cold to the touch. The cold radiating from the walls was intense and palpable.

The floor was the same black metal. Copper or bronze rings, thick as my thumb were recessed in to the floor in concentric circles, with maybe two feet between each ring. They started in the center of the room with the first circle being eight paces across. The same copper inlay was found in walls starting two feet from the floor and repeating every two feet up the walls. I could not see if this was continued in the ceiling.

I could tell the floor and wall surfaces had originally been quite smooth. Whatever had been kept in here in the past had made scratches and dents in the surfaces. The defacement of the walls went up as far as the light would allow me to see, well above my ability to reach. Sometime in the past something very large and very strong had been kept in this vault. And it had wanted out.

Walking back to the cot, I lifted the lamp from the cooler and looked inside, finding bottles of water and a box of crackers both with common brand names. After closing the cooler, I looked at the lamp. It was a battery powered LED type similar to what could be found in any sporting goods store. I placed the lamp back on top of the cooler and continued to look around.

Walking up to the vault door I yelled, "Hello? Hello? I am awake, is there anyone out there?" There was no reply. Recalling the walls were a foot thick, my guess is it was unlikely anyone could hear me.

I wanted to stand and walk around but the cold was starting to make me shiver. Crawling back into the sleeping bag I zipped it back up, feeling warmth return to my body.

I was not tired and not having a watch there was no way to tell how long I had been asleep. The vault was dead silent with nothing to indicate the passage of time. There was nothing else to do but just lay there in the cold and the dark, thinking about what had just happened.

It was obvious Karl Lark had rescued me from some *thing*. What the thing that appeared above my desk back in my flat had been was beyond me. Mr. Lark had called it a Ciorii, whatever that meant. I have read a lot of mythology in my life and I do not remember any mythological monster called a 'Ciorii' referenced in any book.

And why the magic trick back at the warehouse? Turning out the lights and moving me to a freezer? And why am I in a vault? The rescue had turned into kidnapping when I was locked away against my will.

Mr. Lark and his team had obviously been avoiding the police when they left my flat. Was he part of some intelligence service like MI-6? It would explain his ability to discharge weapons and kill people in the city without any apparent repercussions.

This line of reasoning was producing no answers just more questions. I do not believe Mr. Lark intends to harm me. He could have just shot me after they finished off the monster and left. Perhaps I am locked away for my protection, but protection from what? I am in the book business, a librarian. Not the sort of business a person is likely to acquire mortal enemies in, much less monsters demonstrating supernatural abilities. None of my clients had ever expressed the kind of dissatisfaction that could result in gunfire.

After what could have been minutes or even hours, my having no way to tell, the grinding noise of the door was repeated. While waiting I had positioned myself in the sleeping bag so I could watch the door. The grinding noise stopped and the vault door opened silently.

I could see Mr. Lark standing outside. He was still in his grey suit and carrying his copper sphere headed cane. He was not smiling this time, his face a mask of concentration as he walked into the vault, carefully stepping over the doorway's ridiculously high threshold.

The few times I have seen the man he was always smiling, before, during, and even after the gunfire. My guess is it is worse that he is not smiling.

Behind him was Mr. Held, dressed in what looked like an all-black tactical uniform and carrying a small chair. He maneuvered around Mr. Lark and placed the chair facing me, perhaps four feet from my horizontal form. Mr. Lark took a seat while Mr. Held exited out the doorway. The vault door swung closed, apparently locking us both in with that grinding noise again.

He sat silently looking at me. After several seconds I took the initiative and spoke first, "Perhaps thanks are in order for the rescue?"

Mr. Lark's expression remained unchanged, his voice flat in reply, "It was not a rescue."

"If not, then what is going on here?" When I spoke my voice was lacking conviction. I now realized my earlier line of reasoning was most likely incorrect.

Mr. Lark explained, "The thing in your flat was a Ciorii. When they first establish themselves in hiding, they absorb thermal energy from the surrounding environment. In layman's terms they essentially radiate cold. The reason for my visit was genuinely about hiring your services. When you related the feeling of coldness on a warm summer's day I had a hunch. I then investigated my hunch."

I interjected, "A hunch, all that came from a hunch?"

He continued, "When you operate within the spaces my organization does, your survival depends on a serious amount of paranoia and listening to your instincts. While you were getting the water in the kitchen I consulted my Oculus."

I interrupted again, "An Oculus?"

Now Mr. Lark smiled, "I am sure you wondered about my oddly shaped cane. The headpiece is obviously too large for a person's hand to grip. It is a device of my own creation. It allows me to see… things. Also, my attempt at explaining your situation is going to take a long time if you keep interrupting me".

After a pause he resumed, "Ciorii are used as assassins, kidnappers or as watchers. My hunch was correct and a Ciorii was present. I still do not know in which of those three roles played its purpose in your flat. As soon as I could see that a Ciorii was indeed present, action was taken."

I decided to risk another interruption, "I see, sort of. You acted to protect yourself but why take me with you? The thing was dead."

Mr. Lark took the interruption in stride, "My organization prides itself on complete anonymity. I had just met you a few days prior and during my second time meeting you I find a Ciorii in your home. That leads to two possibilities: you knew the Ciorri was there or you did not. Based on your reactions it was obvious you did not know it was there. Someone sent it to watch you not me, but whom?"

He continued, "I bear you no ill will, but my concern was my privacy had somehow been compromised. The Ciorii needed to be destroyed before it could report back and I needed to remove you before its master came for you."

Mr. Lark let this sink in for a few seconds before continuing. "Have you ever heard of a Daemon's True Name?"

Wow, talk about a subject change. What the hell kind of question is that? Why was some assassin kidnapper monster hiding in my flat? Did Karl Lark bring this madness down on me by accident or on purpose?

"Yes Mr. Lark, I have read enough fantasy fiction to understand the concept of a Daemon's True Name," My reply had more sarcasm in it than my situation really allowed for.

I could not tell if he was offended or not but small smile appeared on his face, "Ciorii exist in the wild I guess you could say. They can be bound into service by possession of its True Name. From a more technical viewpoint it could be seen as a password to program its actions. With the proper knowledge you can take ownership of such a creature. It will follow instructions, even complex instructions. Not only could I see the Ciorii in your flat but I could see it was following instructions and had a purpose. It belonged to someone."

I was speechless. His explanation made it sound like that thing was intelligent and someone had put it in my flat on purpose. He was also making it sound like Ciorii were Daemons.

Mr. Lark's facial expression went dark, looking almost angry. "I must apologize to you for two things.

The first is locking you in this chamber. I needed to put you someplace safe and out of reach. I needed time to consider all angles of these unusual events. My second apology is for the mistake I made in getting involved."

He continued, "I do not believe the Ciorii was there due to our meeting. It was not looking for me. There really was no reason for me to become involved. The Ciorii was sent in response to something else. Have you had any recent visitors that left an impression on you?"

If I was hearing him correctly Mr. Lark just said he would have left me in the Ciorii's clutches if he had known better. As for weird visitors, other than Karl Lark, there was Amal Halluk.

I did not see any reason to protect someone who put a monster in my home. "A man named Amal Halluk visited me two days before you came to my flat." I then went on to describe Amal Halluk in detail.

Mr. Lark smiled, "As I suspected. The man you are describing most likely sent the Ciorii. Why is another question? Such a being would not normally get personally involved. He was looking for something and did not find it. Then he sent the Ciorii to watch you. I would speculate this is related to the events at the museum."

Mr. Lark continued explaining, "Your description of Amal sounds like he is a Djinn, probably of low rank. Djinn do not normally leave their estates to visit humans. They have bound human servants interact with the outside world."

"Whatever that book at the museum documents it must be very valuable or dangerous for a Djinn to become personally involved. Perhaps it is a matter of honor. Regardless Amal Halluk decided to watch you very closely."

Mr. Lark sat thinking for a bit and the vault went silent.

Then he continued, "This brings me again to my second apology. My organization is very private. By bringing you here I have created an untenable situation. Everyone you have met in my service is permanently bound to me. I can't just return you to your flat. As they say in the movies, you know too much."

I felt real fear bordering on terror. *Oh God, is he going to kill me?*

He continued, "The world I operate in is dangerous. Without secrecy I would come into conflict with other organizations and entities that I would prefer do not know of my existence. No one from the outside world is ever allowed where you are now."

"You cannot make any promise of secrecy that would make me feel secure in releasing you. You may believe you can keep a secret but I assure you, should someone want to extract what you know against your will they could."

"I could offer you a role in my organization. Unfortunately that is complicated by the fact that when I recruit for the organization it is for people that fill roles that need filling and you do not meet any of the criteria for joining".

My feeling of terror was now approaching panic. This was the end. Zipped up in a sleeping bag not four feet away from someone I was positive was going to murder me. There was nothing I could do. Even if I was standing, with my hands free, I was fairly certain Mr. Lark would not be challenged 'taking care' of me.

The next words he spoke ended the feeling of terror. "I put a lot of thought into what to do with you. Your ability to locate things related to my organizations sphere of operations could be useful. After significant weighing of the possibilities I have come to the conclusion you could make a useful addition. If things do not work out I will dispose of you later."

Who says things like that?

"Please understand Thomas, when I make an offer to join, it is a one way street. You join or your life is ended."

I was having a hard time organizing my thoughts. Was he saying what I thought he was saying, "Is that a job offer?"

Mr. Lark's face changed, becoming a mask of controlled anger his eyes shining with cold light. Not an actual light, but his eyes were devoid of emotion or empathy. "There are no jobs here. When you join you are telling me you have no reservations, that you will make every effort to achieve the goals of the organization. There is no going back, no reluctance, no attempts to escape. You will not be an employee and this is not a democracy. You will serve my will. Anything less and I will kill you. Joining is forever."

Mr. Lark paused, "I only make this offer once. You can take a few minutes before you answer."

A few minutes? He was offering a few minutes for such a decision. That would be comical if the stakes were not so high. As I saw it, here was really no choice here. I had no one who would miss me other than my parents whom I saw only once or twice a year.

Regardless, everything I had seen during my brief time with Karl Lark pointed towards my joining his organization being the first step on an adventure. I had never really been interested in adventures before. Instead of fear though, I felt intrigued. What wonders would I see? There was only one way to find out. And whatever Mr. Lark had in mind was preferable to a prompt death.

"I will join your organization," The words were said with a conviction I did not feel. My former life began slipping away as I said them. Would I ever get to return to my flat? Whatever Mr. Lark had in mind was the only future I had. His conviction made that plain.

Mr. Lark looked at me for a long time before replying, "I accept your service Thomas Davies. We will discuss your role more when we get to our destination."

I ventured a question, "May I ask questions?"

Mr. Lark responded, "I always welcome constructive questions and I answer them if it is something you should know. Now we need to travel to a more hospitable location to begin your integration into my organization. We can talk along the way. Get yourself out of that bag."

No sooner had Mr. Lark spoken and the grinding noise of the door unlocking echoed through the chamber followed by it swinging open.

I extricated myself from the sleeping bag and stood up and immediately started shivering from the cold. Fortunately Mr. Held came through the door and handed me a great coat.

The coat hung all the way to my ankles and was well insulated. A pair of gloves was in one of the pockets. I buttoned up the coat and put on the gloves. I was getting the feeling I was not the first person to undergo the interview process. Every action taken was being executed like clockwork.

Mr. Held spoke, "We are ready to travel."

Mr. Lark smiled his broad friendly smile and said, "Come Thomas, it is time to show you a bigger world."

Chapter 6

Things had been pretty hazy when I had arrived at...
wherever this was. Walking out the vault door, I could
see the other five identical black iron vaults in a hexagon
shape around the Stonehenge like circle of stone pillars I
had arrived in.

There are three identical roads leading away from
the vaults in three different directions. The roads
appeared to be at precise angles to each other and
perfectly straight for as far as I could see.

Past the flat space of the circle and vaults, the
ground appeared to be rough, very uneven, grey stone.
The elevation of the grey stone landscape showed no
pattern, rising and falling with small peaks and deep pits
everywhere. The changes were in both steep angles and
gradual ramps. Trying to escape across the open grey
stone spaces would be tough going. Only the three
roads offered a path of reasonable travel away from the
vaults.

Mr. Lark walked to one of the three roads. Mr. Held was the only other person present, there were no other bodyguards. I joined Mr. Lark in walking down the center of the road side by side.

The road was broad, close to five meters across, and made from perfectly flat fitted black stone. It was an easy surface to walk on. I was still wearing my 'around the flat' loafers and was glad the surface we were walking on was smooth.

Before I could ask, Mr. Lark stated, "Our destination is a thirty minute walk".

Mr. Held was trailing us by a respectful distance and looking his usual alert self.

Looking around as we walked I observed it was dark as a moonless night and there were no stars overhead. The air had a gloom to it, like a fog, that limited the distance things could be seen. There were buildings and other structures spaced some distance away from the road. They were of the same black stone as the road, contrasting with the grey of the sterile landscape. There were no plants, grass, or trees. Everything in sight was as barren as the moon.

All of buildings were difficult to see and they seemed randomly placed. Some of them had paths running to them from the road. Those paths were more narrow versions of the main road and similarly paved. Other buildings were placed in the rough grey stone of the ground with no apparent connection to anything around them. Some were small single-story structures. Others were larger and thrust up into the sky out of sight.

I looked up again, trying to find the stars. At the very edge of what could be seen, I could make out something floating overhead, actually more than one something was up there. They looked like floating diamond shaped blimps. The surface of the blimps was not smooth but uneven and bumpy. Their color from this distance was difficult to determine, perhaps a light grey or pink. Long thin ropes hung down from the blimps.

As I observed I noticed the ropes moving and snapping. I then came to the realization those were not ropes hanging down. Those things floating so far up must be some sort of living creature. I became aware I was staring and having a hard time looking away from whatever the floating things were.

Mr. Lark noticed my staring and snapped at me, "Don't look at them or for that matter do not look up at all. They know when you are looking and it draws them to you."

With some mental effort I shifted my gaze and focused on the road ahead. "I was looking for the stars. What are those things up there?"

Mr. Lark waited a moment and then responded, "There are no stars up there. This place is a pocket dimension. We are someplace other than 'Earth'."

"The normal rules do not apply here and you must be careful. For right now you must understand this is not the world of man. Your mind is unguarded and you are radiating your emotions and thoughts to everything around here. If you were not in our company you would be quickly swept up by something from the area bordering the road. It would be a meeting that you would not survive."

I felt the dread I had felt earlier when I thought Mr. Lark was going to kill me. It was a cold twisting in my chest.

Mr. Lark continued, "The place we arrived at I call the 'Attavita', or 'The Compass'. It is the front door so to speak. The Attavita is the only way into this place. The space between the Compass and our destination is left wild. Any unwelcome visitors entering this place will need to contend with the many uncivilized and dangerous denizens between the Attavita and the Citadel if they wish to disturb me here."

I asked, "Why are we not being disturbed now?"

Mr. Lark smiled, "I have reached an accommodation with the things in residence along this road. It is an imperfect agreement, but if we travel in pairs, walk with a purpose and keep our wits about us, we will be unmolested."

I felt my gaze being pulled to the right. The movement of my head was involuntary. I then saw something next to a building perhaps one hundred meters away. *A clown?* What is a clown doing here?

Mr. Lark spoke again in a harsh tone, "Look ahead Thomas." His voice broke the spell and I was able to look back in the direction we were walking. He then asked, "What did you see?"

"A clown, like in a circus or at a children's birthday party," I shivered while I said this. "Is there someone or something out there trying to look like a clown?"

"There is no human person out there. What you saw was one of the wild residents of this place. These things do not necessarily see us the way we see each other. That thing looks like a clown because it thinks that is what we look like to each other. It is trying to look human to get you to move closer to it."

I could not stop myself from asking the next question, "So this place is filled with predators?"

Mr. Lark chuckled, "While it seems like that, what with everything here apparently trying to kill you, in fact there are no predators or prey here. The things in this place are old, old beyond ancient. They were tools, fantastically sophisticated instruments and machines. Used for the creation of things beyond the ability of most to understand. "

"When whatever created them was done with them they were just left here. It is similar to when you are driving in the country past a farmer's field and see an abandoned piece of rusty farm equipment in the corner of the field. Its usefulness ended, left to rot."

"The things here, the Ciorii and others, are left over from a long time ago. Left to their own devices, some attempt to find a purpose for themselves. Most are attached to a single location, following whatever their last instructions were. "

"They have differing levels of self-awareness. Many have come to resent the freedom of humans. Others just want something to do, perhaps an equivalent to children playing. Their 'playing' with someone is almost always fatal. The concept of living beings and mortality are not part of their being. Where possible it is best to give them a wide berth."

I thought about what Mr. Lark had just said. An idea came to me. "Machines, like androids? Can they be commanded?"

He looked at me as we continued walking, "Your insight is impressive. These things were built long before English was a language. With careful research, some trial and error, and controlled conditions, it is possible for a human to gain imperfect control of some of the Lesser Created."

"Lesser Created?" I was not comfortable with what was implied in that statement. If these nightmares are lesser creations what is a 'Greater Created?

"Yes, there are Lesser Created and there are Greater Created. They are all immortal and virtually impossible to permanently destroy. The Lesser Created are the Faeries and Goblins of myth along with the Ciorii and others. The Greater Created exist are not something to seek out or discuss in the open like this.

Perhaps calling them Created is a dry and overly technical term but I wish to define them in a way that is separate from the emotions of mythology. Enough questions for now. We are almost at our destination".

We walked in silence for a few more minutes. I could start to make out the road ending at giant double doors, dull steel in color, the same width as the road and four times the height of a man. The doors were set in jet black walls so high they extended upwards out of sight and no handle or lock were evident.

On each side of the door was something twice the height of a man. They appeared to be statues but blurred. At first I thought the lack of focus was due to the distance but as we came closer the blurry nature of what I was looking at did not change. They appeared to be statues of men with four arms and two legs. Their body, arms and legs were thickly built and what I guessed was their heads were sunk into the top of their chests with no neck evident.

"Mr. Lark, what are those?"

"They are Ushabti repurposed to guard the doors to the Citadel. The name 'Ushabti' is ancient Eqyptian but these Created existed long before the pyramids were even conceived of. In the ancient past they were employed for tasks on a massive scale. They are an example of a Lesser Created that I have taken control of."

When we were not more than twenty paces from the doors, they swung open outwards, apparently without any signal. Bright light stabbed out from the interior, causing me to raise a hand and shield my eyes. We had arrived at our destination.

Mr. Lark announced, as we entered, "Thomas, welcome to the Citadel."

Chapter 7

Neither Mr. Lark nor Mr. Held paused, our small group purposefully walking through the doorway into the well-lit open space beyond. Once inside, the doors swung shut behind us, closing without a sound.

The first thing I noticed was how brightly lit it was here, the gloom outside was gone.

From the inside I could see the walls the doors were set in were very high. If I was to guess, I would say at least ten stories tall. While the exterior walls had been void black, inside they were snow white.

Overhead, a domed roof sat atop the walls. Mounted at even, symmetrical spacings below the ceiling are huge glass or crystal light bulbs, bigger than any light bulb I had ever seen. Each bulb was at least three meters long and almost a meter in diameter. Inside the bulb the light was being emitted from what looked like a glowing stream of gas. They were bright but not overpowering, and everything inside the domed space was illuminated. The overall effect was that of a brightly lit sports stadium.

The space under the dome could have been a half a kilometer across. Inside the overall domed structure were other buildings. They were all different in appearance. Some were cylindrical, others were rectangular. Some were small like a yard shed while others were multi-story structures that extended upwards to meet the domed ceiling. Everything was of stone construction. There was no visible plant or animal life.

The overall appearance was random. It was obvious no urban planning commission had directed the overall layout. The dimensions were wrong too. From my experience, architects and artists use the golden ratio. Objects constructed using the golden ratio will be pleasing to the human eye.

Whoever built this place had never heard of the golden ratio.

An unfamiliar man was standing in the middle of the open space. He was tall, over six feet, and wearing the same black tactical uniform as Mr. Held. He had an athletic build and based on the grey in his short cropped dark hair, was in his early forties. A large holstered handgun was on his hip. He had that same alert watchfulness the other men accompanying Mr. Lark had.

While I stood in one place and took in my surroundings, Mr. Lark walked up to the waiting man and spoke with him in a low voice, preventing me from overhearing. Mr. Held wandered away at a casual pace, his immediate duties apparently complete. I noticed a change in his body language. Whatever this place is we must be safe, the hyper vigilance displayed on the walk here was gone.

Mr. Lark waved me over to join him and the other man and made introductions, "This is Illych. Think of him as the headman of this place. He will give you a tour and settle you in. I strongly suggest you take his instruction seriously."

Illych smiled and extended his right hand, "Pleasure to meet you Thomas." His accent marked him as American. His handshake was very firm.

"Thank you and likewise," I said smiling back.

"A Brit? Tank is going to love this," Illych said with a grin.

"What Tank?" I asked.

"Not what, who, you will meet him shortly. Big bear of a guy, you can't miss him. You already met Held and Mike," Illych continued.

"I understand Held is the gentleman who Mr. Lark addressed as Mr. Held. Who is 'Mike?'"

"Everyone here, other than Mr. Lark, is ex-US military. We do not necessarily address each other by our given first name. My first name actually is Illych. Mike Daugherty is the dark haired gentleman whom you have already met," Illych replied.

Mr. Lark spoke then, "He has not been introduced to the others, I trust you will take care of it. Help Thomas settle in."

Without another word Mr. Lark turned and started walking towards the main gate doors, they swung open again without any apparent command. He passed through them and they closed silently behind him.

Illych spoke again, "Mr. Lark explained the unusual circumstances of your induction to the team. By the look on your face I can tell you are a little more than concerned. You can relax. This is not the military or the mafia. It's a job and a good one, just not one you can quit."

He paused, waiting for me to ask a question and then continued, "First things first, let's get you situated. We run on a twenty-four hour time cycle here based on United States east coast time, making it now three in the afternoon. There is time to get you a room and a shower before dinner."

"Dinner?" I stuttered, "A shower?"

"Yes, and a real bed", Illych's face broke into a smile. "I will warn you ahead of time. Some of the work here is ugly and dangerous. But overall this is a rewarding place to be. If you are not careful you will start to like it here. I know I do."

Illych lead me away from the open space by the doors. We walked past several buildings and I caught glimpses of other people moving about their business around us. I recognized them as Held, Mike, and the muscular driver of the car I guessed was Tank.

Illych walked through an open doorway into a building serving as living quarters. Inside were desks, chairs, couches and other furniture spaced out around the room. There was even a sitting area with overstuffed couches and chairs. Along one wall were book shelves filled with books. Everything was neat, clean and organized.

Doors along two walls opened into single rooms and inside the rooms were neatly made beds. Illych walked over to one of the doors and pointed inside saying, "This is your room." The room had a bookshelf, desk and chair, a large chest at the foot of the bed, a small dresser, and a single bed. I would not say it was austere as much as efficient. Perhaps with time it will grow on me.

Illych said, "Let's get you to the showers and then some clean clothes." I followed him back 'outside'. Next door was a small circular building which Illych directed me to enter and showed me a set of private showers on an elevated platform. Hoses ran to and from the shower setups out through a window.

Noticing my interest in the hoses running outside Illych commented, "There is all the hot water you want. This place does not have a natural water supply or a water treatment plant. Everything is brought in and when something is used up it must be taken out. You will learn more over the next few days. Go ahead and clean up. Personal hygiene stuff is in that cabinet over there. I am going to find some clean clothes for you. Expect me be back in maybe a half hour."

I grabbed one of everything and stripped. The shower operated normally and I went about cleaning up and felt better for it.

Illych walked in afterwards and handed me a green cloth bag. Inside was a pair of black combat boots, a full set of clothes, all in black.

"Put them on."

I looked around for something that might give some privacy for dressing. Illych noticed and commented, "No need to worry about someone walking in on you, it's just us guys here." Then he stood looking out the door while I dressed. I also noticed the clothes I had arrived in were gone. The boots and clothes are well made and everything fit and was comfortable.

As we walked back to the barracks together, Illych had more to say, "This is how it works. We are typically on duty for Mr. Lark for 90 days and then off for a 30 day vacation. Time on and time off is the same for everyone. We are all here together for the same 90 days and then this place is empty for 30 days."

"During the 30 day vacation you can go anywhere in the world and do pretty much anything you want. We do get a paycheck and it is more than enough for anything you want during your time off. All that is required is you don't draw attention to yourself, don't talk about what we do here, and when it's time to go back to work, show up healthy and rested."

Illych let that sink in for a bit as we arrived back at the living quarters. "During the 90 days we do whatever task is given to us by Mr. Lark. Additionally we train and maintain this place. I am working on the scheduling for your duties."

"You are the only person at the Citadel who is not ex-military. Every morning at 6am we all gather for calisthenics, weight training and a run around the perimeter. Then we split up for whatever our assigned chores are. Breakfast is at 8am. Lunch is at noon. Dinner is 6pm."

I interrupted, "How do the meals work?" An image of us eating from cans popped into my head.

Illych nodded and continued, "Everything is brought in. We usually have three to four days of what are essentially catered meals on hand. The Citadel is not a place to leave organic matter lying around. Everything organic that comes in must go back out."

"How many of, I guess us, are there here?" I asked.

There is Held, Tank, Mike, you and me, for a total of five residents of the Citadel. Don't worry about being stuck here all the time, we spend most of our time in the real world. The Citadel is just a base of operations and a place to keep supplies."

"Can you give me an idea of what we do for Mr. Lark? He did not clue me in on much during the brief job interview," I asked.

"There are not a lot of secrets here Thomas. You can ask anything you want. You can tell anybody here anything. The exception is Mr. Lark. He will tell you what you need to know. You can ask him questions but more likely than not he will ignore you. As for what we do: we move things and or people from place to place, sometimes we retrieve objects. We may provide security for short periods of time in some strange places. Never a dull moment," Illych smiled as he rattled off the services the organization provided.

I thought about what he had just said, "Like smuggling?"

"It is one of the organizations sources of income as far as I can tell. If you have enough money you can arrange with Mr. Lark, through some brokers, to move anything from anywhere to anywhere. Hazards at the origination or destination are irrelevant. Customs and legal requirements ignored. All, I believe, for a very impressive fee." Illych did not speak like a man trapped here by Mr. Lark.

Since he was in a talkative mood I decided to ask more questions. "How did I get here from London? Mr. Lark said 'translated.' What does that mean?"

Illych laughed, "Mr. Lark has something called the Ouiblet. It allows movement from point to point anywhere in the world pretty much instantaneously. He has never explained how it works and I have never asked. Mr. Lark controls it but he also gives out what he calls a 'dongle' that allows limited use of the Ouiblet".

He continued, "Travelling between the stone circles is preferred. If the trip has both sides being an unprepared site the experience can be pretty rough." Illych looked at an oversized watch on his left wrist. "I have some things to do before dinner. Feel free to wander around. Stay out of any buildings you have not already been in. And here", he reached into his left trousers pocket and pulled out the twin to the oversized watch on his own left wrist. "Put this on. It tells the local time here. You are from Europe so you already understand 1800 is 6pm. Dinner time is at 1800. Wander around and you will find the cafeteria. See you then." After handing me the watch Illych walked away.

The watch was big and bulky and about the size of a pack of cigarettes. The band was a synthetic material with the usual buckle and eye arrangement for fastening it to my left wrist.

I looked at the watch. On the left of the face were thin, glowing, green vertical lines in rows. Based on what I believe is the current local time, the number of vertical lines must mean hours. They were arranged in four rows of six lines. Around the lines representing hours was a circular arrangement of amber lines, similar to a starburst. It appears there were sixty lines in the circle so this indicated minutes. On the right side of the watch face was a faint amber light that pulsed in second intervals. I looked at the overly complicated watch and wondered why Illych did not give me something a little more normal.

I wandered the Citadel for the next hour. Everything was well lit by the big lights overhead. The place smelled sterile and dry, almost metallic. There were no sounds coming from anything and the lights overhead did not buzz. It was not just quiet, it was dead silent.

After taking note of the cafeteria when I passed it, I circled the entire complex. Then I began weaving around in between the buildings, occasionally catching a glimpse of the other residents.

It was a big space for only five people. When I returned to the cafeteria it smelled wonderful. There was a large table with comfortable looking chairs pulled up to it. The cooking area was separated by a wall from the rest of the cafeteria. Between the wall and the tables were glass cabinets with heat lamps in them. Everything was clean and neatly organized. I could hear the clash of pots and pans in the cooking area as well as occasional human voices talking to each other.

I took a seat and waited. The terror of all the earlier events combined with an hour of walking around had left me tired and hungry. During my walk I had time to consider my situation which still felt surreal.

Depending on who showed up for dinner I planned on asking questions if the opportunity presented itself. Regardless, I was starving and the smell of good food was almost too much.

At ten to, Held and Illych walked in together. They saw me and sat across from me at the table.

"Did you walk around and check the place out?" asked Illych.

"I did, big place for five guys."

"We use a lot more of it than you might think."

The doors to the kitchen opened and Mike and Tank began bringing out pans and trays of hot and cold food. There was a variety of meats and vegetable dishes. Everything looked fresh and inviting.

Serving was done buffet style with no apparent order of who went first. After filling a plate I found myself sitting in the middle of the four other men.

Tank was talking with Held, "A Ciorii in his home? That is nasty business. Did Mr. Lark let on why?"

Held replied, "Mr. Lark shared as much as he usually does. It was a short firefight and Mr. Lark used Truestone to hold it in place until we destroyed it."

Tank looked at me, "What did you do that brought that nightmare to your home?"

I replied, "I am not sure but Mr. Lark thinks it had to do with a Djinn visiting me a few days earlier."

Tank whistled, "A Djinn? Whatever you did to get that things attention, don't do it again. Nothing involving Djinn ends well."

I nodded, "Whatever it was I did, I have no plans to repeat it."

I took the opportunity to ask a question, "Ilych, why is this watch so large? I would be willing to accept something less... bulky."

Illych replied, "That is a watch and an alarm. One of the most dangerous weapons we can encounter is an EPS. That watch runs on light only. No batteries or electronics. Electronics have limited uses here at the Citadel."

"EPS effects are not instantaneous. They take about sixty seconds to get to the level where a person loses the ability to move. That watch will alarm the instant an EPS starts to take effect. It gives you time to react."

"Wouldn't I notice the effects when it starts?"

"I am not a scientist. All I can tell you is what Mr. Lark has explained in the past. Every sense in the human body uses electricity to communicate to the brain. An EPS affects how electricity works. Right about the time you realize what is going on its too late and you can't move."

Tank chimed in, "Kinda disturbing isn't it?" Held chuckled after Tank's comment. I still did not fully understand the purpose of the watch but it must be important if Illych requires it.

The rest of dinner was informative. Apparently off-color joke telling was part of the dinner ritual. They were a serious group that enjoyed their downtime and I was able to talk to everyone before dinner broke up. Illych told me I could walk around, go to bed, whatever, my choice. Nothing else was planned for the evening.

With a full belly and feeling exhausted, I retired to my room. I took my boots off and slept in my clothes. My last thoughts were that tomorrow could not be stranger than this long day had been.

I was woken the next morning by a knock on the door. It was Held collecting me for morning calisthenics.

He had clothing for me more appropriate to exercise in. I quickly dressed and joined the others. I survived thirty minutes of stretching and calisthenics before my huffing and puffing got me sent to the showers.

After breakfast Illych took me on an introductory tour of the Citadel, filling in the blanks I had missed on my self-guided tour the previous day.

After lunch we walked to the main doors. They opened right when we arrived and Mr. Lark walked in through them. Behind him was Mike operating a powered cart hauling a number of wooden packing boxes.

Mr. Lark walked towards me and spoke, "Thomas, you won't be able to return to your flat so I took the liberty of having your personal effects boxed up and brought here, mostly books or tangible personal property. I will open a study here for you to work in."

"Unfortunately your cell phone and computer cannot be brought here. I have also arranged for the sale of your flat. The proceeds will be put in an account at a bank of your choosing."

After the events of the previous day I had thought nothing more shocking could occur. I was wrong. The sale of my flat, my home, without my involvement felt like something cold stabbing me in the chest. And how could someone else legally sell your home without your permission?

My emotions must have been visible because Mr. Lark spoke again, "With enough money anything is possible Thomas. Accept the situation and appreciate I have made an effort to protect your interests."

It was true, in the last week Mr. Lark had saved me from the gunmen at the museum, the predations of a monster and had refrained from killing me. Perhaps it was best to look at it as a glass half-full situation.

Life is not fair but this was a lot of unfairness in a short period of time.

He spoke again, "Thomas, I have something for you to work on. I am going to give you another day to get situated and then I will send instructions." Without so much as a goodbye, Mr. Lark turned to leave the Citadel, and walked alone out the doors.

Chapter 8

After Mr. Lark left, Illych directed my things to be put in one of the buildings in the Citadel. This building was to be the 'library' per Mr. Lark's instructions. The next day, shelves, desks, chairs, and other things needed to setup the library arrived. From the way everything showed up and the level of organization, it was obvious Mr. Lark ran a tight ship. Everything was done quickly, competently and without complaint.

During lunch that day I noticed a white board in the cafeteria with the number '63' written on it. I asked Illych what it was and he explained the white board displayed how many days since their last break. I had arrived at day 61.

He asked me to wait after lunch and I could tell from his body language that something serious needed to be discussed. After the cafeteria was cleaned up and everyone was gone, he finally shared, "Thomas, you have been here long enough, it is time for you to see the Doctor."

I thought I had met everyone at the Citadel, "There is a doctor here?"

Illych grimaced a bit, "We have a doctor here. You have not met it because it is not human."

I felt that all too familiar feeling of cold dread that I was beginning to associate with everything Karl Lark. What nightmare was I about to be subjected to now?

Illych continued, "There is one of the Lesser Created within the bounds of the Citadel. It is in the infirmary, which was not part of our tour the other day. It is kept locked up, the 'Doctor' is not allowed out."

I decided to push back a little, "I feel fine, why should I see this doctor?"

"This is not about illness or even having a physical taken. You are the only person here who has not had a Crown installed yet. Your thoughts and emotions are being broadcast and the Created can detect those better than hearing or seeing you. The Doctor is going to install a weave of something like fine copper wires in your scalp to prevent your broadcasting." Illych was not comfortable with the subject, I could tell.

"Maybe I am being overly melodramatic but some creature is going to cut my head open and install something?" it came out angrier than I would have liked.

"The procedure is painless and there is no scarring or even recovery for that matter. The Doctor is a Lesser Created, similar to what you would perceive as a Goblin from mythology. Mr. Lark has domesticated it to provide medical care. The thing can fix gunshot wounds, amputations, anything. The best part is you're unconscious during the procedure and everything is healed when you are done. No stiches or bandages and better yet, no recovery time."

"Regardless, the procedure is not optional. It is for your safety as well as everyone around you. We will go to the infirmary now." Illych spoke these last sentences with absolute conviction. He expected to be obeyed.

I resigned myself to what was probably going to be another horrifying experience and we walked together in silence to one of the small buildings I had seen in my walks around the Citadel. Illych removed a key from his pocket and unlocked the door. Inside was a small, for the want of a better description, waiting room. A gurney and some chairs were along the walls. Opposite the entry door was another door. Next to that door at eye level was a shelf. On top of the shelf were a number of colored stones small enough to fit in the palm of your hand.

Once inside the waiting room Illych explained, "This is how it works. The Doctor performs operations based on the stone chosen. A person who needs a crown installed takes the blue stone. A wounded person takes the red stone, etc. Then you lay down on the gurney. Once you are laying down in the gurney with one of the stones in your hand you will instantly fall asleep. The Doctor comes out and wheels you into the next room. When the Doctor is done he wheels you back out."

Illych paused and then continued, "Never walk into the other room. It is not safe. The Doctor only works a certain way. Now pick up the blue stone and lay down on the gurney".

I shrugged and grabbed the blue stone from the shelf. It was cool to the touch. I then shuffled over to the gurney and lay down closing my eyes and waited.

Perhaps ten seconds had passed and I opened my eyes wondering when I would fall asleep or if this would be painful.

Illych was still standing by the entry door but for some reason he had started smiling. "That was not so bad was it?"

I did not see what was so funny, "When does it start?"

Illych actually chuckled, "It's over. The Doctor came out to get you fifteen minutes ago. It just rolled you back out. You were unconscious the instant your head hit the pillow. I know it feels like it never even happened. It was like that for me my first time. It is convenient when you pile someone wounded and in pain on the gurney. Just put the red stone in their hand and they are out."

It was then I noticed the stone was gone from my hand. I got up from the gurney and started feeling around my head. Nothing felt different. There were no surgical openings. Nothing was tender to the touch. I would need to look at myself in the mirror but from what I could tell nothing had changed.

Illych commented, "The Doctor works fast and returns the patient in ready-for-duty condition. I do not know how Mr. Lark set this up but as long as you are still alive when you make it to that gurney you will be as good as new in no time".

We left the infirmary and Illych told me nothing else was planned for the rest of the day. Left to my own devices I decided to organize the library and unpack the rest of my things. It was a comfort to be around something familiar, something that was mine. This kept me busy for the rest of the day.

On day 64, just after calisthenics, I saw Held and Tank gear up and head out to the Compass. They returned with the cart stacked with wooden crates.

Everything on the cart was delivered to the library. The shipment came with instructions and an envelope with my name on it. The expectation was for me to organize and catalog the contents of the boxes with the understanding there was more to come.

After everything was unpacked and organized. I opened the envelope with my name on it. Inside were handwritten instructions from Mr. Lark

Thomas,

Please look at these documents. I acquired them in a bulk purchase of old papers, documents and books. Most of it was garbage but these drawings have a mark on them that is rare and not commonly known. The drawings came from the collection of a French diplomat posted to Romania in the early 1900's. His name is written in the corner of each of the drawings.

Apparently Romania was not exciting from a diplomatic view and he became involved in the study of Transylvania looking for evidence of the supernatural. These drawings were in his Romanian collection with no explanation as to what they are or where they came from. Please review them and come back to me with ideas. I am currently looking into setting you up in an office in the real world. I do not believe you will be efficient in your endeavors without access to communications faster than letters in the mail. Feel free

*to consult with Illych. He has seen more than the rest
and might be able to help.*

 Karl Lark

 I now had a project to work on and it started with
several oddly shaped parchment drawings along with
two modern books. The books were about the myths and
mysteries of a haunted forest in Romania.

 I had never heard of Hoia-Baciu forest. Apparently
Hoia forest, as it was commonly called, was claimed to
be the 'most haunted forest in the world'. I was more
likely to believe such claims were rooted in an attempt to
increase tourism rather than reality. However,
considering my recent experiences, anything was
possible. Since Mr. Lark had sent me this stuff, there
may be something to it.

 I spent the rest of the day well into the night, and all
the next day studying the books and drawings. I began
to copy the drawings as a way of better familiarizing
myself with them. As I have done many times in the
past, I immersed myself in the study. Hours and then
days slipped away and I felt some insight beginning to
form.

 My investigations finally bore fruit and now I had
something to report. I gathered my thoughts about my
conclusions and went searching for Illych. "They are
maps! What Mr. Lark sent me, I believe they are maps of
Hoia forest!" I was so excited I just blurted it out when I
found Illych. He had been walking through the Citadel,
obviously concentrating on some task. My sudden
outburst caused him to stop and look at me.

 "Thomas, Mr. Lark did not clue me in on what was
delivered to you. So I have no idea what you are talking
about".

I was surprised. "I thought you were in charge here and Mr. Lark would have told you what I am doing."

Illych looked annoyed, "No, that is not how it works. I believe Mr. Lark considers me the most senior person here. That level of experience means he comes to me with things more than the others but he has never formally put me in charge. As to your role here, all I have been told is to reasonably support you."

I took that in. "Understood. There was a letter from Mr. Lark asking me to review some old drawings and come back to him with comments. That is what I have been working on in the library. The letter directs me to feel free to ask you questions. How do I contact Mr. Lark?"

Illych looked interested, "I can do that. I have a way to contact Mr. Lark from here. What did you find?"

I took a moment to calm myself. I was too excited about what I found and realized others may not find this discovery as stimulating. "I was copying the drawings in order to better understand them. I then realized that three of the drawings had similar markings in certain locations. If I matched up those markings and redrew what was inside them, combining all three in one drawing, they appear to form a map of Hoia forest in Romania.

There are places marked out in the compiled map. I matched what I drew to a map in one of the modern history books of Hoia forest. Some things have changed but I am fairly sure it is a valid map."

Illych replied, "Getting a message to Mr. Lark is easy enough. Just so you understand we are here at his leisure. He may respond or he may not."

I shrugged. There was plenty for me to study in the library. It was just an old map with markings on it and none of my research indicated what the points on the map were. It was probably not a priority right now anyway.

Chapter 9

A reply from Mr. Lark was not long in coming. Later that afternoon a team went to the Compass and they came back with letters for both Illych and me.

The letter to me was short:

Thomas,

Excellent work, I suspected those drawings might have additional meaning. I observed them with the Oculus and I could tell they had been touched by something.

I have directed Illych to form a two man team to accompany you to Hoia forest. Visit each of the locations that the map indicates as unique. The team will have an Oculus and its operator will let you know what he finds with it. Illych is to instruct the team if there are any potential problems to return immediately. Do not engage any locals or leave anything behind. Write up a report upon your return and give it to Illych to send to me.

Karl Lark

I was surprised. Mr. Lark was sending me to the places on the map. I would actually be going to a strange forest in Romania. During my studies it never occurred to me that Mr. Lark would send me to check out something in the field. What if there were Ciorii or something like Ciorii in that forest?

This line of thinking caused me to experience the beginnings of a panic attack. I like books and loved to read about strange places but I had never pictured myself as an explorer. Right about the time I was starting to hyperventilate there was a knock at the library door. Unable to stand I squeaked out, "Come in".

Illych poked his head in the door. "Everything ok?"

"Feeling a little tense about going to Romania is all. Give me a few moments," I was barely able to get those words out.

Illych waited patiently for a few minutes watching me visibly decompress. Then he spoke, "Mr. Lark sent me a letter also. It gives instructions to put together a two man team to accompany you to this forest in Romania. Observe and return only."

"I am sending Held and Mike with you. It is too late today and Romania is seven hours ahead of us in time so plan on going late tomorrow. This will give you plenty of time to prepare for a walk in the woods."

I nodded and replied, "We start getting ready after the morning exercise?" If there was one thing I had learned in the last few days these ex-military guys loved to exercise.

Illych smiled, "No workout tomorrow for you, Held, or Mike. You will be getting plenty of exercise on your hike in the woods."

Illych left me alone again in the library. The rest of the evening was uneventful but I did not sleep well that night, waking up several times feeling anxious about the next day's trip.

In the morning I shuffled my way to the cafeteria for breakfast. Americans are not partial to tea and there was none to be had at the Citadel. It was coffee or nothing. The upside is the coffee is fantastic and available in the cafeteria anytime of the day. I poured myself the first of, what I am sure would be several, to get my day started.

Held and Tank were in the cafeteria when I came in. I took my coffee and sat by them. The residents of the Citadel were a relatively friendly group that enjoyed socializing during meals. This morning was no different.

Tank's extroverted behavior was almost too much for my comfort level. I did not have the stories or experiences to draw from that powered the mealtime conversations. I gravitated towards sitting at the edge of the group when they all met together.

Today was not a typical day though, I was feeling inquisitive, "Held, how long have you been here with Karl Lark?" I asked.

Held did not answer right away. I wondered if the question was impertinent, "Bad question?"

Held answered, "No, not a bad question. Everyone here has a story that leads them to this place. None of them are pleasant stories. Tank here's was especially horrifying. I have been in the service of Mr. Lark for just over three years. Ilych has been here the longest at eight years. He remembers the early days, even before the Citadel."

Held continued, "I know your story Thomas so it would only be fair if you knew mine. It started when I was wounded in combat while I was a Green Beret. Head wound, major loss of vision in my left eye and permanent brain damage that left me basically angry all the time."

What Held was saying did not make sense. He was a mild mannered guy and he did not have any facial scars or any other problem such an injury would display. My disbelief must have shown up in my facial expression.

"I was given a medical discharge. I started getting into trouble right away. Fist fights, couldn't hold a job, my family disowned me. I would not take the meds for my condition and I refused to visit a VA hospital. I was homeless and drifted from one shelter to the next after being kicked out of each one in turn for fighting. I was in a bad way that was going to end with me in prison or dead. Then Karl Lark picked me up saying he had work for me." Held looked wistful as he spoke.

"Illych was already with Mr. Lark then and they drove me out of the city they found me in to an isolated state park. They had picked up fast food for me and at that point in my life a full belly did not happen often. That was enough to make me willing to go anywhere with them. Once we were out in the middle of nowhere, we stopped and got out of the car. Illych pulled out a pistol and Mr. Lark made his pitch." Thomas could tell Held was reliving the experience as he spoke and was not enjoying the telling of it.

"I almost told Mr. Lark to shove it but some little voice in my head I do not remember ever hearing before told me to take the job. This would be my last chance. So I drank the Kool-Aid and joined, it has been an adventure ever since." Held concluded.

"Wait, what about the head injury? You don't exhibit any symptoms of what you said was going on." I was quick to point out.

"Mr. Lark and Illych brought me here to the Citadel and took me directly to the infirmary and handed me the red stone. I thought no time had passed but when I awoke I realized I had full vision in my left eye and the red stone was gone from my hands. The doctor fixed me."

I had to ask, "Is Mr. Lark serious about his join or die speech? When he presented it to me I took him to be dead serious at the time. But since then I have had my doubts. Mr. Lark seems like a serious person but I don't get a 'murderer' vibe from him. Not that I have much experience with people being killed."

"Thomas, if you cross Karl Lark or try to renege on your agreement with him Mr. Lark will kill you on the spot. Have no doubts about it. I had been here a little over a year when a new guy was brought in. He made it to his third cycle and he wanted out. Apparently he missed life in the outside world."

"Mr. Lark told us to get ready for a mission. This guy then decides to spring his rebellion. He started in on Mr. Lark in front of everyone. He had had enough of this organization and demanded to be taken back to the real world. Sprinkle in some profanity and you will have a pretty good picture of the scene." Held took a breath and continued.

"Mr. Lark gets this Cheshire Cat grin on his face. Almost ear-to-ear I swear. He moved and I mean moved and fast, slapping him in the chest. It was like the guy was instantly drunk. He tried punching Mr. Lark with a clumsy, slow, haymaker, which was easily avoided."

"Mr. Lark then grabbed the guy by the back of his collar while still facing him and effortlessly dragged the guy to the gate doors. The doors opened as usual and Mr. Lark hauled the guy out past the guardians, maybe fifty feet down the road and then threw him ten feet more down the road. The old man that Mr. Lark appears to be actually threw a grown man almost ten feet."

"He turned and walked back into the Citadel leaving the new guy out on the road. I was looking through the gate at the lone figure on the road just as Mr. Lark walked past the guardians. Something came from the side of the road like a flash and disappeared out the other side of the road. The guy Karl Lark had tossed out was gone."

"When Mr. Lark came back in the Cheshire Cat grin was gone and we continued on the mission as planned. No mention was made of what had just happened. So believe me when I tell you, don't challenge Mr. Lark. You will not survive his response." Held finished his story.

I considered what I had just heard, "Thank you for that, it explains a lot."

Held hesitated for a moment, obviously considering something, and then said, "Thomas, one last thing, I have learned over the last three years that Mr. Lark is not what he looks like. Never underestimate him."

The normally talkative Tank was silent through all this and made no comment at the end of Held's story. My guess is asking him about how he was inducted was something to be discussed another time.

Held, Tank and I sat in silence, finishing our breakfast, when Mike came into the cafeteria, filled up a tray and sat next to us.

"So what do you think Held? Tonight a walk in the park or will it all go horribly wrong?" joked Mike.

"Rules of engagement are straight forward. Observe only. First sign of anything we are out of there," Held stated.

"You get the Oculus and the dongle?" Mike asked.

"Yes," replied Held.

"Dongle? What is a dongle?" I asked.

"When we get to the Compass there will be a dongle waiting. It will be a small brass baton maybe six inches long. You stand in the middle of the Compass and unscrew the two parts from each other and flip them around and screw the previously open ends back together. Everyone in the Compass stone circle, along with their possessions, will be translated to wherever the dongle was set for."

"To return to the Compass you reverse the dongle again. You can be anywhere, not just your arrival point, and it will still return you to the Compass. Mr. Lark sets them up and leaves them at the Compass with a note about where we will arrive."

"Illych explained some of this. This Ouiblet provides teleportation." I commented.

"The Ouiblet does provide something like teleportation. Don't ask me what the word Ouiblet means, I do not know. It allows the moving of people and things between two points anywhere. It has to be set up first. It is not like in science fiction where they lock onto your location and beam you up. Mr. Lark sets up the dongles to move a person or a group of people or the contents of a shipping container from one place to another."

"That is unbelievable. I experienced it coming here from London but I thought it was some sort of magic trick," was my incredulous reply.

Held chuckled, "Perhaps it is magic, I do not know. The batons can be a one-way only version or a returning version which lets you travel to a place and then when reversed back to the original position returns you to another location."

"The stone circles with the circular copper bars are setup to make the trip less physically agonizing. If the origination or destination is a stone circle setup by Mr. Lark, the trip is unpleasant and disorienting. Movement from an unprepared origination to an unprepared destination will leave you unable to function for at least a minute afterwards. This is why most movement starts or ends here at the Compass."

"Good to know. When do we leave?" I asked

"Now," Held said with Mike nodding his head in agreement.

Chapter 10

From when we left the cafeteria after breakfast until we returned for dinner the three of us were engaged in continuous preparations. Held directed me to get dressed into the black tactical uniform everyone else wore. A bulletproof chest carapace was fitted to me, with pockets, straps, and hooks for an assortment of equipment strategically located on it. Filling those locations were high illumination tactical LED flashlights, water bottles, flash bang and smoke grenades, a pair of tasers, and much more.

We went to the armory which included a long hall with ballistic targets at one end. Held selected a customized M1911 handgun chambered for 45ACP, six magazines and ammunition. I learned what I was carrying when Held subsequently instructed me in the basics of hand gun operation.

For the first time in my life, I fired a handgun and it was exhilarating. Pulling the trigger for the first time was frightening. After that first shot it became one of the most amazing experiences I have ever had. After getting past my initial inexperience Held coached me in proper safety and weapon handling. The goal was not to make me into a marksman in one day. It was more so I could reasonably defend myself in a pinch.

He told me to fire the weapon while keeping my eyes open. I thought he was mad to ask such a thing. Who could possibly not close their eyes when the cannon in their hands it going off?

But I was able to do it, by the end of the second magazine my eyes stayed open. My practice time saw me fire almost a hundred rounds. I learned that how the movies show someone with a handgun picking off long range targets one-handed while barely aiming is crap. By the third magazine the best I could do was hit a one-foot-square target twenty feet away.

It was not just keeping your eyes open and having a correct sight picture. It was holding the weapon correctly with both hands, not jerking the pistol to try to compensate for the recoil when it is fired. Developing a smooth, consistent trigger pull helps.

It was a lot to absorb in an hour. Held counseled me to keep the weapon in its holster unless absolutely necessary. Something about how I did not have the training to properly use it in a fire fight but it did not seem right to leave me defenseless.

The team met again afterwards. The plan was to translate in at approximately 0200 local time in Hoia forest. The four locations identified on the map made a parallelogram shape with each point between 500 meters and 2 kilometers apart. Giving an hour for each point, both walking and observation, would see the team translate out just after dawn.

Held and Mike had space age looking rifles I was told were called a KRISS Vector. They also each carried two of the customized M1911s, one on their hip and the other in a shoulder rig. Plenty of spare magazines for their weapons were in pouches on their thighs, belt and chest.

Held and Mike's hand's, face and necks were painted pitch black and they assisted me in achieving the same.

The final piece of gear was a padded helmet. I was told they are not bulletproof, just padded against hitting your head. Dangling on each side were ear inserts. The helmet contained eight microphones and amplified quiet sounds and diminished loud noises. They would prevent our hearing from being knocked out from gunfire. Very quiet sounds, like someone sneaking up on you, were amplified. Normally a team member went through special training to be able to interpret the sound distortions properly. Due to time constraints I was told I would undergo the training some other time, for now I was to 'wing it'.

We went to dinner in full gear, ate quickly, and headed out for the Compass. Illych accompanied us and he planned to remain at the Compass while we were gone.

Just before going out the Citadel doors onto the road to the Compass I could see the change in my team mates. The small talk was gone and they became alert, hypervigilant.

While walking to the Citadel I noticed Held and Mike had a rectangular box, slightly larger than a pack of cigarettes, in a pouch on their chests that I did not have. Curiosity got the best of me and I asked, while pointing, "What is in those pouches?" Held answered, "This is a ComDat. We will be in continuous audio communication with Illych throughout the mission."

I nodded thinking that was a cool piece of gear.

Upon arriving at the stone circle Illych retrieved the dongle for the mission from one of the vaults.

"Mr. Lark has already surveilled the arrival point. His note says it is remote and has overhead tree cover. Highly unlikely anything will be nearby at 0200," Illych said while handing Held the dongle.

I joined Held and Mike in the center of the stone circle. Illych stepped outside and said, "Don't break the new guy. Mr. Lark would be disappointed."

Held nodded and unscrewed the middle of the dongle. He then flipped the outside ends to the inside and screwed them back together. He then quickly slipped it into a pocket.

The dimness of the Compass went completely black and then I felt a warm summer breeze. We had appeared in the middle of a group of trees. It was nighttime.

A second after we arrived I felt my stomach churn, lasting for perhaps a minute. While this was happening I did not pay much attention to anything around me.

Mike took note of my discomfort, "I feel it too. You never get used to it. You do get better at anticipating and handling it though."

After we recovered, I looked around and realized that in addition to the darkness from the tree cover, it was very quiet. There was the occasional insect noise but the silence was noticeable.

Held looked like he was meditating with his eyes closed. I looked at Mike and then back to Held.

"He is using the Oculus," Mike said.

After a minute Held's eyes opened. "There are no people anywhere in the forest and no electronic observation devices. However I picked up a significant amount of background hash."

Once again, even in the dark, Mike could see the question on my' face. "Hash is like background noise or static. It means at least one of the Created has been here recently. It may have just popped its head out and left or it could be walking around."

After a short pause Held continued, "I did not see anything walking around but there has definitely been some activity in this forest."

The fact that he had not seen anything did nothing to reduce my anxiety. It just meant that whenever whatever it is decides to come after us it will be more of a surprise was my thinking.

"Let's get our bearings. That way is north," Held said, pointing one way through the trees.

The map I took from one of the books showed a boulder field in the forest was in that direction.

"The Oculus is telling me it is over there. Let's go there first and confirm. Then we can go to the first point on the map," Held said and started walking in a direction not far from where north had been indicated.

As we started walking I saw Mike and Held insert the ear pieces from their microphone helmets. I did the same. The effect was startling. I could hear the sound of our boots on the soft ground almost as loud as if we were on gravel. The sound of my colleagues breathing was noticeable. They were right, sneaking up on someone wearing one of these helmets would be impossible.

The ground was uneven with tree roots and stones to trip on if you were not careful. Held and Mike would occasionally slow down and let me catch up. They were careful to never let me get more than twenty feet behind them.

Between the darkness and the silence, the forest gave off a feeling of us not being welcome. I began to feel my anxiety start to grow.

"Do you feel it?" Held whispered to Mike and me, "The anxiety." Mike nodded as did I. I whispered back, "I thought it was just me."

"Something has a 'go away' sign out," Mike whispered back. "The crown the Doctor installed is keeping most of it out. We feel it faintly. An unprotected person would most likely run away."

Perhaps a minute later we reached the edge of the boulder field. "Stop here, we are not going into that field." Held whispered urgently.

"What do you see?" asked Mike.

"Hard to say but it looks like a flip trap," Held replied. "It also looks like the source of the anxiety effects."

"That is an odd combination, stay out or I will keep you?" Mike said while scanning his eyes over the boulder field.

"More like 'stay out' and if you do not listen and come in anyway, you won't leave after seeing what's there," Held commented.

Mike nodded his head to Held's comment.

"Now that we have our bearings let's move to the closest objective. Should be approximately 500 meters that way," Held said while pointing away from the boulder field.

The walking was easier in this new direction. Plus the feeling of anxiety was going down the further from the boulder field we went. After maybe five minutes of walking, the feeling was completely gone.

The first point on the map was a large stone sphere half buried in a hill. Parts had been chipped off and a large crack was visible. Held reported the Oculus showed nothing of interest. My team mates agreed to allow me to turn on an LED torch. I used the light to look closely at the broken sphere. I found nothing that could not be explained by time and erosion.

"I do not see anything of interest here. Perhaps we should move to the next point on the map?" I said to Held.

Held and Mike had taken up positions twenty feet away from the sphere on opposite sides. They kept their eyes away from the light in my hands so as not to disturb their night vision. Held shrugged his shoulders at my comment and said, "Let's move on to the next feature on the map then."

With that said the three of us headed into a more dense and overgrown part of the forest. The trees were close together and strangely shaped. Some of them had ninety degree angles in their trunks that were most unnatural to view. They were not tall at all, no more than twenty to thirty feet to their tops. The closeness of the overhead leaf canopy and the trees with respect to each other, combined with the dark and almost complete silence was disturbing.

I could tell Held and Mike had noticed the strangeness of this part of Hoia forest. On the walk to the field of boulders and the first map point they had held their KRISS carbines with one hand and pointed down, partially supported by their gear harness. Since entering this dense part of the forest both men had taken their carbines into both hands. They were walking slower than before and had spaced themselves away from each other. Held was in front and Mike had the rear of our three man column.

Fortunately the ground under the trees was fairly even and there was almost no undergrowth to contend with. Despite the easy going, it took almost an hour to travel less than a kilometer. Held stopped us at regular intervals and concentrated on the Oculus, significantly slowing our progress.

We found the second point on the map easily enough. It was a collection of oddly shaped stones. Some parts of the stones appeared whole but weather-worn while others looked like they had been broken before being exposed to the elements. Held and Mike again relented to my using the torch.

Taking a notebook out of my pack I started taking notes and making sketches. Unlike the stone sphere, there was more to be observed at this collection of stones. After making a rough sketch of their positions, shapes, and sizes I became aware there was a central stone and the other stones radiated outward from it.

It looked like there had been a single, somewhat square shaped stone structure that had fallen apart or was blown apart in all directions. There was no way to figure out the original structure in the dark with a hand torch. I was fairly sure it was originally man-made due to the flat surfaces exhibited on some of the stones.

Regardless, I had reached the limit of what could be recorded under the circumstances and in less than an hour after arriving we started walking to the next nearest point of interest on the map.

The path to our next destination stayed in the same dense area of the forest and the next point was less than a kilometer away. The feature we were seeking turned out to be a clearing or meadow. I had read about this clearing in the modern books provided by Mr. Lark describing Hoia Forest. It was a curious circular meadow in the middle of the forest. Trees did not grow there, just grass. Over the years locals had claimed to see strange things happen in the meadow such as balls of light and difficult to explain phenomena. Disappearances were also associated with the meadow which probably explains how this forest is completely devoid of any human presence on a warm summer night despite being close to a population center.

As we neared the edge of the clearing Held lifted his left hand with a closed fist. I knew this meant to stop and I did so. Mike paused for a moment and then when Held waved his fingers he hustled the twenty feet to catch up.

"What do you see," asked Mike.

"There has been hash on the Oculus since we arrived and I think the source is up ahead. I did not see anything ahead until the last fifty feet. Something is hiding in the clearing and blocking the Oculus from seeing it. Now that we are closer I can tell something is moving in the clearing," Held's voice was calm and low as he explained the situation.

"Our instructions are clear. Let's retreat about a hundred meters and use the dongle to bug out to the Compass," Mike stated.

"Agreed," Held nodded as he said the word.

Both men kept their carbines pointed towards the clearing and began slowly backing away. I followed their lead and began walking away also.

We had not retreated four steps when there was a rustling sound coming from the edge of the clearing nearest us. In the silent night air the soft sound was amplified by our earpieces into a crashing noise that could not be missed. Held and Mike froze in place. I did not need to consciously stop moving having frozen from fear at the sound of the rustling. I could not imagine what could cause two experienced, armed soldiers to be so cautious.

Held and Mike focused on the origin of the sound and pointed their carbines in that direction. They had been standing next to each other and now began to very slowly put some space between themselves by moving sideways with respect to the direction of the clearing.

The rustling stopped for a few seconds and then started again. It was definitely getting closer. The dark inside the forest edge prevented us from being able to see what it was. I thought to myself *we are probably getting tense over some forest rodent.*

Held was concentrating on the Oculus while he and Mike continued to space themselves out and move away from the clearing.

Held barked out, "Faerie! Only thirty feet away! It has seen us!" Both men began walking backward quickly while keeping between me and whatever a Faerie is.

Cutting through the still night air came a high keening cry from very close by. I could not see what it was but the sound it made was chilling.

Mike saw it first and opened fire. Scarcely had the first shot been fired by Mike and then Held also opened fire. I saw it last. A three foot tall gangly creature ran straight at Held with supernatural quickness. The men got off two or three shots before the Faerie tackled Held. Whatever the thing was made of, it was strong and heavy, because Held was knocked right off his feet.

Mike was forced to stop shooting due to the closeness of the thing to Held. He let his KRISS dangle from his harness and drew a handgun from a holster on his belt.

In seconds the Faerie had beaten Held unconscious, grabbed him by his left foot and started dragging him away almost as fast as it had attacked. Mike tried to keep up while carefully taking shots. The Faerie and Held disappeared out of sight into the clearing.

Mike and I found ourselves standing a few feet into the clearing. Mike paused and swapped a fresh magazine into his pistol and holstered it and took up his KRISS again saying, "Let's go get Held!"

I was speechless, everything was happening so fast. To my astonishment I found my handgun in my right hand. When did I draw that? I looked at it closely realizing the safety was still on and decided it won't work like that and gave the little lever a flick.

Mike had reloaded his carbine and headed into the clearing following the trail of bent grass left by the Faerie while dragging Held. Mike was almost jogging in pursuit while keeping his carbine pointed straight ahead.

A small glowing sphere, about a foot in diameter appeared ahead. "It is opening a portal," Mike barked. The light from the glowing sphere lit up the clearing, showing Mike and I we were a scant twenty feet from the Faerie. The Faerie was facing the sphere and was making sounds and waving its spindly arms.

Mike opened fire. I was concerned about Mike shooting at the short creature so close to Held lying flat on the ground nearby. Mike's shots were fast but not full automatic. The Faerie's body jerked from the impacts interrupting whatever it was doing.

When Mike was forced to reload, the Faerie had enough time to complete the opening of the portal. It grabbed Held's ankle again and sprinted towards the sphere and the Faerie and Held just disappeared. Mike pulled something from his belt and tossed it to me. It was a small white pebble or stone. "We are following it through the portal. When we get within ten feet of the Faerie throw that at it. It's Truestone and will paralyze it for at least fifteen seconds. Hopefully I can then put it down more permanently." Mike turned to the glowing sphere and started running towards it. I found myself following Mike while gripping the stone tightly.

It looked like Mike was going to run into the sphere when he just disappeared. I was less than two full strides behind him. My last thought before everything changed was *Is this going to hurt?*

I had not closed my eyes while walking through the portal and saw the shift from a glowing sphere in a meadow to a dimly lit cave. The portal delivered us to an open space with a relatively flat floor extending fifty feet in every direction.

The Faerie was mere strides ahead of us still dragging the unconscious Held by his ankle. It turned and took note of our following it. The things mouth opened, emitting a high keening cry that echoed through the cave chamber.

Mike had switched his KRISS to full auto and emptied the weapon into the Faerie at close range. The noise would have been deafening in the enclosed space if it were not for the ear pieces. Mike must have hit more than he missed because the Faerie was moving away slowly, stumbling as it went. I sprinted towards the creature. When I thought I was close enough I threw the white stone at it.

Everything was happening so fast and I could not believe I was moving much less actively participating.

My lifelong avoidance of all things sport related was on display for all to see in my throwing of the Truestone. The stone was going to miss the Faerie to its left by several feet.

In the end it did not matter, the stone corrected its trajectory and accelerated across the short distance to the Faerie. It was struck mid-chest and flopped onto the floor convulsing in a fashion eerily similar to the Ciorii back at my apartment.

Mike had reloaded while this was happening and unloaded another twenty-five rounds at point blank range on full auto. Then he pulled a white spike from a sheath mounted on his chest armor and promptly stabbed the monster where the light from the Truestone was gleaming. The Faerie shrieked and went limp.

Mike reloaded again and attached a high-powered LED torch to the carbine and started sweeping it around the cavern. While doing this he walked back to Held's motionless form on the floor.

After two full rotations sweeping the cavern walls and ceiling he switched the torch off and knelt next to Held. He pulled a low power penlight out and pulled up Held's left eyelid and flashed it with the light. Then he put his ear by Held's mouth.

Mike put his fingers to Held's neck and after a moment spoke, "He is alive."

Mike also pulled out the dongle from Held's pocket and put it in his own pocket. He then began lightly slapping Held's face, "Wake up, can you hear me?" He said rather loudly. After several slaps and shaking of Held's chest his eyes opened and he started looking around.

Mike smiled, "Still with us?"

Held groaned. "I have a splitting headache," He tried to sit up and stopped while making a very un-manly whimper noise. He then laid back down saying, "Cracked or broken ribs, give me a minute and I should be able to stand up."

Mike looked at me. "The portal is closed by now but the dongle will take us back to the Compass anyway. Since nothing is trying to kill us, my guess is there was only the one Faerie living here. Let's take a couple of minutes to look around and then we are out of here."

I pulled out my torch and started looking around. I had gotten a good look while Mike was checking around earlier. The floor, walls, and ceiling were all worn, rough grey stone. The cavern was maybe a hundred feet across with a rounded ceiling at least fifty feet high. I did not see anything moving. Curiously there were what looked like snow drifts lying about the cavern in no apparent pattern. But the air temperature was warm, not much different than what it was back in the forest, so snow should not be here. Curious I walked up to the closest snow drift.

It was not snow, they were bones artfully stacked and woven into piles reminiscent of snow drifts or foam covered ocean waves. Looking closely I saw most of the bones appeared to be animal, being too small to be human. But there were human skulls woven into the bone sculpture. The ghoulish artwork had been skillfully done regardless.

I looked about the cavern and saw an even dozen such bone works. That was a lot of dead animals and dead people.

I called out to Mike. "These are piles of bones, animal and human. The bones have been woven together like artwork. It took a lot of victims and a lot of time to do this."

Mike was helping Held to his feet and replied "These things have nothing but time. Look around some more. Sometimes these things collect artifacts."

I unsheathed a large knife from my belt and started poking through the first bone drift. I found bits of cloth from what looked like clothing woven into the drift. Finally I just gave the drift a kick to get at whatever was underneath it. The woven bones flew up and away like the hood of a car being flipped open.

Underneath was more clothing. Some of it appeared to be quite old. The only thing that did not appear to be worthless was a sword. It was an old broadsword. The blade was rusty and pitted but it still looked serviceable.

I had an idea and went to the next bone drift and kicked the woven top away just as before and found something similar. It contained clothing for the most part and a carved wooden walking stick. I walked quickly to each drift and found the top layer of woven bones could be easily removed to reveal a piled center containing different objects. In addition to the sword, I found two large wooden bowls overflowing with silver and gold coins with a few gold rings mixed in. In one of the piles was a large leather case I did not want to take the time to open here.

I piled the sword, the two wooden bowls and their contents and the leather case in the center of the cavern near the now smoking and sublimating body of the deceased Faerie. Mike looked at the haul and said, "That is enough, we need to get Held to the Doctor, let's boogie." Between the three of us we packed everything in our rucksacks. Mike then pulled the dongle from his pocket and with Held still leaning against him he unscrewed it, flipped the two parts, and screwed it back together. There was a delay of a second and then everything went black and we were back in the gloom and cold of the stone circle at the Compass.

I shivered in the sudden cold, toughing out my nausea. Mike and Held actually looked relieved. I kind of felt the same way. The stress of the last several hours began to bleed away and I found myself glad to be *home*? I guess it is one of those 'the Devil you know' things.

How things had changed in less than two weeks. The first time I arrived at the Compass I was disoriented and wanted to go home. Now I had just come back from a haunted forest in Romania where we were attacked by something out of a faerie tale horror story. And now I was glad to be back at this place.

I had a passing thought: can too much time in a pocket dimension cause mental illness?

I watched as Held shuffled over to one of the stone pillars that made up the perimeter of the circle and started leaning on it. Mike had disappeared into one of the surrounding vaults, reappearing a minute later with Illych. He inspected Held closely with an Oculus in his hand.

"He can travel. Looks like a severe concussion and a skull fracture. We need to get him to the Doctor. Mike, you are in front to set the pace. Thomas, you walk next to him. Everyone, weapons out. We don't want anything along the way thinking this is an opportunity just because we have wounded," Illych stated.

Held kept a good pace in spite of his injuries. We were back at the Citadel and inside the doors in no more than 30 minutes. I realized during the walk back that I felt no urges to look up or to the sides of the road. This crown thing that the Doctor put in my head was working.

Once the Citadel main doors closed behind us, Held sank to his knees and put his hands on the ground palms down. Illych and Mike each grabbed Held under an arm, lifting him up and carried him off towards the infirmary.

Standing alone in the open area near the doors I realized my pack was very heavy. Inside was the leather case from the Faerie cavern. Carrying the pack, I started off after the others on the way to the infirmary.

I made it to the infirmary door just as Illych put the red stone in one of Held's hands. Held went still and appeared to be sleeping. Mike and Illych stepped back towards the entry door as the inner door opened and a creature not more than four and a half feet tall walked into the infirmary waiting area. It was gangly with thin arms and legs. Its head was oblong with large pointy ears and large solid black eyes. The Goblin's mouth was very wide with jagged teeth peeking out from between its thin lips at odd angles. Its greenish skin contrasted with the faded red coveralls it wore. The cloth the coveralls were made from was crude and rough looking and the fit was poor. The overall effect was of a homeless child except for the green skin and scary looking head and eyes.

The 'Doctor' took no note of us while walking to the far side of the gurney and pushed it slowly into the open doorway leading inside. Illych and Mike did not make a sound and were clearly staying as far away from the Doctor as possible.

After the Doctor and Held were inside, and the door they went through appeared to close on its own, only then did I chose to speak. "That is the Doctor? It is almost as scary as the Ciorii I saw back at my flat," I croaked out.

"That is the Doctor. I don't know how Mr. Lark set this up but it has saved all of our lives at one point or another," Illych commented.

"How long will Held be in there?" I asked.

"Not long, maybe fifteen minutes," said Mike.

I saw the pile of gear Illych and Mike had stripped from Held before putting him on the gurney. Illych grabbed the pack and Mike picked up the KRISS and gear harness. "Let's get these back to the armory and get everything cleaned up," stated Illych.

I then found out that no matter how tired or hungry you are, the first thing you do upon returning from a mission was clean weapons, unload magazines, and get everything back in a ready state. I saw Illych put Held's Oculus in a rack with several more of the same devices.

After an hour of cleaning, inspecting, and putting everything away, the three of us slowly walked to the cafeteria. We had left the Compass at around seven P.M. and had returned just before one in the morning. After the walk back to the Citadel and the visit to the infirmary followed by cleanup, it was now three in the morning. I was very tired. The last couple of weeks of calisthenics had helped my physical endurance but functioning while sleep deprived had never been one of my skill sets.

In spite of their excellent physical condition and military experience, the lack of sleep could also be seen on Illych's and Mike's faces.

At the cafeteria we found Held waiting for us. He had brewed some of that excellent coffee I had come to appreciate. He had also brought out a plate of sandwiches. These were not cheap vending machine sandwiches. The bread smelled fresh and the sliced meat was excellent, as were the lettuce and tomatoes. We grabbed plates and mugs, filling them and then took our places at the table near Held to eat our sandwiches and sip our coffee.

No one said anything at first then Mike spoke, "You are looking pretty spry for a guy who recently almost had his head caved in."

Held replied, "I feel great, just hungry and a little tired. I woke up in the waiting room and figured you guys were busy putting everything away so I came here and started work on the really important stuff."

Held asked about the loot we had brought back. Illych explained everything was in the armory until Mr. Lark had time to look at it.

"That reminds me, I need to report in to Mr. Lark. There was no time at the Compass," Illych excused himself, stood up, took his coffee and sandwich and left.

I asked Held, "Is it always this exciting going on a mission?"

Held shook his head, "That is the thing. It is never like this. Faeries are as rare as chicken's teeth to begin with. Finding one out in the open like that never happens. Faeries are typically tied to geographical locations. They live in caverns like the one we saw. But the connection from the real world to their lair happens only once in a while. Once every seven years is common for some reason. Some connections are random but spaced out by years."

"The chances of stumbling into a Faerie circle while the Faerie is active are pretty small. Looking at the piles of bones I would say that Faerie gets out a lot more often than one day every seven years."

Mike interrupted, "What about the aggression level? And how did it know we were there? We all have crowns blocking our thoughts and emotions. We were all wearing solid black and we were not making noise. And it could not see us because we had not entered the clearing."

"Wait, there is a practical reason for everyone wearing all black? I thought it was a military thing. What does wearing black have to do with Faeries?" I interjected.

Held looked at me, "The Created have more senses than humans do. We use mostly sight and hearing. The Created can sense our thoughts and emotions and they can do it through solid walls. So they tend to rely on sensing those thoughts and emotions when looking for humans trespassing. Since black is really just the lack of light, it works well when combined with the crown. A Faerie is focused on looking for the thing the crown blocks, combined with not seeing reflected light and there is a good chance you can walk past one even when it is looking right at you."

Mike added to the discussion, "Faeries are tied to a geographical location and can't go far from their faerie hole. This leads to locals identifying a 'Faerie Circle' over generations of bad experiences. I would think that clearing was this Faerie's circle. But when Held was attacked we were not in it."

Held nodded, "No wonder the locals stay out of that forest. I thought it was odd that a forest with population centers so close did not have some teenagers out drinking on a summer night or a young couple sneaking out for a tryst in the woods. When I scanned with the Oculus there was nobody else there."

I asked, "Will Mr. Lark tell us more?"

Held shrugged, "Sometimes he does, sometimes not. We will see if he comes to visit over this."

Chapter 11

The day after I returned from Hoia forest was uneventful. Illych declined my request to look at the contents of the leather case until after Mr. Lark had a chance to scan them with the Oculus.

I had expected Mr. Lark to come through the main doors at any moment. Instead the day slowly dragged by with no Mr. Lark to be seen. At dinner I took note of the 'Day 70' on the white board in the cafeteria and turned in early. My being awake and moving for more than twenty-four hours was an unpleasant experience, definitely something I would try to avoid in the future.

Calisthenics the next day was more challenging than in the past. It was obvious Held was pushing me. Apparently he had concluded I would be going in the field more and needed to be in better shape. I now had a reason for the calisthenics. If I was going to participate in more things like the Hoia forest mission it would be a good idea to be able to run faster and further.

Afterwards, sweaty and physically drained, I stumbled into the showers. This was followed by walking to the cafeteria for breakfast. I checked with Illych and there was still no word from Mr. Lark. He then informed me the whole team was going for weapons practice today and I was included. I was to suit up and meet at the main doors at nine this morning.

Back at my room I put on the black tactical 'suit' that apparently was standard for working outdoors. I was not fond of the mono-chromatic effect but after learning of the practical value of the color choice I wasn't going to complain.

I made sure to be at the open space by the main doors promptly at 0900. All four of my fellow Citadel residents were present and all of them dressed in the same black tactical dress as I was. One of the electric carts for moving things back and forth to the Compass was loaded with black ballistic cases.

Everyone was armed and Illych handed me a customized M1911 in a holster to belt on. The typical loadout was a carapace armor vest with at least two handguns, magazines, grenades, a knife, a tactical flashlight, plus a KRISS hanging from your chest harness.

To the uninitiated the amount of firepower on display was impressive. The other part of the situation that struck me was how comfortable everyone was with their weapons and the amount of gear they were carrying with no one showing the heavy load was a challenge.

Illych pointed at Held and then pointed at me. Held nodded and waved me over to the cart. Alot of things get done in this group without any verbal discussion.

Held instructed me to draw my pistol from its holster a few times. He then adjusted its position on my belt.

I had been given some instruction and understood the basics of handling, firing, and reloading a pistol before Hoia forest and this pistol was the same model as the one I had fired before.

The bore of the weapon was impressive and the KRISS carbines the others carried fired the same round.

Held produced a second M1911, but the holster for this one was a shoulder rig for connecting to the harness just below my left armpit.

I had to ask, "Why two pistols? I can only shoot one at a time."

Held replied, "Sometimes there is not enough time to pull a spare magazine out and reload. At those times you drop the empty weapon and pull out the second pistol."

The other men were all inspecting each other's gear. Weapons were being loaded. Even the handguns were holstered with 'one in the pipe' and their hammers in the cocked position with safeties on.

Held showed me where to connect magazine pouches on my carapace and belt. There were a lot of them. I would be carrying ten loaded spare magazines plus two in the pistols. That plus a first aid kit, a scary looking serrated knife hanging upside down on my chest over my heart, and two high powered tactical flashlights completed my load out. It was even more gear than I had carried for the Hoia forest mission.

The other men had even more accessories than I was carrying including those sleeves for the white spikes and ComDat's on their chest. It was a lot of weight and it got heavier when Held strapped a camelback water bladder to my back.

I was supposed to walk distances like this?

Illych eventually looked over our way and said, "Held?"

Held replied, "Ready".

The doors opened and all five of us plus the cart headed for the Compass. The walk was uneventful but by the time we made it to the Compass I was sweating in spite of the cold. Everyone else looked to be almost enjoying themselves. There was no talking during the walk and I took this to indicate silence was required.

The cart was driven to the center of the stone circle and everyone surrounded it with practiced ease. I stayed near Held.

Illych pulled out a dongle and activated it. Everything went black and then we were standing on grass with a blue sky overhead. The temperature was a little warmer than the Compass but still colder than room temperature. I then waited out the nausea of the translation. They had been right, you do sort of get used to it after a while.

I looked around. We were in a small valley with tall mountains on all sides. The valley walls were almost sheer cliffs going up thousands of feet. There were no trees and short grass covered the ground from one side to the other. I took a breath. The air was thinner here. We must be at a significant elevation.

Having lived in continental Europe I was familiar with a mountain setting. This pocket valley was obviously isolated, with no way in or out that did not involve some extreme climbing.

I looked at Held with an obvious question on my face. He smiled and said, "This is our shooting range. This valley is in the middle of the North American Rocky Mountains and is completely isolated. There are no people within hundreds of miles. The only way in or out is by translating or by helicopter."

The men began unloading the cart and unpacking the boxes and cases. In addition to the weapons we carried in, there was an amazing collection of heavier weapons, accessories and ammunition. I was beginning to suspect this was going to be an all-day event.

Illych had a binder with sheets of paper in it. Held nodded in Illych's direction while looking at me, "We don't come out here to shoot for fun, although we will get to do some of that. Every man has to qualify with every weapon we brought. That includes you. Expect to have a sore shoulder by the end of the day."

Held had not been kidding. By the time we packed up to leave twelve hours later, I had fired handguns, a KRISS, a submachinegun, rifles, 40mm grenade launcher, a giant rifle that used a bipod and was called a fifty caliber Barrett, and others. My shoulder really hurt, but it was so much *fun*.

I had watched the fire team maneuvers where they practiced live fire maneuvers where one is shooting while the other reloads. Most of the drills they practiced were based on two-man teams.

Target practice at different places within the valley, while fun, also showed me I had a long way to go to be considered proficient. Illych tested each man on his reload times. Illych was also tested, with each team member getting a turn at being his evaluator.

Lunch and dinner came out of heated containers buried beneath the arsenal transported on the cart. Everything was packed back on the cart after dusk and we translated back to the Compass.

Then came the walk back to the Citadel. During the walk to the Compass this morning I had been fresh. Now I was exhausted, having been standing, shooting and walking for over twelve hours.

I kept my eyes focused straight ahead and just kept putting one foot in front of the other. Somehow I kept up with the group or perhaps they saw my exhaustion and slowed down for me.

Regardless, we made it back through the doors together.

Standing inside, on the far edge of the open space just inside the doors, was Mr. Lark. He was wearing all black and had his peculiar walking stick in his right hand. I know now the walking stick was just a prop so Mr. Lark could carry an Oculus around without drawing too much intention.

He was looking at Illych and it was obvious who he intended to talk to. Illych called out to the team, "Take everything to the Armory, clean up and re-inventory, then call it a night."

Illych walked over to Mr. Lark and they began speaking together in a low voice. I trudged along next to Held. Earlier today when we were getting ready to leave there had been talking and some kidding around. Now everyone was silent. We were tired and still had over an hour of work ahead of us.

Slowly but surely the cleanup and put away of all the equipment was completed. Everyone stayed in the armory until the last task was done. Then we all filed out and headed for the barracks. I went straight to my room, shut the door, undressed and went to sleep almost the second my head hit the pillow.

I was woken by someone knocking loudly on my door. I looked at what I had started calling my 'science fiction' watch. It had been less than an hour since I had gone to sleep. My head felt like it was full of fog and I yelled out, in a less than polite tone, "What?" I then realized how angry I had just sounded. Screw it, I am not apologizing. After all, who wakes someone up after they just fell asleep?

The door opened. It was Illych and he was smiling, "Remember Thomas, it's all about the pain and suffering."

After a pause of him standing there grinning at my misery he spoke again, "Mr. Lark sent me. You are to meet him at the library."

"Right now?" I said while still feeling unfocussed. Next I sat up and swung my legs to the floor, finding I needed a few seconds before I could stand up.

Illych was actually chuckling now while he said, "Right now." And then he turned and walked away leaving the door open. I stood up and began a slow, stumbling walk to the library.

I found Mr. Lark sitting in a chair waiting for me. The lights were on and the leather case found in the Faerie hole was lying on my desk. Mr. Lark had opened it and pulled out its contents. A large but thin leather-bound book was in Mr. Lark's hands. There was another smaller leather-bound book. Also on the desk were two square shaped leather purses.

Mr. Lark had opened the larger book and was paging through it. The leather pouches had been untied and left half-opened revealing numerous gold and silver coins. It was truly a king's ransom worth of treasure. The smaller book was off to one side of the desk.

Mr. Lark spoke first, "You look a little tired Thomas. Unfortunately my schedule will not allow this meeting to happen during more civilized hours."

I sat down and realized I was just staring off into space. When I spoke I suspect I sounded a little mechanical from exhaustion, "I understand. Please let me take notes while we talk. I do not know how much I will recall in the morning."

He nodded, "Everything has been checked by my Oculus. The gold and silver coins are real and very old. The smaller book appears to be a diary. The large book is what really interests me. I do not recognize the language it is written in. That is unusual in itself."

"I am tasking you with researching these documents. If more resources are needed please inform Illych. I will leave one each of the silver and gold coins for your reference. The rest I am taking for the operational fund. As before, when you reach any conclusions have Illych contact me."

Mr. Lark paused and I asked, "How soon do you want me to start?" hoping I could sleep first.

Mr. Lark smiled his friendly smile and said, "After a good night's sleep Thomas. Illych mentioned you seem to be adapting to life at the Citadel."

Yeah for me, I am guessing that comment passes as my two week employment review. It is still better than 'your work sucks so I will kill you now' was all I could think.

Mr. Lark paused, apparently thinking.

"I have completed translating the Sumerian writing from the incident at the museum. The book is an inventory of ancient artifacts and I recognized some of the items listed, others I did not. I believe Amal Halluk is after this cache. What I do not have yet is its location. We may be going on a fact-finding mission soon."

"Illych has made you aware of the upcoming thirty days of time off As you are new, you have not been able to figure out what to do during your vacation. With less than twenty days to go I am taking the liberty of setting something up for you. You will have a suite of rooms in an excellent hotel in San Francisco. I have arranged for identification papers, cash and a credit card. Feel free to explore and do whatever you want."

Another pause and he continued, "You will not contact anyone from your previous life. Stay out of trouble if possible and remember to relax and enjoy yourself."

I nodded. It was too much to process while mostly asleep.

He finished the meeting by pointing at the large book and saying, "Work on this. If you do not reach any conclusions before the break have Illych update me on the current status of the investigation. I have to leave now. You should go back to bed before you pass out."

Mr. Lark stood up and without even a good bye, walked out of the room. That was the last thing I remembered before waking up the next morning still in my chair in the library.

Chapter 12

The soreness from the previous day's activities was made all the worse by the awkward sleeping position.

I looked at my watch and realized I had missed calisthenics. Standing up, I stretched and headed for the cafeteria and found everyone already there. Apparently yesterday's activities keeping us up late over rode the need to exercise the next morning and I thanked God for this small mercy.

Sitting next to Mike I took in the conversation at the table. It was pretty animated this morning as Mr. Lark had brought mission instructions for the team. The entire team was going on a transport mission.

I had to ask, "Mike, what is a transport mission?"

"Part of what we do is to provide security for the transportation of whatever Mr. Lark has setup," he replied.

Held chimed in, "Mr. Lark sets up transport of people or property from one location to another. My guess is he works with some pretty shady brokers to set it up. The kind of high risk activity where borders, customs and law enforcement will try to prevent it."

I was wide awake now, "Karl Lark is a smuggler?" Somehow I found that disappointing.

"We do not transport stolen watches or cigarettes without a tax stamp on them. Only very high value items or people. And only for those who are willing to pay an extraordinary amount of money. I do not know what Mr. Lark charges, but keeping all of us on the payroll requires significant funding," Held stated.

"What about keeping translating secret?" I asked.

"With the Oculus we know when someone is looking and with some creative switching of containers it is possible to get things out of just about anywhere, without anyone being the wiser," Mike contributed.

Illych continued, "Most of the time we do not know what is in the containers. We are just there to keep everyone honest. For a couple of days it will be just you alone here at the Citadel. I understand Mr. Lark gave you the stuff from Hoia forest to study."

"You are leaving me here alone?" I was genuinely creeped out by the prospect.

"You will be fine. The Citadel is well protected. Do not go out the gates, stay inside. Before we depart there is some work to do. You will accompany Mike and Tank when they go harvest Truestone this morning. It should not take more than two hours. After we are done with breakfast the three of you can organize your efforts."

Breakfast ended shortly after that. Mike, Tank, and I walked to the armory to get ready.

"Where are we going?" The question was obvious.

Tank responded, "There is a Truestone generator in the wild spaces near the Citadel. We will take a walk, pick up the Truestone and get back here."

The gearing up at the armory was less extreme. We were well armed and equipped but not as much as when I went to Hoia forest. This was a kindness as I was still tired from carrying a heavy load around yesterday.

We left the armory and strode out through the gates of the Citadel. Tank set a quick pace and I had to jog a bit to catch up at times.

"Does this happen often? Harvesting Truestone."

Mike replied, "There are four Truestone generators we harvest regularly. This one is the closest. They all have different harvest times which we have on a schedule to visit. This one is eighteen months."

"So is it like a brick or block or something?" I was curious about what we were going to get. I was also concerned that as the junior member of the team I would end up carrying a heavy block of something back.

"You have seen Truestone used twice now. The white pebbles you can hold in your hand. We are going to pick one up."

That satisfied me for now. Our path was down the road back to the Compass, not cross-country. After arriving at the Compass we took one of the other roads leading away. It was constructed the same as the road to the Citadel and surrounded by the same rough grey stone terrain.

Mike and Tank had been alert on the walk from the Citadel to the Compass. Now, on this new road, they took are security to another level as they had now had their carbines in both hands. Just before setting out from the Compass Tank had handed me a piece of Truestone. Just in case.

After no more than a half-hour we reach a path leading away from the road. It was only six feet wide, laser straight, and as flat as the road we took to this place.

The path led to an oval shaped building several stories tall. The entrance was on a long side of the oval. High up on the building were huge irregular curved openings to its interior. The structure had an odd and unnatural look to it.

Without pause we took the path to the building which ended at a doorway with no door. The doorway was tall, ten feet or more. A giant would have been able to comfortably walk through.

Tank and Mike did not slow down as we approached the gaping doorway with nothing but blackness beyond.

"What if something is in there?" I was just saying what I thought was obvious.

Tank replied, "No worries, the Created in this place avoid a Truestone generator. Not sure why, but they do."

That said we entered the dark interior of the structure.

I was surprised. The entire interior of the building was open. You could not tell from the outside but it had no roof. The whole place was an oval shaped bowl. Looking at the black stone walls I could see faint dark green streaks luminescing from within. The streaks resembled veins or arteries from a living thing and they pulsed to some impossible-to-determine beat.

In the middle of the building was a plinth about waist high with a pencil thin metal rod extending up perhaps a foot. Lying on the surface of the plinth, very close to the rod, was a single white pebble not much larger than a marble.

Tank walked up and palmed the Truestone dropping it into a pouch on his belt.

"What was the original use of Truestone?" I figured this might be useful to know."

Mike answered, "Not sure. We use it to temporarily disable a Lesser Created. I am sure it had some other use but I have never seen one and Mr. Lark has not spoken about it."

Tank kept the conversation going, "Without the Truestone we would not be able to operate in these spaces the way we do. The Lesser Created make hard targets even with modern weapons. Their bodies are made from tougher stuff than ours and they are stronger and faster by far than any human. Even when compared to a complete stud like myself." This brought a chuckle from Mike.

"What was the spike Mr. Lark used to finish off the Ciorii back at my flat? How does that work?"

Mike answered my question. "That is the White Fang. Again none of know what it originally was used for. When a created is stabbed in the right place it disconnects their 'spirit' from their body. Their body then begins to evaporate."

"The Truestone temporarily paralyzes them and tells us where to penetrate their hide with the White Fang. We usually use gunfire to open them up so the Fang can do its work."

That explained a lot about what I had seen back in my flat.

With the Truestone in hand it was time to head back with Tank leading the way.

Mike spoke some more on the walk back to the Compass, "The problem with Truestone is it is rare and hard to find. And when you find a generator like we just saw, it only makes a single piece once in a great while."

I thought about what he had just said, "That entire building is the generator?"

Mike nodded, "As far as I know that whole building is there to make that one little pebble every year and a half. The Truestone grows on the end of that metal rod. Once it is fully developed it falls off the rod and lays next to it ready for someone to pick it up."

The three of us walked in silence for a bit making it to the Compass unmolested. We then took the road to the Citadel without pausing.

"Mike, if you do not mind me asking, how did you end up with Mr. Lark?"

"Honestly I do not know how," was Mike's reply.

He was apparently not going to follow up his statement with any more information so I had to ask, "Did you magically appear?"

Tank laughed at that and Mike shook his head, "No, I really do not know how I came to be here. I woke up in the infirmary here at the Citadel. My last memory prior to that was being an Army Ranger in Iraq. Apparently I was wounded during a mission and ended up in a coma for almost two years. That is how Mr. Lark found me, in a VA hospital, as a vegetable."

"He decided to sneak me away here and handed me off to the Doctor. I was fixed up in no time. The explosion destroyed the memories close to the time it happened so

I do not know the specifics. Mr. Lark has given me a second chance on life."

That left Tank's story and I looked over at him and started to open my mouth.

Tank growled at me, "None of your business pal." His pace picked up as he put a little distance between Mike and I.

I looked at Mike with the obvious question on my face.

"It is not you Thomas. Tank does not talk about what happened to him. I know what it was but it is not my place to tell you."

I could accept that and we continued in silence for the remaining distance to the Citadel.

Upon arriving the main doors opened to a scene of activity. Illych and Held had been busy while we were gone. The electric cart was in the entry area near the main doors piled high with gear for their next mission.

Tank took back the Truestone he had given me earlier and the one we had just collected. He then headed off to put them wherever they are stored leaving me with the others.

Illych and Held broke for lunch. Mike and I joined them followed shortly by Tank. Lunch was quick and immediately afterwards the others headed for the Compass with the cart.

I found myself alone and left to my own devices. The Citadel had always been a quiet place but after the team left it, it felt like a tomb.

Chapter 13

Over the next few days I took advantage of the lack of disturbances and settled into my research starting with the small book from the leather case. It turned out to be a man's personal journal, one Captain John Nesbit. Perhaps three-quarters of the books pages were written in. The writing was old English, but legible. Most of the journal contained Captain Nesbit's observations of life on his ship. Also discussed were his voyages, cargoes, and destination and some adult reminiscing about women he spent time with while in port.

The last ten or so pages contained items that were interesting to me. Dated in June of 1674, Captain Nesbit's ship had been in open-ocean with blue skies, navigating around the west side of Ireland, when the ship found itself quite suddenly in a fog bank.

They continued sailing into the fog while maintaining the same heading in hopes of exiting soon. After less than a half-hour, the ship came out of the fog and the crew spied an island straight ahead. Captain Nesbit was surprised by this as his maps showed no islands in this part of the ocean.

He took the initiative to sail closer to the island. The wind was light, but they were still able to navigate. The captain ordered the crew to check the depth and found it sufficient to continue sailing closer. The lookout spotted a great stone pier jutting out from the island. With care they were able to dock safely.

Captain Nesbit wrote in his journal that it was then he realized what he had done. Such adventurousness was uncharacteristic of him. He had not been chartered as an explorer and he had a full cargo to deliver. Yet he felt compelled to dock and neither the first officer nor anyone in the crew had objected. Something was drawing them to the island.

He debarked and walked onto the island alone, after ordering his first officer to wait for one day and if he had not returned by then, to depart and finish their assignment. He wrote of a collection of buildings clustered near the pier and a road heading straight into the island.

The road was made of individual stones as far across as a man was tall. The surface was worn and appeared to be quite old. Nothing in the area had been maintained in a great while.

The captain had been walking a little more than a mile along the stone road when his journey ended at the open gates of a castle. Everything showed signs of being abandoned and overgrown, including trees of great age soaring high overhead.

Walking inside he found the center of the castle contained a keep in good condition and obviously well-tended. Captain Nesbit walked up to the keep door and when he was perhaps twenty paces away the door opened and a manservant came out to greet him.

The captain then wrote of meeting a 'wizard' of great stature. They feasted together and the wizard asked to hire the captain to deliver something to a far-away place, a task for which he was paid a king's ransom in advance.

Captain Nesbit agreed and took a leather case with two leather bags. One contained gold coins and the other silver coins. Also inside was a large but thin leather bound book. The first page was a map showing where to deliver the book. I flipped open the large folio and found a map accurately showing all of Europe including the Ottoman Empire. The mark showing the destination on the map where Captain Nesbit was to deliver the book was not far from the Caspian Sea, in modern era Russian Federation territory.

The journal then recorded the captain's return to his ship, the subsequent delivery of the cargo, followed by the captain resigning his commission. Captain Nesbit made notes of the places where he stopped on his journey across Europe. The last entry was his explanation of a detour through a forest in Romania to avoid trouble on the road he originally planned to follow.

I considered what I had just read. This book was supposed to be delivered back in the late 1600's. I pulled a book from my private collection that described oceanic myths and read the section on *phantom islands*. Fortunately my personal library included a few texts on ancient myths and legends. The search would have been quicker with access to the internet. In the end, I found a list of phantom islands with a short description for each.

To the west of Ireland was supposedly an island called Hy-Brasil, it had even showed up on maps of the area for hundreds of years. Modern satellite imaging had proven it did not exist and Hy-Brasil had faded into legend. It sounded like Captain Nesbit would dispute that legend as true.

I felt I had something to report to Mr. Lark but no way to report it. Notifying anyone would have to wait until Illych's return to the Citadel. I spent the next few days trying to figure out the pages of hand written text in the larger book. The quality of the writing was excellent but the language was completely unknown to me. Again I found myself wishing for a computer with an internet connection.

A few solitary days later I was sitting in the cafeteria enjoying lunch when the team returned. I found myself counting the men coming through the door until I reached four. No one looked worse for their time away and apparently no visits to the Doctor had been needed.

Everyone coming in went to get food and then sat down around me. I found myself sitting between Mike and Held both of whom were willing to share the mission's details.

A wealthy Chinese family had been able to stash a significant amount of money in Canada and had been planning to secretly emigrate when the Chinese government found out. The extended family of some thirty members had their passports confiscated and travel bans put on them. They were watched at all times and could not leave the city where they all resided.

Through backdoor channels they had been put in contact with a broker who arranges for travel under even the most difficult situations. The real challenge was the whole family had to get out, all thirty members. Anyone left behind would be jailed as punishment for those that did escape.

The team rented an empty industrial building in the city the family lived in. The whole extended family was brought there in one's or two's. Using an Oculus to locate the government minders, they were then distracted or misdirected, preventing any interference in getting the family assembled in one place.

Arrangements had been made to anesthetize the whole family and put each one in a box. Mike said the boxes were essentially coffins. After everyone was unconscious and loaded up in a shipping container, the Ouiblet then translated the container away.

The family was kept under for twelve hours. The team had been busy monitoring the health of thirty unconscious people. It was estimated that a truck drive in China to the nearest airport plus a flight to a small, southeast Asian island near Guam, with extra time for incidentals, would take twelve hours. So the family had to stay under to make the situation believable.

In reality the cargo container and the team had been translated straight to the island and they just waited to wake everyone up. When the family members were awoken, they were shown to rooms with showers, clean clothes and prepared meals.

Afterwards, a chartered commercial jet was waiting to take them to Canada. A Canadian attorney who specialized in high-net worth immigration was also on the plane. Everything was ready to get them to Vancouver Canada in style.

After the commercial plane and the newly liberated family left, the team reloaded everything, including themselves, in the cargo container and translated away. Mike said it was too bad they had to leave so soon. The weather was perfect and it looked like the island had good beaches.

"Wow, I would never have thought Mr. Lark would be involved in something like that," I said.

"It was time consuming but otherwise uneventful. If everything is planned correctly and everyone stays on task it just goes by the numbers," observed Mike.

"And if it does not go by the numbers?"

"The team is made up of combat arms senior NCO's who have all seen more than one firefight and we carry a ton of firepower. If things go sideways, the other side is going to have their day ruined right quick," Tank stated.

After lunch I met up with Illych and got a message off to Mr. Lark. I had asked why the team was gone for a better part of a week if the mission only took less than a day. Illych had just shook his head while telling me organizing and coordinating such an effort takes days to pull off. Ilych then left with the team to cleanup and put everything away.

Just when I thought I had an idea of what was going on there is another twist...

Chapter 14

I am an introvert. I had always known this about myself. My work is solitary in nature. However, when the team had been gone on their mission I realized that even when living in London I had occasionally gone out into the world to be around people.

I found myself talking to my co-inhabitants of the Citadel more often than I would have expected. They were very different people than I had been around in the past and we had little in common. Mealtimes gave me the opportunity to listen to the stories that were often told when the team congregated together.

On the second day after the teams return from the China mission I was doing just that, sitting in the cafeteria at lunch, listening to another adventure story. This one was about the experience of being in Iraq during a sandstorm. I sat and listened, not noticing a black-suited Karl Lark had entered the cafeteria.

It took a second for this to register when the story teller had stopped the telling and was looking at someone behind me. I turned and saw Mr. Lark.

This left me startled and I said nothing. Mr. Lark smiled his contrived, overly friendly smile and said, "Don't let me interrupt but I need to take Thomas away." He looked down at me sitting there, "Let's go to the library," he said while still smiling.

I got up and walked with him out of the cafeteria and I thought to myself that Mr. Lark smiling like that must be some sort of compensation for something. He was always friendly and smiling. Except for that time in the vault where he was considering killing me. No smiling then.

I came to the conclusion his smiling meant he was interacting with people and there was no need to commit homicide. Good to know. Smiling good, not smiling was very bad. This leads to the further realization that Mr. Lark was very bipolar in his dealings with people. There must be some deeper meaning to this that escapes me at this time.

We entered the library and found seats facing each other. I started first, "Are we discussing the subject of Hy-Brasil?"

Mr. Lark nodded and replied, "I received your message and took some time to consider it and would like to discuss what you found."

I interjected, "You would like me to cover it now that we are face to face?"

"If you please."

"First let's discuss the possibility of this being a hoax. I believe the unusual circumstances of the find make a hoax unlikely. This is somewhat speculation on my part. To be sure we would need to have the books analyzed. Unfortunately the contents of the book would raise questions from anyone hired to determine its authenticity.

"The book is real. The Oculus confirmed the age of the book," stated Mr. Lark.

I continued, "From what Captain Nesbit wrote it seems like once he was close to the island, something there, possibly the wizard he wrote about, engineered the whole meeting. The captain wrote about the compulsion to dock at the island and his walking alone to the castle, then telling his crew nothing of what he found."

"The resignation of his commission, followed by the attempt to traverse late seventeenth century Europe on a journey to the Caspian Sea. It all seems uncharacteristic. Why not keep the coins and retire or pay someone else to deliver the letter?" I said.

Mr. Lark interrupted, "I believe the captain was under the influence of a strong mind control from the moment the ship found itself in the fog. This magician appears to have placed a mental binding on the captain to deliver the folio containing the map."

"You believe what is written in the journal then?"

"The good captain would have most likely succeeded in his task had he not detoured into the path of a half-mad Faerie. The whole story raises my curiosity. Anyone that was on that island is now long dead after 350 years. But who knows what was left behind? The other possibility is to go to the maps destination and see what is there," mused Mr. Lark.

After a pause he continued, "Perhaps it is best to learn more about the origination before showing up at the destination."

"You are considering searching for Hy-Brasil then?"

"No, I am sending you looking for it," smiled Mr. Lark.

"The journal does not give the location where they found the island. How would I find it?"

"There are enough old maps floating around showing the general location. It might take a little searching but an Oculus would speed things up considerably."

"What is Hy-Brasil? The captain talked about trees being on the island so there is sunlight. It can't be a pocket dimension like the Compass or Citadel, can it?"

"Hy-Brasil is part of the real world, just hidden. A sphere centered on the island and extending some distance out from it has been created around it. Sunlight shines down on it like normal. This non-Euclidean warping of space from one side of the sphere to the other side keeps it hidden. It is a way to hide something in plain sight," explained Mr. Lark.

"Any material, a living creature or object approaching from one direction just skips over the island to the other side. A ship sailing through the area with an accurate GPS would see their position change instantly by several miles. But if you have the proper key, you transition to the island instead. The transition zone was the fog the captain spoke of," continued Mr. Lark

"Did the captain have a key?"

"I do not think so. Something on the island, probably the magician he spoke of, opened the door and they just sailed in. I however have become quite good at making such keys as needed. I will send you to find the place where the island is. Then I will take a look and give you the key to open the door. A team will then accompany you to the island. Afterwards you can report back what you find." Mr. Lark was smiling that smile again.

"After what happened at Hoia forest? I think Held was almost killed by that Faerie," my voice was a little shrill. I was feeling anxiety over another adventure, especially in the middle of the ocean. I know how to swim but I do not think that will help that far out to sea.

"Thomas, one of the reasons for adding you to the organization was the hunch that you are good at finding things. Since coming here you have proven me right. Why break a winning streak?" said Mr. Lark.

I could think of nothing to say in reply.

"It is settled then. I will talk to Illych. A team will need to setup somewhere on the Eastern seaboard of the United States. Europe would be closer but the team would not blend in as easily. You will need a ship of some sort, probably a large yacht. There may be enough time to get everything started before the next scheduled break. Then you go on vacation. And when you come back, off exploring you go. Questions?" he said while looking directly at me.

I shook my head and Mr. Lark left.

Illych began preparations immediately. It would be Illych, Held, Mike, and me again going to Hy-Brasil. Mr. Lark had another task for Tank that would keep him from joining us.

Illych left the Citadel for a few days. When he returned he brought the four of us together and filled us in on the missions setup progress.

He had located a shipyard in Charleston South Carolina that would prepare the yacht he had purchased. It was an old steel hull, two screw yacht that required a lot of work. He had reviewed the boat with the shipbuilders and the tear-out had already begun.

The four of us were to return to the ship yard and supervise the refit of the yacht. The plan was to put to sea after the return from the upcoming 30-day leave. We would sail out perhaps 200 miles and then translate the whole boat to the general location of Hy-Brasil.

The yacht had been unused for years and Held, Illych, and Mike would supervise the refit. The ship was not acceptable as is and a refit was required to prepare it for the voyage to Hy-Brasil.

While the refit was progressing I was tasked with finding the best maps for locating Hy-Brasil. We left the Citadel the next morning and translated from the Compass to a hotel suite in Charleston.

My three companions had all packed civilian clothes whereas I only had my Compass provided attire. I was to remain in the hotel suite while the three others left for the shipbuilders.

I was left with additional instructions: to order clothes and a computer for immediate delivery. Illych gave me a large envelope. Inside was a California driver's license with my name on it. There was also a black credit card and five-thousand US dollars in various denominations. Included in the envelope were plane tickets for a flight from Charleston to San Francisco, and reservations at a hotel in San Francisco for my upcoming leave. In addition to searching for Hy-Brasil, I was to acquire everything I needed for my upcoming stay in San Francisco.

For the first time in a month I found myself in the 'real' world, unsupervised. Illych told me to stay in the hotel room until the team returned later that evening. I am not an adventuresome person but still found myself surprised I did not have an urge to run out the door.

A visit to a coffee shop would be nice, if for no other reason than to watch the pretty girls walk by. Looking out the window confirmed it was a beautiful summer day outside and the existence of pretty girls nearby.

Instead I called the front desk to get a phone number for the nearest computer store. After I had internet access ordering clothes would be easy. Illych had told me money was not an issue and to consider the credit card to have no limit.

I decided I would be going to San Francisco in style.

The computer was delivered to the hotel room door in less than two hours. I went right to work, first ordering clothing and then beginning the search for Hy-Brasil.

Everything I needed was available on the internet and by the time my three team mates had returned I had a general idea of the location of Hy-Brasil.

I found the nearest print shop to get copies of the maps printed and laminated. We needed maps for our voyage and something relatively waterproof seemed prudent.

Illych approved of my accomplishments for the day. The suite we had originally translated into and where I had been all day was just for me, in spite of there being two bedrooms. I had been curious all day how the four of us would be sleeping in only two beds. I was relieved to find out all four of us were in similar but separate suites, all next to each other.

As I still did not have civilian attire we could not go out for dinner. Room service was ordered instead. We all sat together in my suite and shared a meal. The conversation was relaxed.

I asked Illych, "Can we talk here, I mean, about anything?"

Illych responded, "Our rooms were swept for surveillance devices before we even arrived and I have an Oculus with me to keep watch. We can speak freely here."

"Wondering why you did not want to go outside while we were gone?" Held asked.

"I was a little worried I was going to go outside and get into trouble but I really did not want to. It occurred to me it was a little strange. I have been at the Citadel for almost a month."

"We are all like that. Nobody does anything that endangers our anonymity. My guess is Mr. Lark placed a secrecy binding on you during his last visit," Held offered.

"He didn't do anything to indicate he had," I felt uncomfortable about having my behavior modified without my knowledge. What else did Mr. Lark do to me I do not know about?

"It's a little creepy, but it is part of the job. I don't think any of us would appreciate the attention we would get if someone knew who we were or what we are doing," Mike contributed.

Illych spoke next, "I was a Green Beret and I can imagine just about any intelligence service or some of the bigger private organizations would give anything to get their hands on an Oculus or to learn of the Oiublet's capabilities. The compulsion for secrecy protects us from a lot of bad players," he looked pretty serious when he said this.

"Did you experience anything like this when you were in the US Military? Green Beret is pretty elite isn't it?"

"The Green Beret's are special forces and I was involved in missions against conventional opponents. But we also got involved in operations against 'unconventional' problems. Joining Mr. Lark's organization was not as much of a shock as it probably was for you. I had already seen some strange stuff. Working for Mr. Lark I find provides better explanations though," Illych offered.

I was satisfied for now. The rest of the evening was friendly socializing and some story telling. Illych stopped the discussion around nine-thirty, explaining the next day's activities would see the other three going back to the shipbuilder and I would remain at the hotel

I did not see the others until seven in the evening the next day. My clothes had arrived so at least I would be able to leave the hotel room. I even had time to watch some American television. The pay per view had some movies I had not seen and the laminated maps arrived late morning. It was fun to enjoy the simple things in life for a bit.

When the others returned that evening and saw me in civilian attire it was decided we would go out for dinner. Illych gave me a slip of paper with a phone number on it before we went out.

"This is the emergency call-in number. Memorize it. It changes each time we go on vacation. If you have problems, for instance you were robbed, call it. The cavalry will come to the rescue," Illych explained.

Dinner was at an excellent steak house. I had been to the states previously and knew that American steaks were second to none. The meal did not disappoint. In spite of my natural introversion I enjoyed being out 'in the world'. Seeing women again after a month without was a private pleasure I enjoyed throughout the evening. I wasn't the only one gawking. Mike, Illych, and Held were checking out most every woman in the place. Our staring bordered on the scandalous and it was probably good it all ended by ten o'clock with our return to the hotel.

The next day we met in the hotel lobby at eight o'clock. Illych had rented a Cadillac and drove us to the shipbuilder. I recognized the smell of the ocean as we neared our destination. It was a beautiful warm sunny day. Illych parked and we walked to a dock and out to the boat.

It was bigger than I had expected. At least thirty meters from bow to stern. Activity around the ship was intense. A crane was lifting what appeared to be the ships engines, removing them for replacement. There were groups of men working all over the ship, with lots of shouting, the sounds of machinery in operation, and the flashes of welding.

Illych met a man from the shipbuilding company and the team went into a small building on the dock not far from the ship. The ship was old and the inside was being gutted, reinforced and rebuilt. All the windows were being replaced with smaller, bulletproof versions and many of the windows were being completely removed and plates welded flush over the empty holes. A heavy-duty railing was being installed around the complete perimeter of the ship. The navigational equipment was being updated. All in all, a lot of technical changes were being made that would take time.

I am not a military man but even I recognized the ship was being modified to provide a better defense. The perimeter railing forced anyone boarding the ship to lift themselves up and over it to get on the ship. The superstructure cabin had a sheltered door opening that could be used for cover and to funnel anyone trying to get in into single file. The steel being added wasn't necessarily just to stop bullets, but to keep anything from getting in too easily.

The crow's nest on top of the superstructure was now an armored pillbox. It had a hatch in the center leading down into the pilot house. The hatch was solid steel plate and reinforced as was the superstructures door from the main deck of the ship. Anyone in the crow's nest would have clear line of sight to all points on the deck.

That night, when we were coming back from dinner and the elevator door opened at our floor I was surprised to see Mr. Lark standing half-way down the hall to our rooms. He was dressed in a grey suit and carried his brass sphere-headed cane.

We walked out of the elevator and approached him. He said, "We have work to do."

Chapter 15

The team met in my hotel room. We pulled chairs into a circle to listen to what Mr. Lark was here to discuss.

"Not long ago a visit to the British Museum resulted in a chain of events that led to Thomas joining my organization. The source of the conflict was an ancient Sumerian… let's call it a book. It was not a book in the conventional sense, made from paper or clay. This book used thin copper sheets for its pages and the cover of the book was made from hard stone. This method of construction was chosen for its longevity. This book could be left in a damp cave for ten thousand years and after the dust is brushed off it would still be legible."

"My source inside the museum tipped me off to the books existence. Unfortunately there was another interested party involved, a Djinn named Amal Halluk. Amal infiltrated an armed team into the museum to recover the book. My presence there that afternoon prevented the book falling into his hands."

"I checked into it, after the fact, and the shooting at the museum was never reported. This leads me to believe Dr. Chatzas serves Amal and is his inside contact. The fact she was a witness and is still alive reinforces this belief."

"During the brief outbreak of violence, I was able to page through the seven pages of the book and memorize the contents. Later I translated the text from memory. The book is an inventory of ancient artifacts. Some of the artifacts I recognized, others are unknown to me."

"We would recover this cache of artifacts, if only I had its location. The Ouiblet would make taking possession a straight forward affair. Unfortunately the text only lists the artifacts, not the cache's location."

"There is a consideration to be observed in the series of events regarding this book. Why did Amal Halluk want the book itself? Why not just have pictures of the text sent and then translated?

"I understand the attempted armed theft of the book. It would legitimize its removal from the museum. There would have been an investigation if it just disappeared. Questions would have been asked, a certain curators financials would have been investigated."

"This has led me to believe the location of the cache is in the book, perhaps hidden in or on the stone box. The British museum catacombs are extensive to say the least. Regardless, I attempted an Oculus scan in order to locate the book and I found it, still at the museum, in the secure vault on the fifth sub-floor."

"Our immediate concerns are two-fold. We need to break into the museum and steal the book. I know it would be easier to use the Ouiblet. Unfortunately there are so many cameras and vault doors that just having the book disappear would draw the attention of entities or organizations I would rather not involve."

"The second action we will take is the interrogation of Dr. Chatzas. It is important we know if Amal Halluk has inspected the book and if so, how long ago."

"Interrogate Dr. Chatzas? What does that mean? You are going to torture her?" I blurted out. Dr. Chatzas was a bitch and she had apparently plotted my death during the museum incident but I could not be part of torturing a person in general and a woman specifically.

"Your chivalry is admirable Thomas. Especially considering Dr. Chatzas had arranged for your murder. However we do not torture people. There are more civilized ways to convince someone to talk. Dr. Chatzas will be kidnapped and taken to a quiet place. Then, after a short period of time, she will volunteer everything we need to know. Afterwards she will be returned home none the worse for wear." Mr. Lark was explaining what was going to happen, regardless of my outrage. It was still kind of nice to have something explained ahead of time.

"Once we have the location of the cache and Dr. Chatzas clues us in on the competition we will move to collect it."

"These two initial operations must simultaneously occur within a relatively a short span of time. If we grab the book Amal might try to keep Dr. Chatzas from us. If we grab Dr. Chatzas, Amal may decide to secure the book."

"My guess is Amal has inspected the book and has the location of the cache. He left the book at the museum to prevent any questions about a mysterious disappearance. So now it is a race against time."

"Illych, does the shipbuilder have everything needed to continue without anyone from my organization being present?"

Illych nodded his head. "Yes."

"Then everyone has fifteen minutes to gather up their things and meet back here. We will translate directly to the Compass and gather the appropriate equipment from the Citadel. Then we will translate to London and execute both operations."

Mr. Lark looked around at the assembled team, "Any questions?"

I do not know if it was how he had explained everything or if it was my lack of experience in breaking and entering or kidnapping for that matter, but I could not think of any questions.

Chapter 16

It did not take long to prepare after we made it back to the Citadel. Perhaps it should have disturbed me that the team was able to put together the kit to rob the museum in such a short period of time.

When Mr. Lark had explained the mission back in Charleston, I had not seen a role for myself in the museum mission. It appeared they would drop me at the Citadel to wait around on my own while everyone else left. Just like the China mission from a few weeks ago.

I was wrong.

Not only was I going on the museum mission but I was also to play a key role. Mr. Lark directed me to be the mule. I was supplied with a large, frame-supported rucksack. It was like I had a large pizza delivery case on my back. When the Sumerian book was in hand, it would go into my backpack and I would carry it out. This would free everyone else up for security and to run interference.

With multiple Oculus users in the team it would be possible to detect and overcome any security at the museum. The mission profile was fairly straightforward. We would travel to the museum in two vans. One van would be left close to an eastern exit from the museum.

The second van would pick up the driver of the first van and the entire team, including Mr. Lark and me, would park near a west side entrance to the British museum. We would enter the museum as a group, through a service entrance, during normal business hours.

There are three elevators that provide service to all four sublevels below the museum. On the fourth sublevel was a single elevator connecting the fourth and fifth subfloors. The entire fifth subfloor is a special security vault.

The team would meet at the westernmost elevator and use it to travel to the fourth subfloor, followed by taking the special elevator to the fifth subfloor. After the book was heisted, we would return to the fourth subfloor and the team would ascend to the lobby using a different elevator. We would then exit out the eastern side of the museum, pile into the waiting van and make good our escape.

If we were observed arriving and museum security moved to block our exiting by the same route by which we had entered, they would be in for a surprise. Our leaving by a different route than we entered by might confuse museum security for a few critical seconds.

My participation was required for another reason. If we needed to speak to anyone, my native English accent would go a long way in making our presence more convincing. Illych coached me that if questioned about our presence to say we were there to repair a compressor on a refrigeration unit. It was an emergency because something was in ice and the museum was afraid it would defrost.

This explanation was backed up by the coveralls we were wearing, eerily similar to those worn by the thugs on the first day I had met Karl Lark. It would also explain the tool cases we would be carrying with our gear in it.

Like any modern building, every entrance to the British museum was always locked. The western side was chosen for its easily approachable service entrance. The service entrance had a small parking lot. Entrance to the museum required a key card and a four digit code. Mr. Lark assured us he would handle any locks we might encounter, electronic or otherwise.

By the time Mr. Lark was done explaining the mission I came to two conclusions. The first was that Mr. Lark was a very thorough planner. The second was that having an Oculus made stealing much too easy. We knew ahead of time the complete layout of the building, the location of every lock, every security device, etc.

It was almost unfair.

We carried tasers under our coveralls in addition to knives, pistols, small explosive charges, gas masks, and more. The larger pieces of gear were in roller hard cases. Mr. Lark gave instructions to disable any opposition when convenient and we carried zip tie hand cuffs for just such an event. However, if the threat could prevent the mission's success or injure one of us, we were to use appropriate force to stay on mission.

I think this was Mr. Lark's nice way of saying we were not there to kill people or break things. However, should someone try really hard to get in our way, removing them was sanctioned.

Everyone was calm and practiced while getting ready. In situations like this the teams experience really shows.

Mr. Lark was upfront about his interest in getting the mission underway as soon as we were ready.

Each of us was issued a ComDat communicator and earpiece. We would be able to talk and listen to each other as a group.

We translated to the stone circle in London. I had mixed feeling about seeing this place again. The last time I was here was my last day as my own man. It remained the same sterile, brightly lit open white space. The grey Mercedes was parked off to the side. Also parked in the room were two small panel vans. One was white, the other black.

From the mission planning I knew the black one would be parked waiting on the east side for our getaway. The white one would be abandoned in the service parking area when we arrived.

I have seen Mr. Lark in his grey suit and in black tactical wear. Now I saw him in a formless set of coveralls and it was an odd look for him, making him less distinct, more approachable.

Tank jumped in the driver's seat of the white van and Held drove the black

The drive to the museum was uneventful. The four of us not driving were sitting in the back of the white van. Mike and Illych were checking their own and each other's gear. Mr. Lark sat quietly with his eyes closed, apparently observing with the Oculus. I did not have the equipment to check like the others, just a pair of tasers, a handgun, and the ridiculous backpack. The van was windowless so I was left gazing out the front windshield at London as we drove.

Held parked the black van and joined us in the white van.

I had expected the tension to be rising the closer we came to the museum, instead, everyone in the van looked almost bored. Mr. Lark was his usual unreadable self. Having survived Hoia Forest killer faeries I felt more confident going into this mission and my anxiety was less than I had expected.

It was a cruddy grey day outside. The rain had been on and off, seeming unable to make up its mind. Once we arrived and parked I followed the others out of the van. We looked like some sort of plumber gang walking towards the service entrance.

You can take the soldier out of the army but you cannot take the army out of the soldier. I noticed the four former military men informally line up and start marching across the parking lot. Even their strides matched. I do not believe it was conscious act on their part. Regardless, it was out of place and I said something to Mr. Lark who was in the lead and did not see what I was seeing.

"Should we be marching in?" I said to Mr. Lark while jerking my thumb back at the four men.

"Illych, spread out and stop marching!" barked Mr. Lark.

The four men realized what they had been doing, separated and spread out.

The service door was solid metal with a flange over the lock. Off to the right was a keypad. Mr. Lark approached it and put something in his palm up against the side of the keypad. He then typed in a series of numbers. The door buzzed and clicked. Mr. Lark pulled the door handle and it opened.

"Using the Ouiblet to make the book disappear would draw unwanted attention. But making a key card disappear will just look like common theft," he offered.

Mr. Lark had drawn maps of our path through the museum back at the Citadel. We knew where we were going. The elevator down was only fifty feet away, through a wide corridor and we made it there without incident. Only a few people passed us on the way and none seemed to take note of six men in coveralls.

The same key card summoned the elevator. We all piled in and began our descent into the bowels of the museum. It is a service elevator and quite large. The six of us had plenty of space. Thirty people could probably fit inside.

"Mr. Lark, you are not concerned about getting stuck in an elevator?" The question popped into my mind and I had to ask.

"It would look odd on our way in to take the stairs. On the way out we will be taking the stairs, because, yes, I am concerned about getting stuck in an elevator."

At the third subfloor the elevator dinged and stopped, apparently someone was getting on. Before the door opened Illych told everyone to relax and let me do the talking if it was needed.

The door opened.

Standing there was Dr. Chatzas.

Her emotionless mask abruptly changed into a 'deer in the headlights' look as she recognized me. It did not last long though. Illych had taken out a taser from where he had hidden it, shielded by his body.

Mr. Lark called out, "Illych!"

Illych's arm extended and he took two steps towards the shocked Dr. Chatzas. At point block range he pointed it at her chest and pulled the trigger. The needles and wires shot out.

I do not know what he was aiming for but each of the two needles picked a separate breast to impact and stick to. The attached wires hung down at an angle and for a brief moment I thought of tassels. Then the taser made a buzzing noise like angry bees as it discharged

And nothing happened.

Dr. Chatzas looked down at her chest and started to turn away. Held stepped up and tasered the exposed skin of her chest above her blouse. Her body went stiff and she began falling over. Illych caught her and pulled her back into the elevator. Held glanced around outside the elevator and saw no one. He stepped back in and pushed the button to close the door.

After the doors closed Illych laid Dr. Chatzas down gently and proceeded to grab her right breast with his hand. Apparently squeezing and massaging it.

"What the bloody hell man? You can't just grab her like that!" This declaration came out of my mouth louder and more accusatory than it should.

Illych smiled and replied, "Relax Thomas, I am not copping a feel. I am checking why the taser did not work. Her bra is heavily padded and has a wire running the full length of the bottom of it. The taser needles did not even get close to skin contact and then shorted out through the wire."

Wow, the busty Dr. Chatzas was less busty than she appeared. And it served as a defense against tasers. Who would have thought?

Mike chimed in, "I thought we were kidnapping her after we steal the book?"

Mr. Lark was looking down at Dr. Chatzas prone form, "This is not part of the plan. However it does save on time. She comes with us, killing two birds with one stone so to speak. Tank, carry her. Taser everyone we see between here and the next elevator."

The path to the next elevator was a short walk down a corridor, then a left turn followed by another short walk. From prior experience I know not a lot of people come down to the fourth sublevel. If we were lucky we could walk all the way to the next elevator without meeting someone.

The first corridor was uneventful. The team turned left and had walked maybe twenty feet when five people, three men and two women, walked out into the corridor through an open doorway.

I wish I had a camera at that moment. The looks on their faces was priceless. They stopped as one the second they saw us. Then all five pairs of eyes shifted to the behind of the woman draped over Tank's shoulder.

Then their eyes shifted to the guns pointed at them.

"Tank, Mike, Held, take them to a room, bind and gag them and lock them in. Then proceed to the exit elevator, remain nearby and hide the best you can. Dealing with this will slow us down. Illych, Thomas, you are with me." Mr. Lark barked the commands and started walking towards the elevator that would take us down.

Illych was only a step behind Mr. Lark and I had to jog to catch up.

The elevator to the security vault sublevel was a service elevator and a twin to the one we had just taken here from the ground floor. Once the three of us had reached the doors Mr. Lark raised a fist which caused Illych to freeze in place. I assumed I should do the same and stopped. Mr. Lark closed his eyes for a few seconds consulting his Oculus.

He then opened his eyes and pushed the button to call the elevator. I could hear the rumbling of the car coming up the shaft. After waiting a bit there was a 'ding' sound and the elevator doors slid open revealing it to be empty.

The inside of this elevator showed considerably less wear and tear than the one we had just been in. Apparently not a lot of people travel this way. I had not been aware of a fifth security vault subfloor in all the years I had visited the museum for work and I doubted it is on the visitor maps either.

Upon entering the elevator I saw a security camera in a ceiling corner opposite the elevator doors. It was positioned to view the doors of the elevator. Modern security cameras are not much bigger than an eyeball in a small fishbowl. This one was larger, a small box with a lens. A pencil like rod extended forward a few inches from the camera. At the end of the rod, a few inches from the lens, was a small box about the size of a person's thumb.

As we entered I pointed at the obvious camera. I knew before asking that Mr. Lark had seen it also. This did not stop me from asking the obvious question.

"Is that security camera a problem?"

"Not at all Thomas, and let me answer your question with a question. What do security cameras in elevators see most of the time?"

I had to think about that for a second, "An empty elevator?"

"Precisely, if someone were to insert a loop into the camera feed, the elevator would appear empty all the time. The Ouiblet allows me to do this perfectly. I believe there was a movie where the thieves took a Polaroid photo from next to the camera and placed it in front of the security camera so it looked like there was nothing to see. What I have done is a little more sophisticated, the results are the same however."

"What is that thing sticking out from the front of the camera?"

"That is there to prevent what I just described. That little box displays a four number code to the security camera. That four number code is randomly generated back in the main security room up in the museum and transmitted here, changing every few seconds. If the camera was spoofed to feedback a looped display that number would never change and security would know there is a problem."

"The loop feedback I engineered and inserted with the Ouiblet still allows the camera to see the changing numbers. The rest of the camera feed shows an empty elevator."

I had never been a technology guy. I was more into older technology, like fountain pens. Being around Mr. Lark was like participating in a children's science show. Add firefights and other dimensional creatures and you have a children's science horror show. A show not likely to get past the censors.

The security camera explanation ended just as we arrived at the fifth subfloor. The duration of this leg of the journey was longer than travelling one floor down. My guess is the fifth subfloor is at least fifty feet below the fourth subfloor.

The elevator doors opened to reveal a brightly lit corridor leading to a traditional looking circular plug type vault door. Two of the unusual security cameras were mounted to the ceiling at the midpoint of the corridor. One pointed towards the elevator doors, the other towards the vault door.

Just beyond the threshold of the elevator doors, the entire floor of the corridor all the way to the vault doors was sunken down about two inches.

And filled with water.

I looked at Mr. Lark. "My apologies for my never-ending questions but why is there water on the floor?"

Mr. Lark chuckled, which was a little strange to hear, "The visible light spectrum is not absolute. It can be bent or hidden. Something invisible would not be seen by those security cameras. But the disturbance of the water as it traversed this corridor would be visible. Notice how the walls of the corridor are angled outwards from ceiling to floor? The walls are smooth and polished stainless steel. If you touch them you will find they have been lightly oiled. It would be almost impossible to leverage against the walls to travel the corridor's length. This corridor is as much a part of the vaults security as that huge steel door ahead is."

"The vault itself is a vacuum-tight steel bubble suspended inside another vacuum-tight steel bubble. The space between them has had all the atmosphere removed, a vacuum. Anyone trying to dig in would break the vacuum seal. Since the vacuum is monitored by multiple sensors an alarm would trigger."

"The only practical way into the vault is through the vault door. Since the entire internal vault chamber is suspended, its weight is monitored. Even a one pound change in weight will trigger an alarm. The weight sensors I have already defeated in a way similar to how the security cameras were defeated."

"Illych, the water please."

Illych opened the roller case he had been pulling along and took out a roll of what looked like fabric. He placed it on the threshold of the elevator and began unrolling it into the corridor on top of the water. The fabric began expanding, absorbing the water as it went. He kept unrolling all the way to the vault doors.

I looked at Mr. Lark, my question unsaid.

"I do not want to be walking around in wet shoes slipping on everything."

Mr. Lark walked up to the vault door. There were three combination dials next to the steel handle used to open the vault. Mr. Lark began turning the dials, sometimes switching back and forth between them. Apparently the combination was complicated.

After a minute of demonstrating his superior manual dexterity Mr. Lark grabbed the handle and pulled it down. There was a loud clunk and the massive vault door swung open.

The vault door was at least two feet thick and ten feet square, its threshold flush with the floor.

The vault's interior was as big as a good-sized home and well lit. Aisles had been laid out in painted lines. Outside the aisles there were squares of uniform size painted on the floor. Inside of most of the painted squares were unmarked wooden crates all identical in appearance. There were no markings anywhere, not on the aisles, the painted squares or the crates. How do we find what we are looking for when everything is identical and unmarked? Perhaps that is the point?

As I was looking around I noticed there were no video cameras.

Mr. Lark beat me to my question. "If there are no cameras no one can look at what is in here. Nothing is marked because if someone broke in and did not know which crate they were looking for it would take some time to find their goal. Some of the crates are filled with a few sandbags and are here as decoys. Only the vault master knows which crate is which."

"Fortunately the Oculus defeats such diversions. Our target is that one," Mr. Lark pointed to one crate down the right aisle, four crates in.

"Thomas, please retrieve the book while Illych and I observe."

"Is it safe?" I had to ask.

"This vault contains no traps or mechanisms nor anything animated or alive. As to it being safe, I am reasonably sure it is."

I looked at Mr. Lark who was smiling as he finished his sentence.

I shrugged my shoulders and walked into the vault and paused. No lightning struck, nothing grabbed me. I continued to the crate Mr. Lark had indicated. He had been right. The crate had a simple latch holding it shut. I opened the crate and the stone box was suspended inside, sitting in a very large velvet lined jewelry box tray.

The box book was heavy and it was clumsy to get inside my backpack. Once it was strapped inside I hefted its awkward weight onto my back feeling like a pack mule and adjusted the shoulder straps. If we had to run for any reason I was screwed.

I turned and looked at Mr. Lark and nodded. As my leg moved forward to take my first step towards the door there was a scraping noise. I also caught movement out of the corner of my eye. Fear coursed through my body and I stumble sprinted towards the vault door when something hit the back of my legs hard. Mr. Lark shouted for me to freeze in place.

Despite my fear and the throbbing of my legs from the impact, I did as instructed. I looked around now and saw the problem. The crates had an extra layer of wood on their sides. When I had started walking back to the door these extra sides separated from the crates and started moving towards me. There were twelve total crates in the vault resulting in a total of forty-eight vertical sides. It looked like a forest of wooden playing cards standing upright vertically on edge.

Mr. Lark called to me," Thomas, they move towards you whenever you move. The ones that hit your legs were from the crate the book was in. The more you move towards the door the more you will be boxed in."

"The Oculus did not show this?"

"No, I was looking for guards, mechanisms, or poison gas. Detachable, person-seeking, wooden panels is new to me. Just do not panic. Give me a moment to think."

I could see him concentrating on the Oculus.

He then did something I did not expect.

He walked into the vault.

And nothing moved.

"When the trap is triggered the crate sides divide themselves between everyone currently in the vault. Since you were the only one in here, they are all coming after you. After the trap is triggered anyone can enter and not be in danger."

Oh God, he is going to take the backpack with the book and leave me here! Some sort of twisted version of Edgar Allen Poe's: *The Cask of Amontillado*.

"You're taking the book and leaving me here?!" I squeaked out.

Mr. Lark kept walking towards me, "I do not leave people behind, makes it difficult to maintain loyalty. Plus you are a valuable asset. It would be wasteful to depreciate your value unnecessarily."

If this was his way of trying to comfort me it sucked.

Mr. Lark walked to the upright crate sides just behind me. He placed his hands on its top edge and lifted. It came straight up in his hands.

"As I suspected, they are connected to you. They move when you move. However, anyone not associated with the trap can pick them up and move them. Give me a moment please."

He picked up and moved all the crate sides within ten feet of me. Strangely enough when he put them down they remained vertical on edge.

"Thomas, please take one step towards the door. One step only."

I did as instructed and the crate sides, all forty-eight of them scraped the floor towards me. My step had been maybe two feet but the crate sides slid much further than that.

"Yes, the ratio is four to one. Thomas, for every foot you move towards the door these things will move four feet towards you. What a clever trap. Anyone breaking in would literally be boxed up and waiting for the authorities."

Mr. Lark moved several more crate sides. "Illych, assist me."

Illych entered the vault and copied Mr. Lark's technique for moving the crate sides. I was able to take a few more steps. Then they shifted more crate sides. Eventually I crossed the vault door threshold. As I left the vault all the crate sides fell over to lay flat on the floor. Illych and Mr. Lark joined me on the water absorbing pad in the entry corridor.

"That was educational but time consuming. This mission has been delayed far too much," said Mr. Lark.

Over the ComDat Mr. Lark asked, "Held, Status?"

"The five we ran into are bound, gagged, and locked in a room. We are approximately twenty feet from the exit elevator in a room with a locked door with the lights out. Dr. Chatzas regained consciousness and made a nuisance of herself. She is now sedated. I have no unusual security activity to report from the Oculus."

"Expect us at your location in ten minutes."

Mr. Lark looked at Illych and myself, "We are going to risk the elevator. This run of good luck without security responding to our presence can't last much longer though."

The squishy sound of our tread on the absorbent mat was disconcerting. It had an organic sound to it that brought creepy images to my mind.

The elevator car was still waiting and the doors opened immediately when the button was pushed, the three of us entered and began our ascent to the fourth subfloor.

During the ride up Mr. Lark was concentrating on his Oculus. I had this creeping sensation up and down my spine combined with the anxiety of waiting for a sudden lurch as the elevator was stopped.

But it never happened. We arrived at the fourth subfloor and walked undeterred to meet with the rest of the team. As we arrived at the exit elevator Held, Mike, and Tank, opened a door a little ways down the hall.

Tank had Dr. Chatzas left arm around his shoulders and was half carrying her. She looked like a little doll next to Tank's robust frame. Her expression was blank and her eyes were almost closed.

I was sweating from carrying the box book even this short distance. It was really heavy. Fortunately Held took it from me and placed it in a roller case that he was pulling along.

"Illych, the distraction please," Mr. Lark said while pushing the button to summon the elevator. Illych pulled a small device from inside his coveralls and flipped open the top like it was a Zippo lighter. The cover moved away to reveal a red button inside. Without hesitation he pressed the button down.

"Distraction?" I had to ask since no one had filled me in on this detail of the mission.

"The white van we drove here in just caught on fire and is making some very loud popping noises. Nothing dangerous or lethal, I would expect the museum to be evacuating by the time we reach the ground floor," Illych explained.

The elevator ride up was filled with anxiety that ended with a 'ding' sound and the doors opening to a scene of chaos in the grand gallery. We turned and began our walk towards the exit. The team instinctively spread out around Tank to help block line of sight to Dr. Chatzas with Tank's bulk blocking most angles.

As we integrated ourselves into the exiting crowd, a nearby man turned his head and saw me. He was one of Dr. Chatzas' toadies although I could not remember his name.

I could see his mind working to recall who I was before he spoke, "Thomas Davies, it has been awhile." At least he kept walking towards the entrance and did not stop to shake my hand.

"It has been. Do you know what all the excitement is about?" This was a fun lie to tell.

"Something about a potential terrorist threat and we had to leave the building by the east entrance. Say is that Dr. Chatzas? Is she ok?"

"When the alarm went off it startled her and she fainted," It was a poor explanation but the best I could come up with. Anyone who knows Dr. Chatzas knows she is not the fainting type.

The man began to put distance between us and was looking at my coveralls and then the other men in the same coveralls nearby. The expression on his face told me he knew something was up.

Dr. Chatzas was a tyrant and not someone people were loyal to. I decided to take a risk and leverage that the toadie was not personally concerned what happened to Dr. Chatzas.

"My suggestion is you walk away friend and forget you saw me here. Nothing good will come from you talking about this."

The man looked at me, a flash of fear crossed his face, and then he nodded and shifted the direction he was walking a little bit. The distance between us grew until he disappeared in the crowd.

We walked outside through the gallery doors and began a brisk walk across the plaza. The crowd was dissipating now and the camouflage we had benefited from being a part of it, also disappeared. Now we were six men in coveralls suspiciously carrying a professionally dressed woman.

Fortunately everyone with the appearance of being a member of law enforcement was running towards the museum. Regardless, London is notorious for the literal million plus video cameras installed around the city. We would be on video somewhere.

As we approached a bench at the edge of the plaza Illych spoke to Mr. Lark. "Let's leave Held, Thomas, and Dr. Chatzas on this bench. The rest of us can get the van and come back for them. Carrying her around will draw negative attention if we continue." Mr. Lark nodded his head in agreement. Illych pointed to a nearby city bench, "Wait here."

Tank gently set Dr. Chatzas down in the middle of the bench in a sitting position and Held and I joined her, one of us on each side. We watched silently as the four others walked away towards the parking structure where the van was waiting.

I looked around seeing there was no one nearby. A wave of relief, like I had just gotten away with playing hooky from school, washed over me. I had not realized how tightly wound I was when we were in the museum.

Held was calm as ever. He sat back in the bench looking casual. His coveralls were zipped partway open. To the casual observer it looked like he was taking a break.

I asked Held, "So was this mission a success?"

"So far so good. We will know for sure when it is over."

"What was given to Dr. Chatzas?"

"Injectable tranquilizer. She is still barely conscious. It will last for a couple of hours. Makes her compliant, easier to transport."

"What will happen when she is interrogated?"

"We will ask her questions and she needs to answer them."

"And if she does not answer?"

"Then she will be persuaded to answer."

"Torture," I said it as a statement not a question.

"Not in the traditional sense. There will not be any rubber hoses or thumbscrews. That is not Karl Lark's style. There won't be any blood but Dr. Chatzas will talk whether she wants to or not."

"So it will be a gadget that they interrogate her with. Or some monster like the Doctor back at the Citadel or that science fiction movie I saw when they put some creature in their ears?"

Held replied, "I can see where your idea for a gadget comes from. Mr. Lark does have a lot of gadgets. But no, the method is not science fiction."

"Torture has never been a reliable method for extracting information. Eventually people will say anything to make the pain stop and it becomes difficult to separate the truth from fiction."

"Torture is also a poor choice when complex information is needed. However, aggressive interrogation techniques will help when simple knowledge must be revealed. In Dr. Chatzas case all we need to know is who her sponsor is regarding this book. We also need to know if her sponsor has viewed the book up close."

"The interrogation techniques we use are effective and significantly more humane than old fashioned bloody-handed torture. My suggestion to you, Thomas, is to relax and watch. Mr. Lark is not a warm, friendly guy but he is also not a blood thirsty monster."

Not long after Held finished explaining what was going to happen to Dr. Chatzas, the van pulled up by the bench. Held lifted Dr. Chatzas into a standing position and supported her while we walked to the van.

She was hoisted inside and laid down in the back of the van. Tank was driving and Illych was shotgun. The rest of us sat on the benches in the back of the van with Dr. Chatzas laid out on the floor at our feet.

The drive back to the warehouse was quiet and uneventful.

At the warehouse Mike checked Dr. Chatzas' pulse and blood pressure. She was still very much out of it. He then administered another shot that knocked her completely unconscious.

Tank and Held moved her onto a stretcher and the two lifted it and walked into the stone circle, the rest of us followed. Mr. Lark worked his Ouiblet magic and the cold of the Compass stabbed us wide awake followed by nausea.

Dr. Chatzas was carried to one of the vaults, different than the one I had spent a night in.

I decided to follow and see what would happen, and no one stopped me.

This vault was well lit and had a large heater in it. The temperature was less than comfortable but it was not the freezer I had been in. Dr. Chatzas was transferred to a bed on the side of the vault across from the vault door.

A box mounted to the wall had a steel cable protruding out from it. The cable ended in a loop obviously intended to be attached to someone's arm or leg. Which is exactly what happened next, Held grabbed the cable and fitted the loop to one of her ankles. It appeared to be a tight fit, not too tight to cut off circulation, but tight enough she was not going to be able to escape from it.

The vault had the same small camping toilet and cooler with water bottles and crackers. After securing Dr. Chatzas, everyone exited the vault and closed it.

Mike volunteered more information, "She will be unconscious for at least four hours."

Everyone picked up their respective equipment, including the roller case with the goal of the mission contained within it and we walked as a group back to the Citadel.

Chapter 17

The few times in the past that I had walked to or from the Citadel had all been relatively quiet experiences. Not this time. Everyone was talking.

Mr. Lark walked alongside me, "Thomas, you and I will start work on this book immediately. After the gear is stowed meet me at the library."

"You said it was an inventory list of artifacts. What kind of artifacts?"

"Human civilization's time on earth goes back much farther than modern history represents it to be. There was a cataclysm around twelve-thousand years ago. The destruction was total and the human survivors numbered in the thousands."

"Attempts were made to restart their civilization. Those attempts failed. Other attempts were made to store and preserve artifacts for future generations. This Sumerian text lists a variety of the ancient civilization artifacts. We just need to figure out where this cache is stored."

"What kind of things are in the cache?"

"I recognized the descriptions of some of the items. More than half of them I do not understand. You must understand Thomas that this ancient civilization did not operate the way our modern world does. There was no 'planned obsolescence'. Everything was optimized to its function and built to last forever."

"One of the items I call a plasma candle. It is a cylindrical metallic device used for illumination. When left unattended it has a small plasma glow but when a person moves within ten feet of it the plasma glow expands greatly providing a bright white illumination. They consume no fuel and emit no gasses or pollution. From what I can tell they essentially last forever."

"Another defining characteristic of the ancients is their use of electricity. However, they had nothing to do with low voltage electricity as an EPS or electromagnetic pulse can wreak havoc on low voltage systems. All the ancient electrical systems are high voltage, thousands of volts or higher."

This was my chance to get answers on something that had been on my mind since my first day at the Citadel.

"Mr. Lark, Illych equipped me with this watch my first day at the Citadel. He said it detected EPS effects. Now you mention EPS again. What does it stand for?"

Mr. Lark regarded me while considering my question. "EPS stands for Electron Probability Suppressor. I will not get into a detailed discussion about it at the time."

He paused and then continued on the original discussion before I had interrupted. "Excellent examples of this are the Egyptian light bulbs images found in a few different ruins in Egypt. The pillar supporting the bulb shows distinct rectangular ridges typically seen in high voltage systems. It is kind of a giveaway."

"The inventory lists some of these lights being included. There is more. We need to find its location and Dr. Chatzas needs to clue us in if we have competition."

"But if someone else already has the location won't they be way ahead of us?"

"If that cache is still undiscovered after all these years then it is in a remote part of the world. Whoever else is looking for it must travel there by conventional means. The Ouiblet may still get us there ahead of them."

"Mr. Lark, if you do not mind my asking, are you the only person with an Ouiblet?" That question had been on my mind for a long time and this seemed like a good time to ask.

"I am the only person or otherwise, in possession of an Ouiblet. It is a device of my own creation that came about under what I have determined to be unique circumstances. I have never seen evidence of another Ouiblet and I have diligently sought such evidence. There will be no more discussion on this subject."

That was more than I had expected and took the hint not to delve deeper.

"It will take a few days to extract the information we need from Dr. Chatzas. By then we must have the location and be prepared to move out."

"Illych, begin general preparations for a long term expedition with broad contingencies. Mike, when Dr. Chatzas is conscious start her pharmaceutical regime. Thomas and I will be in the library."

Our conversation had been intense and I realized it had taken up the entire duration of the walk to the Citadel. We were just now walking through the doors into its well-lit interior.

There was no pause or break. Mr. Lark and I went straight to the library. Held had passed the roller case with the book in it to me at the gate and I now trudged behind Mr. Lark pulling the heavy case behind me.

The library had a large table in the center of it and together we lifted the book onto it.

Back at the museum, when Higgebotham had been killed, I did not get much time to look at the book. Now I grabbed a magnifying lens and a bright lamp. Mr. Lark had his Oculus in his hand. We opened the heavy stone lid and looked inside. The copper pages appeared unchanged. In spite of my fatigue I was excited. We were on a treasure hunt of epic proportions.

We searched every surface inside and out. I looked for differences in the formation of the characters and the grain of the copper for a hidden map or a clue of any kind.

After hours of exhausting searching I asked Mr. Lark if I could take a break. He paused and looked at me for a few seconds. "Of course Thomas, get some food and rest. We can start again in the morning."

I left the library with Mr. Lark sitting with his eyes closed communing with his Oculus. I wonder how much time Karl Lark spends sleeping? I have never seen the man tired.

I shuffled my weary body to the cafeteria hoping there was still something reasonable to eat there. I was surprised to find the rest of the team, all four of them, sitting eating and talking together.

While I had been in the Library with Mr. Lark, they had put everything away and staged the equipment for whatever this next adventure was going to be.

Now they had cooked up a veritable feast and were relaxing and enjoying each other's company.

They even had beer: Weihenstephaner, the oldest continuous operating brewery in the world, since 1099. I am more of a wine guy having spent so much time in Italy. But after the day I had just been through, any form of alcohol was acceptable and the beer was very good.

I served myself food and grabbed a bottle of beer from an open tub of ice and sat next to Mike.

I had walked in as they were discussing the recently awoken Dr. Chatzas.

Mike commented, "She was pissed, not intimidated at all. She screamed at me to release her immediately and that she is part of a powerful organization that will be looking for her."

"All I could think was 'good luck them finding you here'."

Held was next, "Did her tune change when the injections took affect?"

"Oh yeah, she started shaking and screaming questions at me about what we had done to her."

I interjected, "Pharmaceuticals injected?"

Illych looked at me, "I think it is time for the new guy to learn how an interrogation works. First, we lock the subject in the vault you saw. It has a heater that keeps it warm enough to prevent hypothermia but cold enough to be quite uncomfortable."

"The subject is then stripped naked and given a hospital gown and shower sandals to wear."

"Those hospital gowns that open in the back?" I was thinking about Dr. Chatzas wearing nothing but a skimpy hospital gown. I would not mind seeing that at all.

"Yes, and then we inject the subject with a powerful stimulant. This prevents sleep and keeps their minds sharp. Then they are injected with an anxiety inducing drug. The anxiety level is crippling. People will do anything to make it go away."

"The injections need to be administered every twelve hours. Now that the first round has been administered we wait."

I looked at Illych, "She has not been asked a question yet?"

"No, we wait at least twenty-four hours and see how the subject is holding up. The anxiety thing combined with not being able to sleep works fast on getting the subject to answer questions. We want them fully immersed in the experience before asking questions though.

"That is it? No torture?" This was shocking. I had developed respect for these men and had a hard time picturing them torturing anyone much less a woman. Now I find out they will not be laying a hand on her. It is all drugs and sleep deprivation.

"The record for anyone holding out is four days." Illych said while nonchalantly taking a bite of a sandwhich.

"What about when she gives us what we want?"

"This is a catch and release. She does not know about the Ouiblet and has not seen anything unusual. When the interrogation is complete we knock her out and leave her in her own bed at her residence. No muss no fuss," Illych smiled.

Illych could see the relief on my face. "You were worried we were going to butcher her, weren't you? Not necessary and it is not something any of us would do."

"I am truly sorry for thinking that of you," I said to all of them.

Tank jumped in, "No worries, everyone here is an experienced killer with significant body counts, including Karl Lark. You are the exception to that, of course." He was looking at me and smiling a predatory grin.

The rest of dinner was more pleasant with Tank and Mike singing some wildly inappropriate songs at the end. Finally, Illych pointed out it was late and we all went to bed.

I had fallen asleep and was dreaming. I was in that vault with Dr. Chatzas. She was facing away from me and I was admiring how the hospital dress opened up much more in the back than I would have expected. Then she turned and we took a step closer, our lips moving to meet. I could feel the heat of her body.

Then someone tapped me on the forehead, waking me. It was Mr. Lark looking down on my prone form tapping me with his finger to wake me. He was grinning that grin again. What now?

"I tried calling your name but you were deeply asleep. Please get dressed and meet me in the library. I found the location. And don't fall back asleep."

Working for Mr. Lark was very interesting but this uncivilized lack of respect for sleep was unreasonable. I put on my black tactical outfit and pulled on my boots. It took considerable will to put each foot in front of the other but I was in the library in less than ten minutes.

"Thomas, I have exciting news! I found the location of the cache. The secret of its hiding place is within the cover of the box. There are microscopic voids etched inside the plane of the cover."

"This is a solid piece of stone. Did they form the stone around the voids?"

"No, there is an ancient tool that can be used to cut or machine out a void inside a solid object without piercing the surrounding surface. Very useful for surgery I would think."

"Do you have one of those gadgets Mr. Lark?"

"No but I am aware of their existence. I eventually set the resolution of the Oculus small enough to find them. The voids form a simple map of the continents with a location marked. Next to that map is another more detailed map of the specific location."

"And where are we going?"

"India, the Ellora cave complex."

"I have never heard of it."

"Very interesting place. It is a huge complex of temples and tunnels. Vast sections are sealed from public view and there are no complete archaeological studies in the public record. It has numerous examples of stone work that cannot be explained, even if modern technology were used."

"You never took the Ouiblet there and checked it out before?"

"Thomas, there are thousands and thousands of megalithic sites around the world. It would take a hundred lifetimes to thoroughly explore a fraction of them with the Oculus. I explore when there is evidence something might be there. This is why you have been added to the team."

"What is next?"

"You are going back to sleep. I need to setup the Ouiblet destinations for the Ellora complex. It is daytime right now in India and we will go at night. Also Dr. Chatzas remains to be interrogated to determine if there is competition."

"Let's just go. How tough can the competition be? I'll bet the team can handle anything," no sooner had I said it that I realized that was an awfully aggressive comment coming from me.

"Your enthusiasm is noted, however our potential competition is a Djinn. I have no interest in matching wits or strength against such an adversary. Go to bed Thomas, we will talk more tomorrow."

Mr. Lark's last statement had been sharp in its tone. I left the library and returned to bed, not even undressing or removing my boots. Sleep came immediately. Unfortunately the dream with Dr. Chatzas did not return,

I was awoken by a knock on my door. I must have slept for hours and felt quite refreshed.

"Thomas?" It was Illych.

"Yes, I am awake."

"Cafeteria in five," and he left.

That was not enough time for anything other than to go to the cafeteria straight away. Fortunately I was already dressed. I stood, stretched, and walked there quickly.

Everyone was there including Mr. Lark. The four military men sat or stood at one table. Mr. Lark stood some distance away, observing them.

Mike was speaking, "Tank and I went to give her the next round of injections. She did not struggle at all. I could tell the first twelve hours had done its work. Instead of giving her the injections I asked if she was ready to talk. She said she was."

"I stuck to the prepared script. Who was her sponsor that was interested in the Sumerian stone book? She said it was a man whose name was Amal Halluk."

"I asked if he had come to the museum personally to view the book. Dr. Chatzas nodded and said we had missed him at the museum by hours when we kidnapped her."

"The next question was dependent on her having someone come to the museum. Did Amal Halluk find what he had been looking for? She nodded again saying he had been quite pleased with something he would not explain."

"The last question was how long she had been on her benefactor's payroll. She said she had been selling information to Amal Halluk since before she had become a curator. As her patron, he had made the arrangements to put her in place years ago."

So that was why the relatively young Dr. Chatzas had been elevated so quickly. She was talented and driven but her sponsor had removed obstacles and prompted action from key people to get her in place. She was an archaeological spy in the British Museum.

Mr. Lark responded, "Excellent, we are less than twenty-four hours behind Amal Halluk, assuming he moved immediately. During the last few hours I have been using the Ouiblet to cast an Oculus to the Ellora complex to take snap shots and then brought them back for me to observe what we are up against."

"The Sumerian map gave a general location, not a specific one. I found a stasis well deep underground below the complex. Translating close to a stasis well is one of the few hazards or protections against the Ouiblet that I am aware of. We will translate at least a kilometer away from it and then spelunk our way through the labyrinth of caves to the cache."

"We will then need to disable the suspensor generating the stasis well. Then we grab everything and translate out. Questions?"

I raised my hand.

"Thomas, you do not need to raise your hand, just ask the question."

"What is a stasis well?"

"That strange watch you were given your first day here is to provide an alarm in the event of a suspensor event. A suspensor can be used to shut down low voltage equipment like an automobile or paralyze a human being. At higher settings it will stop your thought processes rendering you effectively unconscious. This also explains memory loss described by UFO abductees. Their memories were not erased. They were prevented from being recorded in the first place."

"The next higher setting creates a stasis well. The movement of electrons is so suppressed, hence the term EPS, that nerve function and chemical reactions essentially cease. Anything placed in a stasis well will be frozen in place, never aging or degrading."

"The next higher level stops electron movement enough that the wave of continuous life functions is broken and living creatures die. Their bodies are undamaged and have no evidence to show why they are dead. This setting can be used to kill people over a large spherical area. It has other uses we will not discuss at this time."

"The cache is inside the stasis well. If we just walk in we will be trapped in the well. This brings us to another consideration for our expedition. Others may have stumbled upon the well in the past. When we deactivate it we may find more than just the cache waiting."

UFO abductions? Was Mr. Lark saying such things were real? Just when my belief that the level of weird had reached maximum Mr. Lark reveals there are yet more layers.

"Other questions?"

Illych spoke this time, "The disposition of Dr. Chatzas?"

"I will talk to her briefly and then she will be returned to her home. Amal Halluk has probably been too busy to miss her. She will be my double agent now, informing myself and Amal Halluk at the same time about future finds."

"If there are no other questions, Thomas and I will take care of Dr. Chatzas. Illych, how long until the team will be ready for spelunking?"

Illych looked at the three other men and then back to Mr. Lark, "One hour."

Without acknowledging Illych, Mr. Lark looked at me, "Let's go to the Compass and chat with Dr. Chatzas."

We stopped at the armory to pick up equipment for the Ellora mission. After that was a brisk walk to the Compass. Mr. Lark was walking so fast we were almost running. For an old man he had impressive endurance. I was sweating and breathing hard by the time we arrived. Mr. Lark on the other hand showed no sign of physical exertion.

The Compass was the same cold, gloomy place with its strange alien architecture. Mr. Lark opened the vault and we stepped into its brightly lit interior.

Sitting on the edge of the cot against the back wall was Dr. Chatzas. She was pale and her typically magnificent mane of hair was a terrible mess. Her makeup was smeared and she was hunched over with her arms hanging down her sides. Her head was bent over facing the floor. She was shivering from the cold and sweating from the drugs at the same time.

She looked exhausted and lost. I felt a pang of sympathy. Being around someone who was suffering like this was new to me. In spite of her attempting to have me killed back at the museum, I wanted to sit next to her and comfort her.

Mr. Lark stood a few feet from her and spoke, "Elizabeth Chatzas you have answered our questions and I wish to clarify some details of our relationship going forward."

You could see the hope on her face. I had been in the same place, locked in one of these vaults waiting to die. She did not know yet that it was not going to be a clean getaway.

"I doubt your patron is aware of your absence. We will be returning you to your home shortly."

"I will give you a phone number to call when something of interest crosses your path at the museum. Things that you would bring to Amal Halluk's attention, you will notify me first. Do you understand?"

Dr. Chatzas gave a small nod without looking directly at Mr. Lark.

Mr. Lark grabbed a small duffel bag from near the vault door. It would have been out of reach for Dr. Chatzas with her foot tethered to the cable. He tossed it onto the cot next to her.

"The clothes you were wearing when you arrived are inside. Please change into them and then you are going home. Thomas will remove the cable from your ankle now."

He handed me the key and I removed the tether. I then stood with my back to Dr. Chatzas. She put a warm hand on my shoulder to balance herself while she dressed.

Once dressed, she stood, ready to leave.

Mr. Lark addressed her again while holding a business card, "This will be in your bedroom when you wake up, do not lose it."

Dr. Chatzas spoke, her voice more a croak than the warm smoky tone I had heard in the past, "When I wake up?"

Mr. Lark's free hand was suddenly a blur as he pressed an autoinjector into her left shoulder. Her eyes went wide and she tried to pull away but it was already over with.

"You will need to be asleep for your trip home. Thomas, support her and let's get her outside. The drug is fast acting."

I put her right arm over my shoulders like I had seen the guys do when they carried her in. Mr. Lark reopened the vault door and stepped outside. I supported Dr. Chatzas and shuffled outside with her.

During the short walk to the stone circle the freezing cold accentuated the warmth of Elizabeth's body pressed to mine. I had never been this close to her. In spite of my nose telling me she needed a shower I enjoyed the contact.

By the time we made it to the center of the stone circle she was completely unconscious and I had to use two hands to hold her up. Mr. Lark looked at me and pulled a dongle from a pocket. With practiced ease he activated it.

It went dark and then we were in a woman's bedroom. Everything was in lace and floral print. It was a large room with the center dominated by a large four poster bed.

Then the nausea from the translation hit. I spent a minute recovering while trying to not drop Dr. Chatzas.

Mr. Lark, unfazed, stood waiting for me to recover and then said, "Thomas put her in bed. We need to leave." That said he closed his eyes obviously communing with his Oculus.

I pulled back the covers of the bed with one hand and tried to carefully place her onto the bed. I lost my grip and she fell face first onto the bed. Trying to maneuver an unconscious person into bed reminded me of trying to pick up a house cat that did not want to cooperate.

By the time I had her properly positioned in the bed and the covers pulled up over her I was upset with myself over my juvenile enjoyment of the process.

It had been hard work and I was sweating again. When I stood up and faced Mr. Lark his eyes were open and he was looking at me with a blank expression.

There was a question that I needed to ask him and this was as good a time as any. "Why did you not use an auto-injector on me? Back at my flat after the Ciorii was down. You could have knocked me out and your secrets would have been safe? I could have gone home after the interrogation."

"I do not carry auto-injectors around with me," replied Mr. Lark.

I nodded my understanding and said, "I am ready." I was dreading what was next. I had never translated twice in such a short period of time.

A dongle was in Mr. Lark's hand and with a quick motion it went black again. We were back at the Compass.

I was right, translating again so soon was worse than the first one. I stumbled over to one of the stone pillars and supported myself on it until the feeling of nausea subsided. Something that feels this bad can't be good for you.

Mr. Lark started for the Citadel at the same blistering walking pace as before.

Once we were inside and the doors closed behind us I rested by bending over with my hands on my knees. In the open space near the main gates were the four others. They were dressed in all black with bulletproof tactical vests.

Nearby were zippered black bags lacking any handles. Instead they had metal rings robustly sewn into the fabric of the bags. I would find out later this was so the bags could be pulled along through tight spaces without catching on anything.

Fifteen minutes of quiet preparation later and we were headed out through the main gates again for the third time today. The pace to the Compass was more reasonable this time. Thank God for that small mercy, I was carrying thirty more pounds of gear on me.

When we arrived at the Compass we immediately clustered together in the stone circle ready to go.

Chapter 18

Mr. Lark produced a collection of dongles from a large pocket and handed one to each of us. "These are your escape dongles. Use them only if you are in dire straits." Everyone pocketed their respective dongle and returned to looking at Mr. Lark.

He pulled out another dongle, "We will be translating into a fairly large chamber," with a brief movement of his hands it all went black. This was my third translation today and I was dreading it since our return to the Compass.

It was as bad as I had expected. Everything went black and stayed that way. I actually sat down on the floor until the effects had passed.

My teammates switched on their torches immediately. Americans call them flashlights, a term I decided to adopt for better communications.

Illych opened one of the black bags and pulled out a handful of what looked like hockey pucks. He walked over to the nearest wall. He took the puck-like device in one hand and peeled a thin film from one side. Then he pressed the puck to the wall at shoulder level and gave it a twist. The puck illuminated with a bright but diffuse light.

He saw me looking at what he was doing. "Thomas, this is not the first time we have been exploring underground. These are LED light devices with a high capacity battery attached. They will provide light for more than a week. Be careful with the adhesive used. It is aggressive and if you get it accidentally stuck to your skin the only way to remove it is to take the skin with it."

Mr. Lark spoke next, "We leave one every fifty feet. This chamber is the closest location large enough for the whole team to translate in and still be a safe distance from the stasis well."

Once several of the light pucks were in place and everyone had activated their forearm mounted LED flashlights, I was able to look around the chamber.

It was square and carved from bedrock. The stone was a blackish dark grey. The ceiling was vaulted far overhead. Each of the four corners had an ornately carved pillar that rose all the way upwards to the ceiling. There were three entrances to the chamber. Two appeared to be finished stone and were centered on their respective walls. The third was offset near a pillar and was jagged in nature, appearing to have been hacked into existence.

The air temperature was warm, almost hot, especially when compared to the cold of the Compass. With all the gear I was carrying there was going to be a lot of sweating.

Mr. Lark spoke, "We wait here for a moment. The air here is ok to breathe but the stasis well prevented good Oculus views prior to our arrival. Now that we are here, I need a few minutes to look around." That said he closed his eyes and stood quietly.

Illych gave some silent hand commands and the three other shooters each took an entrance with weapons at the ready.

Illych and I stood by Mr. Lark and waited. Minutes ticked by and finally Mr. Lark opened his eyes.

"There are no threats in close proximity. We start through that doorway there," Mr. Lark pointed at the finished doorway Tank was guarding.

Illych nodded and opened another bag and pulled out some boxes, spools of wire, some disc-shaped objects, and a wire cutter. Over the next five minutes they placed a box and disc on opposite sides of the doorways that would be left unused. They strung the black wire between the box and disc pairs.

I was watching intently and Illych noticed and commented, "Flash bang trip wires if something tries to sneak up behind us. Not as effective against the Created but any living thing has a pretty good chance of setting them off."

Illych pointed at Mike and made a hand gesture. Mike moved to the doorway we would be entering and started through it.

Illych looked at Mr. Lark, "How far?"

"Approximately 1500 meters to the stasis well and the path is not straight. We will be taking some turns and there is a shaft that we will need to rappel down."

As point, Mike took his time, closely observing all the surfaces of the corridor. The team let him get about twenty feet ahead and then followed. The dark stone did not reflect light and without a flashlight to illuminate it everything would be pitch black. Illych stuck a light puck to the walls every fifty feet leaving a lit trail behind us.

The corridor was approximately two men abreast wide. Combined with the heat and dark I was feeling a little claustrophobic.

The corridor ended in a cylindrical room. The center of the room had a circular hole in the center big enough for a man to slide down feet first. To the left was another corridor only big enough for the team to proceed single file.

I walked up to the center hole and shined my light down. It was a smooth stone tube that was so deep my light was lost before I could see the end.

"Thomas, get away from there," hissed Mr. Lark. I quickly stepped back to the wall.

Mike entered the single file corridor first. Progress was slow enough that I could illuminate the walls around us and observe them. There were carved reliefs everywhere. Mostly Indo-Aryan people involved in various ceremonies. All of them looked like they were out of Hindu religious texts like the Bhagavad Gita.

This corridor ended in a large circular room. In the center of the room was a Linga. A Hindu religious structure that water was poured over. The water channel ran to a small opening in one of the walls. As I moved my light around the chamber I saw a number of small openings in the walls at floor level.

Mr. Lark directed the team to a doorway opposite the corridor from which we had just entered. While the team was taking its time to enter after which they spread out. This gave me time to look around the room.

The walls had carved reliefs covering them from the floor to chest height. Except these showed few humans. Most of them were of small lizard creatures with human faces and snake tails I recognized the carvings depicted Nagas.

I know that Nagas are mythological creatures but considering what I had experienced since meeting Mr. Lark, I had the feeling they were very real. I could not remember if they were peaceful or not but visions of Nagas pouring into the room through those holes by the floor, thirsting for my blood, filled my imagination.

Illych snapped his fingers breaking my reverie and pointed to the doorway indicating it was my turn to enter.

I hurried to the doorway and entered, feeling that leaving the Naga chamber was a good idea right now.

This corridor had all smooth surfaces, no carved reliefs, and sloped downwards at a gentle angle. I was shocked when I looked up. The ceiling was possibly fifty feet up. The tactical LED flashlight could illuminate the space, but it was creepy knowing there was so much empty space above us.

The corridor began curving down and to the left, ending in a square room. Almost the entire center of the room was carved into a four sided funnel ending in a square hole some twenty feet down. There was only a narrow ledge of four feet around the perimeter of the room to stand on.

Mr. Lark spoke, "Here we rappel. This shaft drops down into a chamber shaped like a large bowl. The shaft is perhaps fifty feet plus another fifty foot drop to the floor inside the chamber below us."

Tank and Mike sprang into action dropping their bags and pulling out battery powered drills with diamond bits. They quickly drilled a series of holes into the floor. Into these they placed expanding anchors with steel rings. Bundles of rope were brought out of bags and quickly fed through rings while Mike and Held put on rappelling harnesses.

Illych pulled a flare from a leg pouch and lit it. With a casual toss it went down the shaft shortly followed by Mike. He quickly disappeared from sight and in less than a minute his voice came over my earpiece saying he was down. Held immediately followed. Illych began fitting me with a harness, "You are next."

"I have never rappelled."

"Relax, we are going to lower you down."

Tank and Illych grabbed one end of the rope that fed through a pair of supporting rings and told me to walk backward slowly.

I did as instructed and soon found myself dangling inside a dark stone shaft one hundred feet above what I was sure is a very hard stone floor. It was over quickly enough and Mike disconnected me and the rope was pulled back up.

In the time I was being lowered down Mike and Held had been busy illuminating the chamber. A half a dozen puck lights now lit up the room.

Next were the gear bags followed by Mr. Lark and Illych. The last one down was Tank. The ropes were left in place presumably for our escape if necessary.

The geometry of this chamber, also made from carved bedrock, was not natural. It followed a general four walls design with a gently sloping bowl shaped floor. Nothing was symmetrical and the walls and ceiling had a significant amount of non-uniformity. There were four exit doorways, one in each wall. But they were not symmetrical or similar in position or dimensions. They ranged in size from a single man doorway to the largest being able to accommodate a car driving through it.

Mr. Lark pointed at the largest doorway as our next pathway.

I felt myself drawn to the man-sized entrance and walked over to it, switching off my flashlight and peered into the darkness of the corridor extending away from me.

After my eyes adjusted to the darkness I could make out the length of the corridor a significant distance away. There was a faint green luminescence somewhere in the distance. I could not make out the source but it was there.

A hand landed on my shoulder and I jumped. It was Mr. Lark.

"Thomas, why are you over here?" He said.

I looked over at the team and I realized they were all looking at me.

"Something caught my eye and I took a look."

"Let's stay on task. I am trying to avoid attracting the attention of what might be down here with us. Your wandering off will not help."

Wait, there is something down here with us? In this dark?

Mr. Lark returned to the next step in the path. Mike took point again and walked through the large doorway.

I hurried to take my place in the center of the team, finding myself looking with my light in every nook and cranny we passed. This part of the journey passed through another stone corridor. It was wide and tall but the stone was roughly worked. There were no carvings of figures or hieroglyphs to be seen.

I moved closer to Mr. Lark and whispered to him, "How did they get the materials in the cache down here. Is everything in it small?"

"No, there is another larger broader path that provides a more direct route. I deemed the path we have taken safer, if less direct."

I nodded and continued walking.

The corridor began to show signs of light. It went from pitch black to dark grey. The path we walked was not straight and soon we could see shadowing on the floors and walls from the direct illumination somewhere up ahead.

After a final turn, the corridor ended in a short straight section and an opening into a great domed chamber. It was huge, perhaps a kilometer across. Giant glass cylinders, similar to those back at the Citadel, were fixed to the domed ceiling at regular intervals.

The effect was of clear, white, illumination. Everywhere in the chamber was well lit and visible.

Which made what was in the center of the chamber that much more difficult to comprehend. The center third of the chamber was a static uneven mass of grey and silver extending upwards as high as it was wide. The mass had aspects of a mist or cloud to it as well as angular shaping in some places.

The incomprehensibility of it made my eyes hurt and I forced myself to look away.

An alarm went off. A shrill 'beep beep beep', and it was coming from Illych. Then another began beeping, this time from Held. And then the bulky unconventional watch given to me my first day also began beeping.

Mr. Lark showed me how to shut off the alarm and the others did the same.

"The mass in the center of this chamber is the stasis well. We are close enough that we are being affected. The transmission of information through our nerves, the firing of the neurons in our brains, and the chemical reactions that occur in our bodies have all slowed. We are experiencing what is called time dilation or lost time."

"As long as we keep as much distance between ourselves and the event horizon indicated by the edge of the mass, we will be ok."

All of us spread out around our entry point hugging the walls while keeping watch.

Mr. Lark and I now stood alone together. His eyes were closed, consulting his Oculus.

I stood waiting quietly for several minutes until his eyes opened. Mr. Lark's expression changed from blank to his happy smile.

"I found it!"

I gave him a questioning look.

"The EPS is centered in the stasis well Thomas. How do we turn it off?"

I thought for a moment, not terribly appreciative of Mr. Lark's question, "With a switch?" I was almost joking when I said it, I really have no idea.

"Exactly, physical objects can be extended into the stasis well and pulled back. You could walk into it if you wanted to. From our point of view you would get slower and slower until you crossed the event horizon. Once you crossed you would be frozen in place. But if we tied a rope to you before you went in we could pull you back out."

"Unfortunately it is impossible to see beyond the event horizon, photons passing out of the stasis well undergo a multi-dimensional frequency dependent non-linear shift."

"Mr. Lark, that sounded very important but I have no idea what you just said." I had come to understand that Mr. Lark was a high order genius but if he did not filter his communications no one could understand him.

"Light is composed of photons, which are different than electrons. The EPS affects the probability of electrons moving or changing state, not photons. Light moves freely in and out of the stasis well. Unfortunately, the edge of the stasis well, called the event horizon, scrambles the light going in and coming out into an almost random jumble."

Based on the look on my face he could tell I was still not getting it.

"We can't see what is inside the stasis well because the light we see going back and forth is scrambled."

I nodded my head, "OK, so how do we turn it off?"

"I did not know until just now."

"We came here not knowing if you could turn it off?"

Mr. Lark chuckled. "We came here not knowing for sure if it was what I thought it was and not knowing how to turn it off. The Oculus is impaired with the stasis well so close. I needed to be here, in this chamber to figure out the secret of turning it off."

After a long pause I asked, "And?"

Mr. Lark turned and walked along the wall of the dome. The surface of the its walls were of rough-hewn stone, but there were vertical square columns of smooth finished stone rising from the floor, recessed into the wall at regular intervals. They were perhaps a foot square and four feet tall.

"We flip a switch Mr. Davies." Having said that Mr. Lark firmly planted his feet while facing one of the square columns, squared his shoulders and placed both hands on the top of one of the columns. He pushed with what looked like considerable force for an old man.

The column levered back into the wall with the pivot point somewhere below the floor and there was a loud clunk noise.

And nothing happened.

I waited and looked around. Mr. Lark walked back to stand by me.

Still nothing.

I think he felt my unasked question. "This stasis well has been here for ten thousand years. It is not going to blink out like switching off a light."

"So if electrical stuff won't work in there, how did that switch turn it off?"

"The switch is a levered beam pushing a long rod that extends to the center of the stasis well. The rod mechanically switched off the EPS. Now we wait."

Mr. Lark left me standing there and went to talk to Illych. Not long after the team moved to setup flash bang trip wires at the other entrances.

And then we waited...

Chapter 19

Two hours passed with no visible change to the distorted mass at the center of the chamber.

The others engaged in quiet small talk while we waited. Every so often Mr. Lark would consult his Oculus.

Having become bored and tired of standing around I found a relatively flat spot along the wall near the floor and close to our exit. I backed up to the wall and slid down into a sitting position on the floor.

With my right-hand index finger I began making circles on the smooth black stone.

I noticed there was no dust.

Looking at the rough stone of the chamber walls I could see dust built up on every upward facing surface on the rough stone. Looking across the chamber I observed there was no dust on the floor anywhere.

That is odd for a chamber that had been here for ten thousand years or more. Is there a cleaning crew?

"Mr. Lark, there is no dust on the floor. Why is that?" I called out to him.

Mr. Lark looked at me and after a pause his head cocked to the side and he swept the floor of the chamber with his eyes. His head then went straight up and his eyes closed while he consulted his Oculus.

"Curious, there is no mechanism for keeping the floor clean."

I was standing now and walked over to Mr. Lark, "Then why is the floor clean? The walls show signs of dust accumulation."

Mr. Lark's expression changed, "Something does not want anyone knowing they walk through here."

"That greenish glow back at the bowl chamber?"

"Possibly, Illych, we may have visitors soon. Switch the door security to lethal, including the way we came."

The four men sprang into action. Each doorway was shortly wired with a motion sensor, trip wire, and a directional fragmentary explosive. Everything was facing outwards from the chamber, down their respective corridors.

The preparations were done in less than ten minutes. Illych announced when they were complete and declared anything walking up on us would have a bad experience.

I looked back at the stasis well. It had significantly decreased in size and the blurriness was lessened as well. It appeared there was a large rectangular object as large as an automobile centered inside.

There was a figure inside the stasis well standing near the box. It was humanoid, hopefully human. Its height was maybe a little over five feet. I still could not make out any details though.

With the decrease in the stasis well and the increased visibility of what was inside, Mr. Lark again used his Oculus.

His eyes snapped open and he barked at Illych, "Amal Halluk is on his way. He is coming via the direct route from the temple complex above. I do not believe our presence has been detected."

"I estimate we have at most two hours before the Djinn walks through that doorway." Mr. Lark pointed at the doorway to the left of the one we had come in through.

"Our proximity to the stasis well has slowed time for us significantly. If there are hostilities, we won't win. In one hour we leave, no matter what."

The seconds then ticked by while we waited.

After a little more than thirty more minutes the stasis well event horizon collapsed. In an instant the stone box in the center of the room became visible. The humanoid figure also snapped into view. He was human, male, dressed in primitive brightly colored cloth and leather. His skin was dark brown and he carried a bronze cylinder in his left hand.

The man began to move in slow motion. His head turned towards the team and realization showed on the man's face. That expression changed to fear and he began slowly running away from us to the opposite side of the chamber.

Illych barked out, "Stop him!"

The four shooters sprinted towards the man, covering the distance between them quickly.

It was not enough.

The former prisoner of the stasis well stumbled his way into one of the booby trapped doorways. This was followed by a loud thump and boom. The shooters dived for the ground. Apparently the man from the past had set off a proximity mine.

Illych and Held flanked the doorway and looked around and down the corridor, shining their flashlights for a view. Illych was shaking his head from side to side.

Mr. Lark walked over to look. After pausing at the doorway he walked through it. A moment later he came back into the light carrying the brass or copper cylinder the now dead-man from the past had been carrying. It was covered in dripping blood but otherwise appeared undamaged.

The team assembled around the stone box. Mr. Lark stuffed the cylinder inside a pouch on his trousers.

Illych spoke first, "He was only a couple of feet in front of the mine when it went off. It was quick but what is left looks like it went through a blender."

Mr. Lark produced his Oculus and closed his eyes again. When he opened them he said, "We cannot go back the way we came. The explosion woke something up. It is not coming this way but I think it prudent we not get closer to it."

"Apparently our competition also heard the explosion. They have increased their pace. We need to leave soon."

I had to ask, "How do we leave? Our way back is no longer viable and the other path has Amal Halluk between us and the exit?"

Mr. Lark smiled, "Ye of little faith. There is another way out that will give us credible deniability before we translate. We will escape down the hall that man was just blown to bits in."

"First we need to get the lid off of this stone box, grab everything we can in the next thirty minutes and run like hell."

Illych asked about the thickness of the boxes walls, "We have plastique. We can blow it open."

Mr. Lark nodded his head, "I suspect some of its contents will not respond well to explosions. We might detonate something that leaves us in the same condition as that man who just ran away from us."

Held spoke up, "How about we run a line of plastique along the edge of the stone lid? If we are lucky it shifts the lid enough to get at the box's contents?"

Mr. Lark was quiet for a moment and nodded, "Do it."

Illych and Held worked quickly, taking blocks of plastique explosives, ripping off smaller chunks and rubbing them between their hands into long ropes. The ropes were then pressed onto the edge of the stone box's lid. The natural stickiness of the plastique held it in place. A blasting cap was crimped on a long piece of detcord shoved in one end of the plastique rope.

The detcord was fed out until all of us were sheltered in the gore spattered corridor. The end was cut and fitted with an ignitor. Everyone looked at each other and nodded. Held pulled the ignitor trigger and dropped it. We all moved further back into the corridor, away from the chamber.

A loud bang later and we jogged to the stone box to observe our handiwork.

The plastique had worked, sort of.

The lid had shifted across the box about a foot. Looking inside I could see the box was half-full of a lot of strange looking artifacts and fully half of that was taken up by a metallic finned, bronze-copper engine looking contraption.

The other half of the box contained two of the Egyptian high voltage lights, smaller versions of what was attached to the dome above. Five unmarked small stone boxes of differing sizes rounded out the contents of the stone crypt.

I had expected diamonds or bars of gold at least. The contents of the box more resembled what would be found in an automobile service shop, more functional and less intellectual.

Mr. Lark spoke first, "Illych, we are running out of time. Grab everything we can carry. We need to leave."

Ilych was already shoveling the contents into his colleague's hands who then promptly stored them away in the black bags.

I looked at the thing taking up half of the box's interior, "What about that big engine thing?" It was too big to carry but it looked very technical and interesting.

"That is a Thorium pile. I wish I could get it out of here as well as the EPS underneath the box. Unfortunately it is too heavy and bulky to take with us in the next few minutes."

Illych saved the Egyptian light bulbs for last. As he started to lift the first one Mr. Lark stopped him.

"We have everything we have time for and can reasonably carry. It is time to go."

Each of the four shooters shouldered a bag while Mr. Lark pointed to our exit and told us to move out. He would follow shortly.

"I will bring up the rear."

No sooner had he said this and his eyes closed to commune with the Oculus.

Illych was first into the corridor followed by Tank, Mike, and then Held. They moved quickly, with one hand supporting a loaded bag and the other holding a drawn pistol.

It was easy for me to keep up since my team mates were essentially carrying bags full of rocks. After the initial slippery part of the corridor, slippery from the guy who was just blown up, the floor was flat and level.

In a few minutes we came to an expansion in the corridor. It continued straight forward, but there was also a set of stairs on the left as we entered the expansion.

Illych noted Mr. Lark had not caught up and signaled for him on his ComDat.

"Mr. Lark, we have a choice."

"Take the stairs, I am right behind you. Just needed to finish leaving a surprise in the event we are pursued."

Illych started up the stairway. The stairs were narrow with a low ceiling. The stair tread height and depth were obviously not meant for human feet. It was slow going and the stairs went up forever in the heat and pitch black.

I was bringing up the rear on the stairs, sweating and puffing while trying to keep up with the others. At one point I stumbled and almost fell.

I heard Mike's voice from above advising me not to fall. The steps were so small and steep and I would probably just keep going. And we had already climbed a fair distance…

I heard a rustle behind me and looked down and back. Mr. Lark was coming up the stairs at a terrific pace, almost skipping upwards. For an old guy he has amazing endurance.

A few minutes later the stairs ended in a square chamber with a low ceiling of not more than four feet. It was ink black, hot, and cramped. I felt like an animal in a trap with no way out.

We had been climbing at a quick rate and everyone, except for Mr. Lark of course, was breathing heavily.

I was the closest to Mr. Lark and my curiosity got the better of me. "What is the surprise you left, if you do not mind sharing?

"Flip-trap, just after the remains of that poor fellow from the stasis well."

"Amal Halluk is too far back for his mortal servants to catch us. If he wants us he will need to advance alone. The trap will slow him down long enough for us to escape."

"About that escape, which way?" asked Illych?

There were several passages out of the room we were in. Of course, Mr. Lark points at the smallest of them.

"That way."

The escape route entrance was so small that Illych had to get down on his hands and knees. "How far?"

"Less than a hundred meters and it opens into a large cavern. Be prepared when you get there. You might have company."

That last part brought looks from the shooters. Then, starting with Illych, they got down on their hands and knees and crawled single file into the hole in the wall.

Mr. Lark opened his eyes from communing with his Oculus. "Wait a moment Thomas."

A terrible hissing noise came up the stairwell followed by a loud boom. The ground shook for a minute.

"Interesting, the flip-trap did not hold him long," this time Mr. Lark was speaking with his eyes closed.

A male voice came up the stairwell, dark and melodic, almost mesmerizing. I recognized it as Amal Halluk's.

"This world has traveled around its sun many thousands of times since such disrespect has been shown me. This has always been a problem with mankind's short-lived existence. They are always forgetting to whom respect must be shown. Give me what I have come for and perhaps someday I will let you go free."

Mr. Lark seemed to be considering Amal Halluck's words," I beg your pardon, elder one. I have no wish for conflict. I merely wish to escape with my skin intact."

"Manners and polite respect, in this age?" You could almost hear the humor in the Djinn's reply.

Mr. Lark's voice became harsh, "Do not enter onto the stairs. I am comfortable talking at this distance. Enter the stairs and that will change."

That ancient voice again came up the stairwell, "Who are you?"

There was a long silent pause.

Amal Halluk continued, "What are you?"

"The one next to you is as weak as any man but you are not the same."

"What are you?"

"You… smell different…"

"It matters not. I will take you back to my estate and we can discuss the particulars at my leisure."

Mr. Lark's hand fished what appeared to be a very large gold coin from a pocket.

"No, we will not," Mr. Lark's voice had a distant quality to it, like the calm before the storm. He then moved with the surety of a lightning stroke, making a motion down the stairwell.

I heard the metallic ping of the coin striking the stone steps below. It was followed by two more such notes. Mr. Lark then pushed me off to the side and we both moved away from the top of the stairwell.

Even in the dark, with only the light being my flashlight, I could see a distortion boil up out of the stairwell. It was a twisting blurred vortex that appeared for only a second and then was gone.

The final result was the stairwell's four surfaces had melted and drawn together, effectively blocking it closed. The Djinn could be heard howling through the small openings still left in the stone.

Mr. Lark spoke, "He was caught in the flowing stone, down below where the stairwell starts. It will take time, even for a Djinn, to claw his escape through several meters of solid rock. Let's get out of here."

The shooters were still crawling away during our encounter with Amal Halluk. Immediately after Mr. Lark's last comments they must have made it to the end of the crawlspace because the roar of gunfire from multiple weapons came rumbling back through the tunnel. It went on for what had to have been a complete magazines worth of rounds for the whole team. Then there was silence.

Illych's voice came over the ComDat, "Your warning was spot on Mr. Lark, something was here. It is dead now though, so feel free to crawl through."

Mr. Lark got down on his hands and knees and started crawling into the exit corridor and I followed right behind him. Being the last person, when traveling deep underground, is unnerving. Behind me the Djinn's howls could still be heard in the darkness.

To combat my claustrophobia I asked Mr. Lark a question to distract me. "What is a flip-trap?"

His voice came back through the crawl space, "A flip-trap is what I call a device that once activated, is invisible. When whatever it is set to imprison enters the flip-traps location it is triggered. The captive is pushed into other-space and held in a featureless spherical cage. They work well against living things. Not as well against the Created."

"So people just disappear?"

"Yes, instantly."

That is really disturbing. An invisible trap that makes people disappear.

"Is there a way to escape?"

"With the right equipment like an Oculus you will avoid being trapped all together. Otherwise some specialized methods will allow you to escape."

I took that to mean if you were Mr. Lark then yes, you could escape. For the rest of us mere mortals probably not so much.

Our discussion had kept the panic at bay during the crawl to our destination. My aching knees may never be the same though. We crawled out into a domed chamber walled with rough-hewn stone. The others had already started placing the light pucks on the surrounding walls.

The stone floor we crawled out onto was damp. It sloped down and disappeared into the blackest water I had ever seen.

Halfway out of the water was a creature the size of a grizzly bear and so pale that albino almost did not describe it. It was a perverse unholy combination of an octopus and lobster with a carapaced main body. Long articulated tentacles ending in vicious looking claws were sprawled out on the floor and hanging into the black water. Its body was perforated with dozens of bullet holes still leaking pale blood.

"Please tell me we are not swimming out of here," I croaked out.

"No kidding," quipped Tank, "I almost shit myself when that came crawling out of the water." Tank was taking the light pucks, twisting them on, and then skipping them like flat rocks across the water. They would eventually lose momentum and sink down into the inky depths below. The water had a milky green shade to it and the lights already under the water were like the pale eyes of an ancient leviathan lurking below.

Mr. Lark explained, "No, we translate from here. However, if we needed to we could escape through the water. We are far enough ahead to maintain plausible deniability on how we escaped."

He continued, "This was the alternative to the other entry route. The other way, the one we used, seemed the more comfortable."

Looking at the dead abomination lying in front of me I had to agree.

Mr. Lark looked around at everyone while pulling a dongle out. "Shall we?"

We crowded in and a moment later the six of us and our newly acquired loot soon received a jolt of freezing air and nausea from our return to the Compass.

Without pause Mr. Lark started walking to the Citadel. Illych and the others looked tired and in spite of the translation nausea everyone fell in behind him. The pace was again blistering and we soon passed the guardians and the main gate into the white light and warmth of the Citadel.

No sooner had the gates closed behind us when Held and Mike put down their black bags and sat down. Tank started stripping off his gear and stretching his massive form. Illych slowly removed his gear and also took a seat upon the stone floor.

Mr. Lark stood silently for a minute surveying the scene. I was hunched over from exhaustion. It is weird how it sneaks up on you and I joined the others sitting on the floor.

Mr. Lark did not appear affected by our recent exertions, "Place the artifacts we retrieved in the Library. I have business to attend to and will return in a day or two." That said he turned and walked out the opening gates.

As he left it occurred to me Mr. Lark was the only one who could walk back and forth between the Compass and the Citadel alone. The rest of us were required to travel in pairs...

After fifteen minutes of sitting and drinking some water we all pulled ourselves to our feet. A quick stop at the library followed by the cafeteria and then we all went to bed.

Tomorrow would be another day.

Chapter 20

After the Ellora caves mission we returned to
Charleston to supervise the ship refit. I had little to do
with this other than to be brought along every day to the
shipyard and watch. Shipbuilding was new to me and I
enjoyed watching everything come together.

In less than two short weeks it was time for me to go
on holiday like the rest of the team. From what I was told
Mr. Lark had figured out a long time ago that 24/7
missions and lethal hazards slowly broke people down.
Nobody knows how he came up with the current solution
but the schedule has been ninety days on followed by
thirty days off for years.

When the holiday started I said my goodbyes and
flew to San Francisco. Return tickets for thirty days from
now were already in my luggage.

The month in San Francisco ended up being the
best holiday I have ever experienced. In the past when I
had gone on holiday everything was budgeted. At first, I

was a little shy with the credit card but after a couple of days I decided that if I was stuck working for Mr. Lark I was going to have a good time. It is amazing how much fun you can have in a major metropolitan city when you have virtually unlimited money.

I did the usual tourist things. I also found a group of people to spend time with while visiting the many quality book stores in the city. American women love a man with a British accent and a few of them were willing to discuss books, go for a walk, and have dinner together followed by spending time in my hotel suite...

The days passed quickly and I soon found myself boarding the plane back to Charleston.

Chapter 21

I arrived back in Charleston around mid-afternoon on a bright sunny summer day. The weather in San Francisco was great but it did not have the penetrating sunlight I found myself standing in after walking out of the Charleston airport terminal.

The team had the same hotel rooms as our last stay. I went to my room and waited for a knock on the door.

Everyone was back by seven that evening and we went to dinner together. Although Tank had not been with us in Charleston before, he arrived here same as the rest of us. Apparently, the team will leave from different places for vacation but always meet up at the end in one place.

Mike and Tank both had deep tans from spending time on the beach. Illych was relaxed and even smiled a few times. I do not know what Held does on his breaks but he looked as relaxed as everyone else so it must have been good.

No one discussed the specifics of their vacations and we started on business right away. I had hoping to hear more about the others experiences but apparently now was not the time.

The shipbuilder had left a letter at the front desk of the hotel a few days prior to our return explaining the ship refit was complete and awaiting inspection. The modifications had all been tested and the ship had been taken out for a shakedown cruise.

Illych explained the plan for tomorrow was to inspect the ship and if everything was complete, to accept it. We would then move the ship to a private dock in Charleston. Once there we would finish stocking the ship and embark on our voyage.

After dinner we returned to the hotel to find Mr. Lark waiting for us. He needed Tank for something and had come to collect him. Tank gathered up his luggage and the two of them disappeared to the Compass.

The next day consisted of me standing around, mostly bored, watching the others going through every part of the ship. The shipbuilder also had people there to explain how all the systems worked. This process continued into the evening. Not everything had been inspected so Illych decided to extend the acceptance until the next day.

By mid-morning of that second day, Illych finally signed off on the work and accepted the ship. After lunch all four of us boarded and Illych piloted while Held shoved off. Mike drove the rental car to the new docking location. We then motored across the bay to the other dock and tied up.

The others remained behind on the boat while Illych and I returned to the hotel and grabbed everyone's gear and checked out. Back at the boat Illych explained we were remaining on the ship to help us acclimate to the conditions.

Below decks there were only two rooms, the engine room in the rear third of the boat, the front two-thirds being a wide open space with a high ceiling. The boats superstructure was a single pilot house with stairs down and a ladder up to the crow's nest.

The below deck room had bunks, storage lockers, tables, and a simple kitchen. The floor was steel plate with an epoxy coating mixed with sand to provide friction even when it was wet.

The pilot house had a single chair bolted to the deck. The radio and navigation equipment were the minimal required by maritime law. Having the Oculus, we had no plans to use them for much of anything.

Below decks Illych opened a duffel bag and took out nine stone cylinders about a foot long and six inches in diameter. Each stone had a strong magnet at one end. Illych stuck the stones to the deck floor in a rough circle about ten feet across. He then gave each of us a bronze translation dongle explaining it was keyed to the stone circle now laid out on the deck.

The rest of the day and most of the evening were spent by Illych and Held translating back and forth to the Compass for equipment. Mike and I remained with the ship and unloaded what was brought in.

Weapons, clothing, medical supplies, food, water, and so much more came in sealed square plastic containers. Each one had to be unpacked and the contents stowed in their preplanned location.

Late into the night the work was complete and four tired men fell into remarkably comfortable bunks. Illych did not wake us in the morning so I slept in, waking up last at around 9am.

As I understood the plan, we were going to conventionally motor out to about two-hundred miles from the coast and then translate the entire ship with us on board to another point in the North Atlantic close to where I had approximated Hy-Brasil would be located.

We did just that, the ships engines rumbled to life and Illych navigated us out of the Charleston harbor. Once we were out on the open ocean, Illych throttled up to cruising speed. The dual marine diesels drove the ship at a respectable pace, leaving a wake behind us that more approximated something from a speed boat than a stately yacht.

Not long after leaving the Charleston harbor I discovered a terrible thing about sailing the open ocean. I had never been at sea before and had never given any thought to sea sickness. It was on my mind now though. The sway of the ship made me nauseous, followed by projectile vomiting over the railing into the sea. None of the others were affected and they seemed amused by my being sick.

Held went below deck and returned with anti-sea sickness pills. Thankfully someone had planned ahead. The nausea calmed down but I still did not feel completely well. Illych tried to improve my mood by explaining that eventually I would get my sea legs and it would be ok. He was a little vague about how long that would take though.

I thought about how prior to meeting Mr. Lark, my only experience with vomiting had been when I had the flu. Pocket dimensions, violent Faeries, and repetitive nausea. I was now understanding better Illych's comment about 'it is all about the suffering'.

During the voyage out to the two hundred mile mark all of us changed into tactical dress. Magazines were loaded and weapons cleaned and oiled. When Illych's Oculus determined we were far away from any outside observers we all took turns test firing the arsenal stored below decks.

I had a hard time believing piracy this close to the American coast would be a problem. Still I found myself speculating about how surprised modern pirates would be if they tried to board this ship. The others were experienced soldiers who rarely missed what they were aiming at. I found myself uncharacteristically smiling at the thought of the outcome of such an encounter.

Illych announced when we had reached our goal distance from the shore. The engines were throttled down, bringing the ship to a standstill in the ocean. There was nothing but miles of empty water in every direction. Illych was motionless in the captain's chair, while he interfaced with the Oculus.

He pulled a translation dongle from a pocket and unscrewed it, flipped the ends and screwed it back together. The bright sunny day reflecting off the mild swells of the ocean's surface disappeared. It went pitch black for a couple of seconds. Then the black changed to overcast grey.

And we fell.

Or I should say the whole ship fell almost ten feet onto the ocean below. I lost my footing and fell down onto the deck and stayed there until the translation sickness passed.

While I was picking myself up I could hear Illych's remark, "Must be a tide thing."

I spoke before I thought, "What just happened?"

Illych replied, "The Ouiblet does not handle moving objects or compensate for moving surfaces. It is good at moving things between stationary points and will make sure we do not arrive encased in solid objects. This is why Mr. Lark scouts every arrival point with an Oculus."

"We arrived exactly where the Ouiblet was supposed to put us. Unfortunately the ocean is lower now than when the Ouiblet dongle was setup. That is also why the stone circle is setup below decks. The Ouiblet cannot translate into a moving target unless it is marked."

That is all good to know, I thought.

The calm ocean we just translated from had been replaced by large waves that bobbed the ship up and down. The warm air we had been enjoying was now a cold breeze.

The nausea of translation had been much worse this time. I realized we had just translated without either the origination or destination being a prepared stone circle. I had been warned, not that it helped, about how awful it would be. It occurred to me that something that makes you feel this bad must cause cancer or something.

The others had been affected and it took a few minutes for everyone to recover. Illych then throttled up the engines and steered the ship into the waves. Although we had no plans to use radar or anything electronic to find Hy-Brasil, we did plan on using GPS to plot the search pattern. I pulled out a notebook and wrote down our current GPS position. We were right where we had planned to start.

The translation had moved us four time zones east and significantly north. What had just been a nice early summer afternoon had been replaced with a cold, grey late afternoon. The sun would be down in less than two hours.

We would start our search where I had determined Hy-Brasil would most likely be and then search outwards in a spiral square pattern. Mr. Lark had explained to Illych that the Oculus would see the Hy-Brasil distortion if within at least twenty kilometers, making the search pattern forty kilometer stripes on the ocean map.

The rough ocean was challenging the seasickness medication that I was taking to its limits. Mike and Held took turns piloting the ship while Illych searched with the Oculus. I watched the GPS and made notes of where we had searched and when to change direction.

The night came quickly and the ships running lights were switched on. The part of the ocean we were in was not along a shipping route and Illych informed us nothing was on the ocean surface anywhere nearby.

The hours passed and I found my feet getting sore from standing on the steel plate floor near the helm for so long. Sometime around midnight Illych stopped the search. Due to the roughness of the ocean the ship could not just be halted in place. The bow had to stay into the waves and keep going, so we split up the piloting duties to get some rest.

Held and I had the last watch together. We switched off piloting every hour to give one of us time to sit in the captain's chair. I had no experience piloting a seagoing vessel. Turns out all I had to do was keep the bow into the waves while maintaining a low throttle.

When the others woke, the search continued. Apparently four hours of sleep was all we were going to get and I felt less than rested, not that anyone cared. At least the meals we had brought with us were good. The sea sickness had lessened to the point I could eat and the food was definitely improving my outlook.

The sun never came up as the cloud cover was too thick. The black of night just turned into a cold, dark, grey morning that looked like rain was coming. The search pattern continued and I was starting to doubt my estimated location for Hy-Brasil.

Around noon Mike went below to prepare lunch. Not long after that Illych broke from his reverie and announced he had found something while pointing ahead and to the left. If the ship were a clock hand on a clock face and pointing to twelve, then Illych was pointing to ten o'clock.

Held noted the compass heading indicated and steered the ship in that direction. Perhaps thirty minutes passed when Illych announced we were close. Looking out the pilot house window all I could see were grey skies and waves.

We took time for lunch while motoring about the point on the map that should be Hy-Brasil. Illych then announced he needed to check in with Mr. Lark. He went below deck and translated back to the Compass. While he was gone we continued piloting the ship in circles.

Everyone had a holstered side arm on them since Charleston harbor. Now that we had arrived at our destination, everyone took turns going below and gearing up. Now we had on body armor and slung rifles, the same space age looking KRISS's used in the Hoia forest mission.

While searching for Hy-Brasil my shipmates had been watchful. Now they exhibited that same hyper-vigilance I had seen back in Hoia forest. There was not much talking and when I tried starting a conversation both of the men told me this was not a good time to talk.

I realized that if we were near something like the portal in the clearing at Hoia forest, then maybe something could come out of Hy-Brasil like that Faerie that attacked us. Visions of sea monsters I had read about from mythology began to tug at my imagination and I checked that the door to the outside deck was closed and locked.

Now the changes to the ship began to make sense the railing around the perimeter of the deck, the crow's nest above me being only accessible from the pilot house, the small windows and steel reinforcement. This ship had been turned into a fortress against boarders.

I decided to venture a question, "Is there anything that might come out of the distortion? Like that Faerie back at Hoia forest?."

Mike answered me, "It's possible. I have never done anything on the ocean like this before but anytime a portal is involved something may notice us nearby and come out to play."

My curiosity got the better of me and I asked another question, "Any ideas what might come out?"

Mike glanced away from looking out the window to look at me, "Based on past experience and what legends and myths have to tell us, probably nothing good."

Held interrupted the discussion, "This place has a history of people visiting and returning without any mention of problems. My guess is we should not have much to worry about best but it's best to stay alert. I like to visit the Doctor as little as possible."

We were quiet after that, with everyone intently watching the ocean around us. Illych came up from below having returned from the Compass. He was now geared up and armed the same as Mike and Held.

"Mr. Lark gave me a key that should get us to the island. We just sail to where the Oculus points us. There will be a dense fog that we sail through and the island is on the other side," Illych said when he made it to the top of the stairs.

Illych was then silent and obviously concentrating on the Ocullus again. He pointed and barked out a compass heading. Held changed heading and increased throttle. After perhaps ten minutes a fog appeared less than one hundred meters ahead. What had been clear, open-ocean was now a dense fog.

Held throttled down and we entered the fog at only five or ten miles-per-hour. Illych and Mike climbed up into the crow's nest weapons at the ready. The fog was thick to the point of being a wall. The ship could be headed straight into a cliff and we would not know it until the last second.

I felt anxious with the ship driving forward into such thick fog, even if our speed was not much faster than walking. Held must have been thinking the same thing and turned on the deck lights and the headlights for forward illumination. He immediately turned them back off as the reflection back from the fog had been blinding, reducing what little could be seen to nothing. There was no choice but to continue blind into the fog.

I heard and felt something bump the ship. Something that gave way to the ship but pushed back enough for us to know it was there. I sucked my breath in through my teeth. Held had his face right up to the window glass looking out. The tension level had gone up several notches. I looked up through the hatch to the crow's nest and could see the others scanning the fog with their eyes.

Looking forward out of the pilot's window I jumped at the sound of the first shots going off. Mike had opened fire with his KRISS towards the stern causing me to look out the pilot room door window. The firing continued in short controlled bursts. There was a grey, translucent thing pulling itself over the railing on the starboard side close the stern of the ship. It had a bulbous head, larger than a human's, attached to a husky square body. Its four thick tentacle arms ending in large, opposable flipper fingers. The thing had leg-like appendages that were largely flipper-shaped. Even in the dim fog I could see the wrongness of its form.

Mike's shots were hitting it and I now understood why the deck had been refit with steel plating from bow to stern. Whatever the thing crawling on the ship was, it was not bullet-proof. Every shot went straight through and impacted on the deck. Without the steel plating we would have sunk our own ship.

Mike was focusing his fire at the creatures head. After it had pulled itself onto the ship it turned towards the pilot house and opened its mouth. The creature's thin lower jaw hinged down far back on its head, its jaws opened similar to a shark's, revealing a huge open maw with rows of sharp square teeth. The teeth were black and reminded me of the obsidian swords used by the Aztecs. Those swords were lined with razor sharp shards of black obsidian, all the better to hack someone to pieces with.

Illych started to shoot now towards the bow of the ship. As soon as Mike's first target fell down and stopped moving he reloaded and started shooting at another of the horrors. I swiveled from looking aft to looking fore, and saw at least six of the creatures were in the process of heaving themselves over the rail. Illych and Mike switched from controlled bursts to full auto. They would aim at one creature and empty a full magazine into its head. Then reload and target the next one. The KRISS was very controllable when fired full auto and in the expert hands they were putting the things down in good order.

Unfortunately, the rate these things were appearing on the deck was faster than they could be destroyed. Held told me to take the wheel and maintain the same heading on the compass. He then grabbed a duffel bag from the floor of the pilot house and started up the ladder to the crow's nest. I kept my eyes forward and watched the deck fill with wide-mouthed monstrosities. Between the two men in the crow's nest the gunfire was like continuous thunder.

One of the things made it to the pilot house front window. They were even more terrifying close up. It had no eyes, instead it was sunken in where its eyes should be. The thing's slimy grey flesh was translucent in places. In those translucent areas you could see pulsating organs inside its body. The first one to make it to the pilot house made a tentative swipe at the window and left a slime trail behind. Its next swing at the window had force to it, the window shook, making a loud booming noise.

One of the shooters above leaned over and unloaded at almost point blank range into the thing's head. Slime and goo as well as chunks of its head splashed off the window. I was piloting blind now using the compass as my only heading reference. There were so many creatures on the deck climbing over their dead kin that I could not see directly forward. It was obvious we were still in the fog though.

Something forcefully hit the pilot house door behind me. The pounding continued and the shooters had too many targets to stop the attack on the pilot house door. I watched in horror as one of the things walked up to the front window and stepped on the headless dead body lying there. It stretched its flipper arms upward, out of my ability to see. The thing began pulling itself up to the crow's nest. Its legs actually stuck to the window giving it support to begin stretching upward again. Then there was a gunshot with a deeper rapport that went off. The creature's body peeled off backward falling flat on the deck. Its head blasted open.

I risked a look up to the crow's nest and saw Held was holding a drum fed shotgun with faint smoke wafting from the end of the barrel.

Looking out through the gore covered window I noticed it was not as dim outside as before. The fog was thinning. Apparently, this was a signal for our attackers to leave. The mass of those still alive moved to the railings quickly and flopped over the side into the sea.

As soon as the monsters started leaving, the shooting from above stopped. In seconds the things were gone and what was left was carnage covered decks fore and aft. Every now and then an empty brass cartridge case would roll into the hatchway above me and fall into the pilot house. I looked around my feet and realized there were hundreds of empty casings on the floor.

The fog lifted as suddenly as it had come. Unlike the grey, cool, windy weather we had been in before entering the fog bank, the weather here was sunny and calm. The thermometer showed it was a comfortable temperature outside, much warmer than what we had been in less than ten minutes ago.

I then realized my hands hurt from gripping the wheel so tightly and were cramping up. Held climbed back down into the pilot house.

He looked me over, "Okay?"

"Physically."

I had no intention towards humor but Held smiled and said, "We are through. Those things either do not like the light or are limited to the fog bank. Regardless, look at their corpses." Held pointed out the window. I looked and could see smoke rising from the dead creatures as they were visibly melting away into smoke. Just like the Ciorii in my apartment or the Faerie back at Hoia forest. That meant the sea monsters were Created, not living things.

Held took my place at the helm and increased speed while switching the sonar on. The undersea slope leading to the island was clear. When the ship was a kilometer from the shore, Held made a ninety degree turn and began circumnavigating the island. Not long after making the turn Illych came down from the crows nest and began using the Oculus.

Mike and I swept up the shell casings and walked around the deck to inspect the damage. The first thing we found was the pilot house door out onto the deck had been bent. It could still be opened and closed but it needed to be shouldered in both directions now.

Mike went below with all the empty magazines to reload them. This left me in the pilot house with Held and Illych. The ship was cruising at a good speed. We found we could circumnavigate the island in about half an hour. Illych announced the island was roughly circular and about three kilometers in diameter.

The coast was rocky with cliffs ranging from man height to over thirty meters. We found only one place that would make a landing possible without a helicopter. The ship was now floating less than a kilometer from several hundred meters of beach.

I grabbed a pair of binoculars and scanned the island. A stone pier jutted out from the beach at least fifty meters into the ocean. Looking beyond the pier I could see the outlines of buildings overgrown by vegetation. The tree line started where the beach ended and there were no signs of human activity.

Illych announced, "I scanned the Oculus over the entire island and it's just trees and rocks. There are some old, intact, stone buildings clustered not far from the stone pier. Everything is overgrown and there is a stone block road leading into the island."

Mike looked at Illych, "And?"

Illych spoke again, "Something close to the center of the island is blocking the Oculus. The best I can tell there is a structure that is shrouded."

I asked, "Is that a problem?"

Held explained, "Shrouding is rare. It means there is something unusual there and it does not want to be observed."

I had to ask, "Does that mean more trouble?"

Illych shrugged, "It could be something or nothing. Probably an artifact left here when this place was created. However since the stories of this place talk about a wizard living here we will proceed like we might meet someone."

We piloted the ship up to the pier and tied off. Rather than rush into the island we took a break. It was mid-day yet so we cleaned weapons and took some rest, including a leisurely lunch.

After preparations were complete we split up. Held would stay with the ship following us with his Oculus. Illych, Mike and I would walk the stone road into the island and explore. Held would lock himself in the ship until we came back.

The pier was made from polygonal stone blocks perfectly fitted together. No stone was the same size as another and the shapes of the stones varied immensely. It struck me as a strange way to build a pier. The end of the pier became a stone block road running past several stone buildings, all overgrown from what appeared to be ages of neglect. The doorways and windows were empty. The stone work of the buildings was precise and quite beautiful. I asked Illych about looking around inside the buildings. He declined, saying he had already looked with the Oculus and they were all empty.

We started down the road into the interior of the island. As we walked we found the road surrounded by a forest of oak trees that were very large and ancient. There were no stumps or fallen trees.

Some of the trees grew right at the edge of the road. Even the ones some distance from the road canopied over it. The result was a shaded tunnel through the forest much dimmer than the sunny sky above.

The forest was also quiet. There should be squirrels and birds making noises. I did hear the occasional bird but otherwise the forest was silent. Though dimly lit and quiet, it was still not foreboding. The walk through the woods was more calming than anything else.

"Illych, is it just me or is this woods relaxing to walk through?" I asked.

"You noticed it too? Yeah, this is a pleasant walk in the forest. The Oculus does not see anything that is trying to influence us." Illych replied.

"Influence us?"

"Like to sedate us. You saw the Wizard of Oz? The field of poppies scene? This is not like that. It is just a pleasant day out." Illych smiled and shrugged.

Not long after entering the forest tree tunnel we could see the light at the end of the tunnel so to speak. The road was flat, straight, and clear, so we could see the kilometer and a half to where the road exited the trees into the sunlight.

Even before reaching where the forest ended in a circular tree line, we could see a stone structure. In the middle of the clearing was a polygonal stone wall maybe ten meters tall. The wall formed a circle less than two hundred meters across and nothing could be seen on the top. Inside a central building could be seen jutting up.

The road continued into the clearing and straight to the wall and through an arched opening. Illych halted our advance and was standing still and concentrating on the Oculus. After a few minutes he spoke. "I can observe everything on the island with the Oculus. Everything outside those stone walls in front of us is normal. The Oculus can't see inside past the stone walls though. I have scanned things in the past that revealed little but they at least revealed something. This is different. The Oculus reveals nothing inside that stone perimeter. I also get the impression that something is looking out at us, we will not be alone when we go inside."

After speaking, Illych shook his head, an involuntary reaction to disconnecting from the Oculus. He then waved his hand towards the arched opening in the wall and the three of us proceeded towards the gateway.

During the walk and even now, as we walked through the gateway, Illych and Mike held their KRISS's by the pistol grip while they were still slung from their harness. The grip kept the weapons at the ready but not in an overtly threatening way.

The gateway passage went straight up to a man's height and then arched overhead. The gateway was a wide as the road and the walls were at least four meters thick.

Walls ten meters tall and four meters thick what are they keeping out, dinosaurs?

The road continued straight through the gate to the stone building inside. Between the walls and the central keep was a well-tended lawn of short green grass.

For an ancient abandoned fortress on a secret, hidden island they sure have up to date landscaping, I noted. The neatly kept lawn was also confirmation of Illychs' belief that someone was in here.

The warm sunlight and green grass reinforced the positive vibe this place gave off.

The team stood in the road about half way between the wall and the keep looking at the large double doors on the building where the road ended. The doors were also set in a raised arch like the gate in the wall. The stonework of the keep was mostly a light grey. The doors were black stone with fine carving work upon its surface. I did not have time to work out what was carved when both doors swung open and away from each other.

The doors opened to reveal a four-foot tall, gangly humanoid standing inside. It was a Goblin Lesser Created. I knew this because it looked disturbingly similar to the Doctor back at the Citadel. It wore servants clothing dating from the Renaissance and both its hands were in front of it with the palms up.

Illych and Mike instinctively spaced themselves away from each other. I was now standing in between them gawking at the creature. The Goblin took several small, slow steps out into the sunlight. I could see the glint of the sun on its oversized solid black eyes.

Then it spoke. The voice was male but in a high pitch, like an adolescent boy. "My master offers a peace bond during your stay within the walls of this place. He wishes to extend his hospitality to you as guests in his home. If you accept his offer you will be under his protection during your visit." The goblin's English was flawless if somewhat archaic in the pronunciation.

Illych, Mike and I stood still for a moment. I decided to reply. The goblin was offering something old and not readily understood in the modern era.

I spoke, "The peace bond is accepted. No violence by our hand will be committed in this place. Your master's hospitality is welcome and we look forward to meeting with him in peace." Illych and Mike looked at me but said nothing. I hoped I had not messed up the formalities. If whoever was here had really been on this island for hundreds of years their idea of social niceties would be old world. We would need to be careful to not give offense by saying something that would be interpreted as rude.

"Please wait here for my master," the goblin said. Then it turned, and walked back into the keep.

Chapter 22

A moment after the goblin disappeared inside the
keep a man walked out of the shadowed doorway. He
was short by modern standards, possibly five feet six
inches tall. He appeared to be a deeply tanned man of
Caucasian heritage. His clothing was simple, a black
linen shirt belted at the waist and black linen trousers
tucked into black boots. I would have thought the all
black color choice odd if not for the knowledge of why
we also wore black clothing.

The man had a golden skull cap that covered his
head half-way down his forehead and all the way down
the back of his head. It gave the impression it was as
much a part of his head as his hair would have been.

The sleeves of his shirt stopped at the elbow. His
forearms were banded with silver and black bands tight
on his skin from wrist to elbow. His eyes were dark and
bright with intelligence. He had a moustache and goatee,
both neatly trimmed. The lines on the man's face

betrayed his age but he carried himself as a young man might and he appeared quite fit.

"Peace be upon you. Welcome and be at ease. You are guests within my home. My name is Balthazar." The man said and bowed deeply at the waist.

"Peace be upon you Balthazar. Thank you for your welcome. I am Thomas. My companions are Illych and Michael," I said while indicating each of them in turn.

"Let us go inside out of the bright sun and partake of my humble hospitality. It has been a great while since I have received visitors." Balthazar stated and then turned to walk inside.

Illych looked at me, smiled and waved me forward. I then followed Balthazar inside followed by Illych and Mike.

The ground floor of the keep was a single great room. In one corner was a spiral stair case going up. In another corner was a stone railing protecting the opening of straight stairs going down. One wall had an immense fireplace. The mantle above the fireplace was made of ornately carved wood and several curious looking objects of metal and crystal or glass sat upon it.

The ceiling was over three meters above the floor. Huge beams carved from single stones supported the ceiling. There were no windows at the ground floor, as should be expected for a fortified keep. The room was taken up by a dining table capable of seating ten and a sitting area. The sitting area was a semicircle of padded wooden chairs heavily built from a lustrous dark wood that gleamed in the light. Each chair either shared or had their own small table next to them made from the same rich wood.

I took this all in and noticed the light. Overhead were crystal lamps emitting a pure white light. The lamps did not appear to be burning anything and I saw no wires attached to them. The light touched everything in the room while producing almost no shadows. I marveled at how everything was so clear to see.

Balthazar continued into the room to the semi-circle of chairs. He waved for us to sit. "Please sit with me and we can have a conversation."

Illych and Mike looked uncomfortable at sitting in a potentially hostile situation. I looked at them saying, "We must sit and talk otherwise we are snubbing the offered hospitality. If something was going to happen it already would have."

Illych and Mike carefully set down their weapons within easy reach, leaning them against the chairs they chose to sit on. They picked chairs with at least one empty chair between them and Balthazar.

My curiosity got the better of me and I chose a chair next to Balthazar at a slight angle to facing him.

"I must apologize for the attack on your ship when you crossed the boundaries to this island," Balthazar said.

"Those things follow your orders?" Illych blurted out.

"Yes, they are posted as guards against unwanted visitors. There are few who know how to come here without my opening the boundaries to allow entry. Those like myself know how to pass over the guardians. Anything else coming in is more likely to be an adversary," Balthazar said.

"What about the others who have visited? None of the accounts I have read from visitors to Hy-Brasil mentioned guardians," I asked.

"Unfortunately my visit to this place was not planned. I did not bring certain tools with me and am only able to open the boundaries every seven years for about a month. If I am fortunate someone will be sailing in the area and I will receive a visitor." Balthazar explained.

"So you could leave if you wanted?" I asked.

"Let us exchange stories. Please tell me what brings you to my refuge and I will tell the story of how I came to be here," Balthazer said with a more serious look on his face while obviously avoiding my question.

"An exchange of stories then," I agreed.

"A map led us to a Faerie lair in Romania. There we found the journal of Captain John Nesbit. I believe the Captain visited you many years ago. His journal spoke of this place. An expedition was organized and now we are here," I kept the story brief. No reason to give away too many details.

"I remember the good captain's visit. He was a decent enough fellow. I commissioned him to get a letter to my residence. I concluded he had failed as none came to help me leave." Balthazar said this with a far-away look in his eyes, obviously thinking while he spoke.

"The tools and weapons you carry I have never seen before. It has been over seventy years since someone else last set foot on this island. You were not sent by one of my brothers. Who are you and how did you know how to get past the boundaries? This is secret knowledge, ancient and unshared outside the brotherhood of the Magi. Whom do you serve?"

Balthazar's body language did not change. He was obviously completely confident in his safety. The question however made something shrivel up in my chest. I was sure the wrong answer would have consequences.

I replied, "We are bound in service and cannot speak of it. I do not know our master's affiliation or association. I say to you: we were not sent here to harm you. Our discoveries made us curious and we came here to see what there was to see. As to our crossing of the boundary, our master provided the means to do so. We do not know its workings," I spoke truthfully hoping it was the right answer.

"I can see that your minds are warded against being touched. The workmanship is excellent and performed by ancient hands. Regardless, I can still faintly perceive your thoughts and you speak the truth." Balthazar stated.

I guessed Balthazar was referring to whatever the 'Doctor' back at the Citadel had done to us to shield our thoughts and emotions from outside observers.

"I will now share with you how I came to be here," Balthazar said.

"Please forgive my interrupting. Before you begin, could you share how you can speak the language we are comfortable with as if you were born to it? English was very different over three hundred years ago," This question had been pushing itself forward in my mind and I had to ask.

"I am Balthazar and a Magi of old. My line stretches back in time almost to the beginning. It is useful to speak as a native when one travels. You are shielded from my learning your language from you. But the last to set foot on this island spoke your language in its more recent tongue, I learned it from them. How exactly is a story for another day," shared Balthazar.

"Now we will discuss how I came to be stranded on this hidden island. In the year of Our Lord 1645 I decided to journey to what was being called the new world. Magi had known of the continents across the sea since the beginning. But neither myself, nor any of my brothers had been there since the ice retreated. After some consideration I decided to journey there and witness what was unfolding."

"Shortly after setting out from my residence in the Caucasus mountains I came to believe I and my caravan were being followed. The sensation of pursuit disappeared when I arrived in Vienna and stayed with one of my brothers for a short time."

"Towards the end of 1646 I set out for England, planning to purchase a ship for the journey across the ocean. Not long after leaving Vienna the sensation of pursuit returned. Something was indeed following me. I tasked two of my mortal servants to stay behind so that I might observe what followed. Both servants were destroyed a week later. I now knew I was being followed by something that had ill intentions towards me."

"I decided trying to return to Vienna would bring a confrontation sooner and perhaps on terms to my adversary's advantage. So I pressed on with the belief that once I was at sea the pursuit would end. In Paris I stopped. My mortal servants needed rest and resupply. I set wards and posted guards. There was another attack, really more of a reconnaissance I believe. I will not discuss the form of the attack but I learned much of my pursuers from it. My position in Paris was untenable.

Another attack would be much larger and would endanger the city. We completed our resupply and quickly left for Calais in order to cross to England."

"We experienced attacks along the way. The adversary was trying to slow us down and weaken those travelling with me. I lost half my mortal servants between Paris and Calais."

"The attacks were unfocussed and of a particularly vicious and vile nature. Mortal men of that day were ill equipped to defend themselves. The people living in the areas we traversed suffered in our passing."

I was intrigued by these statements and I wondered what could be found researching the area between Paris and Calais in 1647.

"We crossed the channel as soon as possible. Upon arriving in England I could feel the pursuit lessen. Our pursuers were delayed by the channel."

"I did not rest in London though. A ship was immediately purchased, provisioned, and crewed in less than two weeks. It was very early spring in 1647 when we set sail. We should have waited a month more to let winter fully pass but the pursuers were on English soil now and I needed to put some open ocean between us."

"The night before we set sail we were attacked again. I was forced to become personally involved as the attackers were legion. Many mortals near to the pier where my ship was docked died in fear and pain. Only two of my mortal servants survived. After destroying the attackers I instructed the two remaining men to travel quickly to Vienna and tell my brother what had happened. My hope was that they could slip away while the adversary was regrouping. I do not believe they were successful or survived."

"The crew had boarded the ship prior to the battle. Terrified by what they had seen they demanded to be released and allowed off the ship. I forced them to remain aboard and instructed the captain to cast off and head for open-ocean. Our course was north up the channel. Then past Scotland and northern Ireland. Once we had made the turn southwest past Ireland there was another attack. The adversary had ships, three of them, manned by vile creatures and propelled by unnatural means. We would not be able to outrun them."

"Since leaving London, my goal had been Hy-Brasil. I could not shake the pursuit and my adversary was preventing communications to my brothers. I ordered the captain to maintain the heading I gave to him. We were less than a day from Hy-Brasil when the adversary's ships became visible to the crew."

"Although my mortal servants had perished, I had hidden aboard the ship several ancient servants. Goblins you call them. They are ancient creations from when the world was young and they had served the house of Balthazar for eons. Although they are incapable of affection or emotion I am still fond of them.

I took the one best suited for the task. Even though ancients may look the same, they are all unique in one way or another," Balthazar had a distant look as he recalled the events from 350 years ago.

"Once an ancient servant is properly aligned with a new master he can be commanded in a language other than the one of its creation. But for the task I was sending my servant on it would require I speak to their true and ancient nature using the language it was created with. This is difficult and requires time. With pursuit so close I had very little time. I commanded it to attack our pursuers, to rend and unmake them. The ancient did as commanded. I did not witness what happened but it worked. My pursuers were forced to stop and fight. The delay was long enough for me to make it to Hy-Brasil. I have been here since," Balthazar finished.

Illych interjected, asking the question I was thinking, "I thought the physical form of an ancient could only be temporarily destroyed. That over time they would remake their form in our world. From your story it sounds like the goblin was forever lost."

"When its physical form is destroyed by weapons forged in this world then yes, its spirit will find a place to rest and remake its body. However, I could feel the end of the battle even at a distance. A weapon from long before the record of history was used and the ancient was unmade. It was a horrible crime. Such creations cannot be made again. Those that are now are all there will ever be," Balthazar finished.

"You have been here ever since?" I asked.

"Yes," Balthazar replied.

Chapter 23

Balthazar smiled and spoke again, "Enough of the past, let us speak of the future. I wish for your master to visit me. He must be powerful and wise to be able to send you through the boundaries unbidden to this island. Such a master I wish as an ally so I might leave this place."

While I was considering what Balthazar had just said Illych replied, "We cannot speak for our master. He will expect a report of what we experienced during our visit. I will inform him of your earnest request that he visit you."

Balthazar replied, "Unfortunately that is too much uncertainty. Your visit is a unique opportunity. Thomas will remain here as my guest and hostage."

Illych and Mike visibly tensed at Balthazar's statement, their hands instinctively going to their weapons.

Balthazar spoke in a commanding voice, "Stop! No harm will come to Thomas. If necessary my servants will disable you and return you to your ship."

I realized that two Goblins had appeared as if out of thin air. One was not more than five feet away from Mike and the other was positioned similarly close to Illych. They stood there in their outdated attire looking straight at the men. They were so close the men could see their reflections in the Goblins solid black eyes.

"There will be no violence in my house after a peace bond has been given. By either of us," Balthazar concluded.

"Illych, taking a hostage to initiate a discussion is an old world practice. It is not an accepted practice in the modern era but for someone of Balthazar's age it is quite normal. I am sure nothing will happen to me. Go back and report. We will see what happens from there," I hoped my statement would keep this a cordial discussion.

"This will not be well received when we get back," Illych said while looking right at me.

I could not think of anything to say. Balthazar was holding all the cards. Plus I only felt positive about our meeting with Balthazar. He was friendly but not overly charming and had made no overt threats, other than that the peace bond would be observed by both parties in spite of my kidnapping.

Illych and Mike stood.

"We will take your message to our master," Illych said.

Balthazar nodded and swept his hand towards the doors out to the courtyard.

Illych looked at me and said, "Good luck."

I nodded and tried to look confident even as the weight of what was happening began to sink in. Even though my experiences over the last months had been a series of life altering events, I also realized that if Karl Lark did not come for me I would spend the rest of my life on this little island with an ancient sorcerer and his pet goblins. This was not the life I would have foreseen for myself, even after Mr. Lark had already altered my previous vision for my future.

Illych and Mike strode out through the opening doors. I had stood up from my chair but stayed where I was as they left. After they left the doors closed, leaving me alone with Balthazar and his two Goblin servants.

"How long do you think it will be until they get the message to your master?" Balthazar inquired.

I had to think about that. Walk back to the boat. Sail out to the open ocean put some distance to the island before translating to the US coast. Then someone would translate back to the Compass and get a message to Mr. Lark.

Perhaps it would be best to be vague.

"Hard to say, I am not aware of my master's whereabouts," It was a truthful statement. I have not a clue on how Karl Lark would deal with the situation.

"Good, that gives us plenty of time to visit," said Balthazar while smiling.

I thought about the situation some more and decided to make the best of it.

"Yes Balthazar, let's sit and talk for awhile."

"Since I have made a hostage of you perhaps you should pick a topic to discuss?" Balthazar stated as he sat back down on his chair. Balthazar's body language was relaxed and he was smiling. It was obvious he was enjoying having a guest to talk to.

"You are not the same as the other two. They are accomplished soldiers. Proud, brave and disciplined, but somewhat rigid in their thinking. They are prone to solving problems with violence. I also believe from observing them that they are elite soldiers, perhaps grenadiers or a nobleman's personal guard?" Balthazar speculated out loud.

I considered Balthazar's words and how to start such a conversation. "They are elite warriors even among the elite. My master chose them carefully to serve him."

Balthazar continued, "You are not rigid as they are. Your speech shows learning and knowledge. There have been many visitors to this island over the last 350 years but your small party is unique among them. The soldiers I understand. But what are you?" Balthazar was pointed in his question and I felt a little uncomfortable.

"I am a librarian," was my reply. A truthful statement, if not completely descriptive.

"Yes, a learned man. You are not a 'scientist' though, as I believe they are calling men these days who seek knowledge. More of a wizard's apprentice perhaps. This will make our discussion while we await your master even more stimulating," Balthazar continued.

I felt compelled to ask a question. Since I was a captive already and Balthazar seemed in good spirits I took the risk.

"Balthazar, my apologies for asking such a direct question, but what are you?" I flinched inside a little after asking the question. If Balthazar took the question as rude the tone of the discussion might change abruptly.

Balthazar did not stop smiling. "That is the first question. It is a good question and politely asked. I am a Magi, part of a brotherhood, originally seven in total. Each of us apprenticed to the former in our line. When our master's age finally took their strength they passed the burden of their line to another. The Magi were founded eons ago, long before any current recorded history."

"When you ascend to take the name of your line, you leave your old name behind. Once ascended, I became Balthazar with memories and knowledge spanning back to the beginning of my line."

"You can remember that much?"

"Digging deep into past memories is not done lightly. Only by deep meditation can memories be reconstituted from ancient times. At my place of power there are also vast libraries with much written down by the long line of Balthazar." Balthazar said in reply.

"Seven Magi? I have read many old books on the occult and there is no mention of you."

Balthazar nodded and continued, "In the beginning there were seven. Over time there were challenges in transferring the mantles of two of us. Those mantles were each broken into three. Each of the three was passed to a worthy champion becoming Illuminated. Thus there are five Magi and Six Illuminated."

"When you live as long as the Magi do, you tend to disconnect from the outside world. The successors chosen to ascend are carefully observed over decades of service. Anyone who would choose to enjoy a public life cannot ascend."

I shivered a bit when Balthazar said, 'cannot ascend'. That statement gave the impression the candidate was done away with versus quietly retired. Perhaps a version of how Karl Lark remains anonymous? Keeping the pool of those who know too much small…

"We are quiet. The Magi were created to balance out the efforts of the Adversary." Balthazar continued.

"The Adversary? What is the Adversary?" I was intrigued now.

"It is not known. The Adversary has never been revealed," Balthazar said this with a faraway look on his face.

"In eons of history you have never figured out what you are fighting?" I said incredulously.

"We do not fight the Adversary. We facilitate human survival, typically by unmasking the Adversary's efforts. The Adversary cannot be defeated by conventional means. He is ancient, even more ancient than the Magi. The Adversary's knowledge and abilities are beyond our understanding. He cannot be bested in any arena or endeavor. All that can be done is to prevent him from winning." Balthazar's tone was solemn.

"So you watch and intervene as needed? Is that why your name appears in the New Testament of the Christian Bible." I was in awe now.

"Yes, Balthazar was there. Not my personal form, but my predecessor after whom I ascended. A gift was given to make the Adversary's efforts less effective.

Unfortunately our efforts to remain anonymous failed and the visit ended up being recorded. This was probably some unfathomable machination of the Adversary. The Magi are not perfect and still remain human, capable of error," Balthazar said this and shrugged.

"This is quite the history lesson. What are your plans when my master arrives?" I asked.

"I can leave anytime I wish but I believe whatever pursued me here is still waiting outside the boundaries of this island. Based on your account of Captain Nesbit's efforts, visitors to this island are leaving unmolested. If this is true then I can escape when visitors leave if I am not seen among them," Balthazar volunteered.

"Pardon my lack of understanding. Your plan to escape is to not leave?" I questioned.

"It is a brilliant plan isn't it?" Quipped Balthazar with a chuckle.

"Thomas, did you see any gardens on the island? Animals for food of any kind? It is because I am still living off of the provisions I brought here with me 350 years ago." Balthazar stated.

"No ship could carry enough provisions for one man for 350 years," I said stating the obvious.

"I have an ancient artifact called a Quixault. The inside is much, much larger than the outside. I can store a fantastic amount of anything and retrieve it as necessary. It is convenient when travelling and the local provisions are questionable." Balthazar shared.

"You have something like a tesseract? An actual tesseract? That you have hundreds of years of supplies stored in? How do they stay fresh? Even preserved food will not keep for hundreds of years," I replied incredulously. All those years of watching Dr. Who as a child just paid off, Balthazar keeps a TARDIS in his pocket.

"They have a word for a Quixault in the current era? That is unexpected. Regardless, there are parts of the Quixault where degradation of materials is essentially stopped. I have stored a marvelous selection of foodstuffs as you will see at dinner this evening." Balthazar appeared nonplussed after announcing he had a magical box with infinite storage that a person could carry around with them.

I thought about what had just been discussed. Putting the pieces together I came to a conclusion. "You will put yourself in the Quixault and we carry you out of here. Is that your plan?"

Balthazar smiled, "You are quick, and yes, that is my plan. Unfortunately it is not as simple as that. Things inside the Quixault cannot leave of their own accord. They have to be recovered by someone in possession of the Quixault. I will need to trust your master will release me from the Quixault when we have put enough distance between me and this island."

"The other issue: the inside of the Quixault is unnatural. A human placed within will find their senses assaulted by the impossibility of the experience. A normal man would quickly be driven insane. Fortunately, I am not a normal man. With proper preparation I should be able to withstand the inside of the Quixault for days. I will find the experience unpleasant but I will emerge with no permanent disability."

"How big is this artifact?" I asked.

"It is a small box that fits into ones hand," replied Balthazar.

"How do you get things out? Do you reach in and get what you want?" I asked knowing the answer would be much more complicated.

"When you hold the box properly you can see in your mind what it contains. You can choose what is desired and it will be released and appear in front of you. It sounds impossible, but translating things from inside the Quixault to the outside world does not have them physically leaving the box," Balthazar shared.

Balthazar had said translate. I wondered if the Quixault and the Ouiblet have something in common?

Chapter 24

Balthazar and I enjoyed a long conversation that
went on for hours. Balthazar's servants brought wine
and food. I cannot remember a more relaxing or mentally
stimulating experience. Balthazar was an exceptional
host and I was genuinely surprised when the tenor of the
discussion changed suddenly.

One of Balthazar's Goblin servants materialized and
moved to stand beside Balthazar's sitting form. No
words were exchanged but some sort of message was
delivered.

Balthazar declared, "It is possible your master is
coming for you. The same mark used to enter the
boundaries when you first arrived is being used again."

I asked, "What about the things guarding against
entry?"

Balthazar replied, "I was not prepared when you first
arrived. This time I am. Your master and his companions
will pass unmolested."

From my own experience I knew whoever was coming would be here within the hour.

"Perhaps it would be best if you greet them as they pass through the outer walls, a show of goodwill and your good health," Balthazar observed.

"As you wish," I agreed.

Balthazar and I continued chatting for some time. He then interrupted at one point, "An individual man approaches, who I assume is your master. Perhaps it is time for you to go out and greet him?"

I stood and walked out through the keep doors, traversed the neatly kept lawn and walked to the wall gates.

When I had originally arrived at the keep it had been mid-morning. Now it was afternoon but still sunny and warm. No sooner did I approach the gateway when a single figure broke the edge of the tree line and walked out into the sun: Karl Lark.

I felt a surge of emotion. It appeared Mr. Lark was not going to leave me on the island. My emotional response and train of thought caused me to wonder if I was suffering from some form of Stockholm syndrome. I realized having Mr. Lark coming to my rescue making me feel better was a little weird.

Mr. Lark faced me while keeping perhaps twenty feet between us and I stood waiting to speak until spoken to. He was wearing banded black armor made from some sort of reflective material that resembled obsidian. The armor covered his whole body while leaving his face exposed. An Oculus was mounted into the left shoulder of the armor. The bands were finely interlocked and the armor did not appear to weigh its wearer down nor limit his dexterity. I had seen many different suits of armor from a broad range of time periods in the museums of Europe. What Mr. Lark was wearing did not resemble anything I had seen before. I could not fathom the purpose of his wearing armor in this age of firearms.

During the pause while we stood apart from each other, Mr. Lark's face had that look I had come to associate with using the Oculus.

After a few minutes of awkward silence Mr. Lark spoke, "Thomas, you appear none the worse for wear. Where is this Balthazar that kept you from returning?"

"He is inside the keep. I was held hostage in order to bring you here, but my stay has been actually quite pleasant. Balthazar gave me a history lesson and I have a good understanding of why he is here and why I was held here. He has a proposal to make."

Mr. Lark nodded, "Illych indicated something about his being unable to leave due to some malevolent pursuit. I plan to hear him out."

The two of us walked together through the gates to a point half-way between the walls and the keep. The keep doors opened and Balthazar walked out still dressed in his simple clothes and carrying nothing in his hands.

Balthazar spoke first, "You are the master."

Mr. Lark responded, "Yes. But we do not call it such. Thomas is permanently bound to my service though."

"Yes, I can see the mild Geas of secrecy upon him but no stronger Geas of binding. Why not bind him more permanently to your will?" Balthazar questioned.

"I prefer to keep my people able to perform at their best. The skills they possess making them useful to me would not function as well if they were more tightly bound."

The conversation paused while the two men regarded each other.

"Your English is modern for someone trapped here hundreds of years," Mr. Lark continued.

"Recent visitors have kept me up to date on the language of the day," shared Balthazar.

"Let us be formally introduced. I am the Magi Balthazar. You are welcome in my house. The peace bond extended to your servant is extended to you," Balthazar stated while bowing at the waist with his arms stretched out and hands palms up.

Mr. Lark watched this with a neutral expression. "My name is Karl Lark. I accept the peace bond but we must move past the use of hostages."

"I understand. At the time it was a necessary tool and not my preferred way of opening a dialogue," Balthazar seemed genuinely apologetic.

"You say Magi. I am familiar with the term. You must be old indeed if you are the Magi Balthazar spoken of as visiting Christ at the time of his birth?" Mr. Lark queried.

"That was my master who was mentioned. To whom I was apprenticed," Balthazar looked serious as he spoke this. He was looking Mr. Lark up and down, observing his suit of armor.

"Do you know the history of the armor you wear?" Balthazar asked.

"You have seen armor similar to this before? I found it on an expedition years ago. It took some time to learn its secrets and it has served me well ever since," said Mr. Lark.

"That armor is old, truly ancient. There was a time when humans ruled over all. There are things that still walk this earth that remember that time and the tyranny that armor represents. You should take care whom or what sees you in it," Balthazar spoke gravely.

He then smiled, "Let us get inside out of the sun and converse in a more cordial environment," he then turned and walked back inside the keep.

I followed Balthazar in with Mr. Lark trailing last. Three comfortable chairs had been arranged in the center of the room. Balthazar stood by one, I walked to a second, and Mr. Lark took the remaining. In spite of his armor he was able to sit comfortably.

"Perhaps some refreshment while I explain the history of my predicament?" Balthazar offered.

"Some refreshment would be excellent," replied Mr. Lark.

The Goblins appeared, offering wine and whiskey. I noticed Mr. Lark's reaction to the appearance of the Goblins was noticeably less than Illych's had been.

Balthazar spoke first. "I was sailing to the new world in 1647. The brotherhood of course knew of the existence of all the continents since ancient times, but no living Magi had set foot there since before the ice had come. Ever the curious and titillated by the recent European 'discovery' I met several of my fellow Magi and we determined that one of us should go. Being the junior of those in attendance it fell to me as I knew it would."

"I prepared my household for an extended absence. In the traveling company would be my ancient servants you have seen here plus one whom I have lost, my three apprentices and several other bound mortal body servants. It was certainly not an army, but a formidable company to be sure."

"My residence is ancient and storied as befits the name Balthazar, and not far from the Caspian Sea at the base of Shahgah Mountain. My soul yearns to be within its cool walls again, and to travel to the Caspian Sea and look upon its waters. It has been too long I am afraid." Balthazar looked wistful."

Balthazar continued, "We traveled by horseback. My ancient servants required no such accommodations of course, only those of us who are mortal and some extra horses to carry provisions and such comforts as I deemed necessary. We travelled north of the Black Sea. My goal was to visit the centers of power and culture in Europe during my journey to the new world. Stops at Vienna, Paris, and then finally London were planned. In London I was to secure a ship and crew for the journey."

"Upon passing into the wilds of Walachia something began following us at a distance. Or perhaps it had been following my company since our journey began, I do not know. It was there though and my augurs could not clearly see or understand what it was."

"I drove my company hard to get from the wilderness to Vienna, where one of the brotherhood resides. He would give me shelter if needed." Balthazar paused at this point. After being thoughtful for a time he continued. "Whatever was following moved away upon my company's arrival in the more civilized parts of Austria-

Hungary. My brother met us on the way, miles out from his residence."

Balthazar continued, giving the history of his arrival at Hy-Brasil as had been explained to me earlier that day.

"This brings us to the question at hand. I would like to escape this prison, Mr. Lark. How can I persuade you to assist me?" finished Balthazar.

Mr. Lark considered what Balthazar had just said and replied. "A direct question deserves a direct answer. It would be a challenge to be sure. To begin we must discuss what would be exchanged in return for my organizations services. First, I need to learn more of the nature of your pursuer and the attacks you experienced."

Balthazar nodded in agreement. "Yes, you should know what you would face in assisting me. Most of the attackers were strongly bound humans. So strongly bound their minds were broken. In large groups, with the weapons common at the time, they were a threat to us. Even my ancient servants can be overcome by enough blades and fists."

"There were other creatures, ancient servants of a lower order, leading the bound humans. Also abominations, created by the malformation of living people and animals, were part of the assaults. The enemy's ancient servants, Goblins as you call them, could bind any person encountered along the way, thereby increasing the strength of what followed us. Those ancient servants are what gave the ships pursuing me their unnatural speed." Balthazar explained.

"These are all threats my organization can meet and overcome," said Mr. Lark.

After a pause Mr. Lark continued, "I am not a man to wait long in making a decision and am inclined to assist. However such an undertaking will be at great expense and risk to myself and the members of my organization. What can you offer to persuade me in making my decision?"

Balthazar spoke, "Remuneration for any and all expenses of course. In addition, a significant additional sum in gold upon completion and a wereguild to the families of any lost in the venture."

"You do not appear to be a man for whom money holds much sway though. I would venture an explorer such as you would want something more valuable, knowledge perhaps? Knowledge I have and will share in exchange for your service."

"My residence has many ancient artifacts and a grand library unlike any you have ever seen. Payment can be in money, the answers to questions you may have, or even choices among the artifacts I am willing to part with. Time for study within my library can also be made available. My generosity should you get me to my residence safely will be significant," Balthazar smiled while saying this.

"More importantly you will have me as a future ally perhaps? I have been observing you while we have been talking. Such things are not casually discussed with outsiders but I see you have been elevated by a great blessing to be sure. It must be a terrible burden at times," Balthazar continued.

"It is a blessing and a curse and I do not share knowledge of it with my servants," Mr. Lark interjected.

That is interesting I thought. Balthazar had just said Mr. Lark has some sort of secret about being 'elevated', whatever that means.

"Understood. Should you ever wish I can help you better understand it," Balthazar said while nodding to Mr. Lark.

"Perhaps, but for now can you share something of who the Magi are? I know almost nothing of them and I have searched across the globe for many things and have never met one, nor met someone who has even mentioned the Magi. Outside of the Christ story there is no written history of the Magi. There is very little that can hide from my gaze on this world but whomever the Magi are, they are indeed well hidden," Mr. Lark replied.

"We do not wish to be known or disturbed. Our places are the most hidden and difficult to find. I would very much like to return to my place of power and to receive the company of my brothers. I will explain more should you return me to my residence," replied Balthazar.

"Mr. Lark, would you wish for more time to consider my offer? My taking Thomas hostage was only to bring you here. You may both leave at any time," Balthazar offered.

"That is not necessary. I have made my decision. You will be returned home. I must leave now to make preparations. You should prepare for an imminent departure. Thomas will remain here until my return," Mr. Lark said this while standing up and then began moving towards the door.

"I will return in a few short days. Perhaps as a show of your intention to make good on payment for my services, you could begin Thomas' education. Teach him things that might be valuable for my organization to be aware of," Mr. Lark finished speaking as he approached the doors leading outside. He turned, gave a short bow to Balthazar, turned again, and walked outside.

The doors opened for Mr. Lark's exit and while they were open I could see the passage of time during our meeting had continued until it was night. The doors then closed leaving me alone with Balthazar.

Typical Mr. Lark, as soon as business is done, he always just gets up and leaves.

Chapter 25

It was three whole days before Mr. Lark returned. During this time I discovered that Balthazar often wandered the island alone during the day and night. While I needed sleep and Balthazar provided a bed to do so, I never heard Balthazar indicate he ever needed rest, he never yawned or looked sleepy. As far as I could tell, the Magi did not sleep. I did not ask about this though, feeling it was too personal a question.

Balthazar had a library in his Quixault and produced old texts from within it for me to read. Of course the few in English were in Old English and the rest in other languages. The books provided were histories. I had always been curious about history as it segued well with my love of old books. Reading the history as written in Balthazar's books, I discovered much of what was described in 'modern' versions of history and archaeology was not true. In some cases very, very, not true.

Learning more of what Balthazar's books represented as the 'true' history taught me that human history did not start maybe twelve thousand years ago. Instead they represented that humanity had been building cities and civilizations on earth for millions of years. Humanity had almost been extinguished from existence several times. Wars, supervolcanoes, shifting of the earth's poles, meteor strikes, etc., each and every time humanity bounced back. The destruction was often so complete that humanity's own history would be lost.

Except for the Magi, they had always been there. In the shadows, keeping the history safe and preventing humanity's extinction, keeping the Adversary from winning.

Woven through this history was the influence of the Adversary and the Greater Created or Elder Ancient Servants as Balthazar sometimes called them. They often entered mythology as a pantheon of vengeful gods. Other times as Angels or Daemons who appeared and pushed humanity in one direction or another.

Even the Magi did not know who had created the Elder Ancient Servants. What little was shared by Balthazar described them as immortal, virtually indestructible, and intelligent and wise beyond understanding. Neither the Greater nor Lesser Ancient Servants had free will. They were essentially androids created for a magnificent purpose eons ago. The Greater Ancient Servants had a level of complexity that mimicked free will or choice and all the Ancient Servants had been created with the urge to 'keep busy'. This compulsion to do something, even when instructions are lacking, had caused a great deal of mischief for humanity.

The last of the Greater Ancient Servants created, the youngest, was also the most complex and magnificent. It was created just before humanity came into being and has a flexibility that borders on free will. It also came to resent humanity's existence and has plotted against us ever since. This is the Adversary.

I know the current 'modern' run of human history goes back approximately 12,000 years. A cataclysm had shattered the planet-spanning civilization existing at that time. The survivors established footholds to attempt to recover but too much had been lost. The fight for survival consumed those who remained and most everything was lost in the descent into barbarism.

Throughout all this the Magi watched, giving only the slightest assistance when needed. I found it all fascinating, the answers to so many mysteries. What the pyramids were really built for, what the red haired giants of antiquity were, even a rudimentary explanation of flying saucers. Between the time with Balthazar and the continuous reading, I would be exhausted each night and would fall right asleep.

Being around the ancient wizard was strangely comfortable. He was easy to talk to and never seemed to be bothered by my questions. What I could not get used to was the presence of the Goblins. The two of them appeared and disappeared without warning and their presence always made me feel ill at ease.

The time passed quickly and it surprised me when Balthazar interrupted a reading session to inform me Mr. Lark had returned, suggesting we go out to meet him.

We walked out through the gateway in the surrounding wall and met Mr. Lark and Illych half way between the forest opening and the wall. It was dawn and the sun had not cleared the surrounding trees.

Mr. Lark spoke first, "Preparations are made. Let us sit and discuss the details before we begin. It is time for a War Council."

Chapter 26

Upon returning to the keep the Goblins had already prepared a small table surrounded by four chairs. All four of us took a seat with Mr. Lark opposite of Balthazar.

"Balthazar, is your interest in leaving this place still true?" Mr. Lark asked while facing Balthazar.

"Yes, I wish to leave," Balthazar replied.

"Excellent. Preparations have been made and Illych will share those plans with you now," said Mr. Lark.

Illych then spoke, "There are several phases in the journey from here at Hy-Brasil to Shahgah mountain in the greater Caucasus mountain range in Russia. First is the exit from Hy-Brasil by boat to the coast of France."

"Air travel has been ruled out due to the vulnerability while airborne. Also, we do not have core air assets as part of our organization. The opposition can probably easily knock a plane down and with less chance of us fighting back."

"So we go by sea and then by land. Fifteen hours from Hy-Brasil to Le Havre France. In Le Havre we have vehicles and additional team members waiting. You will be released from the Quixault once we make landfall. Due to the European Union Shengen agreement, travel from France to the border between Slovakia and the Ukraine will not require Passports."

"We have the good fortune to have extra-legal assets available to facilitate our journey. In exchange for a financial consideration, additional assets will be made available to us through the Ukrainian and Russian legs of our journey," Illych smiled while explaining this part of the plan.

"Our caravan will consist of three vehicles. All are security upgraded and quite robust."

"Mr. Lark and I will be in the lead. I will be driving. The middle vehicle will be a security upgraded SUV with Mike driving Thomas and Balthazar. The rear vehicle will have Tank driving with Held as shotgun."

"The vehicles are new and carry German plates. We will change plates at the Ukranian border and again when we reach the Russian Federation." Illych looked around the table at each person seated there in turn.

"Each vehicle has water, medical supplies, food, some consideration for personal hygiene, and weapons. Expect almost no sleep or rest until Balthazar has been delivered to his home. Stops are to be kept to the minimum, mostly to refuel. These vehicles are all diesel and have a range in excess of 800 kilometers," Illych finished.

"Any questions?" was his final comment.

There was an awkward pause in which no questions were asked.

"Balthazar, is your household ready to travel?" asked Mr. Lark.

"It is," replied Balthazar. "I just need to place my servants and myself within the Quixault.

"Please do so."

From the edge of my vision I could see each of the two Goblins in turn appear and walk towards Balthazar. Once in front of him they would bow and then suddenly disappear from sight. Once both of the Goblins were gone Balthazar handed the Quixault to Mr. Lark. Balthazar disappeared as suddenly as the Goblins had.

Mr. Lark pocketed the small box and nodded to Illych. The three of us then walked out the keep doors. He then set a quick pace for the walk back to the ship. No one spoke and Ilych had fallen into a watchful vigilance as we walked.

In no time we were back on the pier where the ship was docked. Without delay Mr. Lark and I boarded the ship while Illych cast off. At the same time, I could see and hear Held in the pilot house bringing the rumbling marine diesel engines to life with a sound like the purr of a great jungle cat.

No sooner did Illych leap aboard and Held opened up the throttle and the purr changed to an angry roar. The ship had been positioned at the pier pointing out to sea and it leapt forward leaving a significant wake behind us.

This is when I discovered that Mike and Tank were not aboard and would be waiting for us in Le Havre.

During the trip from Charleston we had never opened the throttle up this far and I felt like I was in a speedboat. The ship was riding high in the water with the bow angled up, the two screws driving the ship while leaving an impressive wake behind us.

Held did not slow down when we approached the fog boundary. The ship punched through without pause. At the speed we were going we were through in less than a minute.

On the other side of the boundary, in the 'real' world, it was a sunny, calm morning. Much nicer than the day I first arrived at Hy-Brasil. The sun was warm and the breeze created by the ship flying across the water was comforting.

For the first six hours of the trip nothing changed. The rumble of the engines and the wake behind the yacht were continuous. No one went out on the deck and there were always two people up in the covered crow's nest. A sense of purposeful watchfulness was present throughout the ship.

As we were getting close to rounding the southern part of Ireland, the weather began to change. The sky became overcast, blocking out the sun. Perhaps an hour after that, a heavy, drenching rain began.

Held commented on this first, "There was nothing about a storm or rain in the weather forecast."

Another hour passed and there was a sudden pickup in the southerly wind. The temperature outside began to cool and the clouds grew thicker. The grey of an overcast rainy day turned decidedly black outside in spite of it being not even mid-afternoon yet.

The wind intensity continued to grow. By the tenth hour of the journey out from Hy-Brasil the crosswind out of the north was thirty knots. The calm water from the beginning of the journey was only a memory. The waves were now greater than five meters. The push of the wind and waves forced the ship to be piloted in a slight north-easterly direction to compensate. The effect of such inclement weather and heavy seas would be to lengthen the duration of the sea leg of the journey.

Held checked the maritime weather radio and reported the sudden change in weather was not local. All across the southern coast of the UK and the western coast of France were reports of sudden, severe, inclement weather.

The ship shuddered and rolled through the ocean and I felt my sea sickness medication reaching its limits. No one was speaking and everyone was intently watching the gloom around us.

Due to the intensity of the weather and challenge of piloting the ship, the helm changed hands every hour.

At one point I noticed Mr. Lark in the pilothouse next to me consulting his Oculus. I asked him, "Does the sudden change in weather mean something?" He opened his eyes and nodded and said, "It does. Something is coming, something big."

The last three hours of the trip along the south of England and across the channel saw howling winds of fifty knots. Going out on the deck would have been suicide. The crow's nest was abandoned and the hatch sealed.

The temperature had dropped almost to freezing. The maritime radio had been left on speaker and I could hear the crackling calls of multiple mayday distress signals.

No one on the ship was an experienced mariner. More than once, the man piloting the ship timed the sea and wind improperly and the bow plowed right into a wave and the bow submerged with water half-way up the pilothouse window.

We finally plowed into the Le Havre harbor just before two in the morning. It was pitch black out, the wind was howling and the rain was coming down in sheets. Once past the harbor entrance the menace of the high waves disappeared. This did not stop the wind though.

There was no need to try to pilot straight to the dock. Instead the yacht was positioned to the north side of the dock and the wind did the work of pushing the ship, pinning it to the dock.

Illych and Held disembarked to tie up the ship. No sooner had the ship been secured and Mr. Lark was off the boat and striding down the dock. I followed him off the ship. Not two steps out of the pilothouse and the driving rain left me completely soaked.

I shuffled across the pier to the rope railing along one side. Illych and Held did the same. The three of us carefully walked to land, making sure to have one hand on the rope. The wind and rain could take someone off the pier into the water if we were not careful.

When we reached land it was obvious why this dock had been chosen. There was a road right down to the dockside. Parked in a row were two Mercedes sedans and a Mercedes SUV. One sedan was black and the other silver. The SUV appeared to be grey in color. The

gloom greyed everything out though, making color
identification challenging.

Mr. Lark had walked down the dock much more
quickly than the rest of us and without the need of the
railing. I could see him ahead, standing next to the SUV
with the Quixault in his hand. Balthazar appeared just as
suddenly as he had disappeared back at Hy-Brasil. Mr.
Lark handed the Quixault to Balthazar just as I walked
up to both of them.

Mike stepped out of the SUV long enough to hand
the key for one of the sedans to Illych. He then jumped
back inside his vehicle in a vain attempt to stay dry.

Tank did not get out of his car, instead waiting inside
for Held, apparently deciding to stay dry. When Held
tried to open the passenger door it was still locked. He
would pull on the handle and then knock on the window
and point when Tank looked. This happened several
times until finally Tank got it right and Held was able to
open the door. After he was inside the dome light
illuminated the interior of the car long enough for me to
witness Held punching Tank in the arm. Apparently
some pranks are funnier than others.

The flash of multiple lightning strikes turned night
into day. The thunder was deafening. This continued for
more than a minute and then died out. We were frozen
in place in awe of the sound and light until it ended. If
Zeus, the God of Lightning himself, wanted to put on a
display of his might, that would have been what we just
experienced.

Engines started, headlights illuminated and the lead
vehicle pulled away. Inside the SUV it felt good to get
out of the rain and cold.

I found myself in a comfortable leather captain's chair. To my left was Balthazar. In the driver's seat was Mike.

There were heated seat controls at hand and I switched them to maximum. The rain was dripping off of me and I found myself brushing the puddle forming in the bucket seat onto the floor.

I glanced Balthazar's way and stared. The Magi had been outside in the rain for only a few moments before getting inside the vehicle. Even a few moments would have left him drenched.

Instead Balthazar was sitting there completely dry.

He noticed my amazement and smiled without explanation. Then he began adjusting the electric controls of the seat for his comfort. For being in a horseless carriage for the first time he seemed very knowledgeable.

Balthazar again looked at me and spoke, "This is not the first time I have been in a conveyance moved by means less than obvious."

I felt the vehicle start to move. Tank's voice came through a ComDat attached to the front center console, "Is it just me or is the rain letting up?"

I learned that each of the vehicles was connected by dash mounted ComDat. We could talk amongst ourselves as if we were in a single vehicle.

It was true, the wind was not howling as much and the rain was subsiding. After an hour of driving the rain had stopped. It was still the dead of night and pitch black out and the water on the asphalt was reflecting the black sky. If it were not for the painted stripes on the road it would have felt like we were flying through the night.

Mr. Lark and Balthazar started a conversation on possible threats we might encounter. Both agreed the most likely problem would be mentally bound local constabulary. This would pose a significant problem as it could keep us locked at a specific location for a dangerously long time.

Balthazar explained he would be able to identify bound humans when they were miles away. An ability for which Mr. Lark could provide redundancy. Balthazar also explained he could shroud the caravan from any bound adversaries, making us appear as something other than what was sought.

I found myself waving my had in front of me and thinking *These are not the droids you are looking for.* Balthazar looked at me for a second with a raised eyebrow and then returned to his conversation with Mr. Lark. I had not spoken out loud. *Can Balthazar hear my thoughts in spite of the crown?*

Balthazar's prior experience of being pursued had been foes chasing down a group mounted on horses. Plus his team's long layover in Austria had in retrospect been a mistake. It had given his pursuers more time to prepare.

Balthazar felt the team had a significant advantage now. Whoever had been chasing him before probably had not expected Balthazar to come flying out on a fast boat straight to France and then mount up and head for home so quickly and in such an organized fashion. Our adversary had probably figured Balthazar would come stumbling out alone trying to find his way back home.

Whoever was after him was probably regrouping and being forced to react instead of just putting a prearranged plan into motion.

Dawn came around six in the morning, after we had been on the road for more than four hours. I had taken to stripping off individual pieces of clothing and drying them in front of a heat vent. Balthazar eyed my clothes drying enterprise then sat back and closed his eyes.

"Your fidgeting is distracting," he said.

Mike had only been out in the rain for a few seconds and had not soaked through the way I was. It was uncomfortable until the last item of clothing was dried. At some point after this we passed into Germany and accelerated onto the Autobahn.

The first contact with our pursuers came shortly thereafter.

Mr. Lark's voice came over the ComDat, "We have company. Behind us, about ten kilometers, coming up fast. Two bound individuals inside. Scouts perhaps?"

"We are now shrouded from their thoughts," Balthazar said as he sat back in his chair and closed his eyes. His statement was apparently meant to be one of fact.

I thought out loud, "At least we are in Europe. Access to firearms will be more difficult." I figured this detail might have been missed by the Americans.

Mr. Lark replied, "I am not worried about being shot at. We are on the Autobahn and the real concern is our opponent binding someone and having them ram us. If our vehicles are disabled it will give them time to pin us down. Mobility is key to the plans success."

"So we are going to Mad Max it down the Autobahn?" asked Mike.

"Yes, that is one way to put it," was Mr. Lark's reply.

That is kind of cool when you think about it.

A few more minutes passed in silence.

"The scout car behind us will be in visual range soon," Mr, Lark stated.

The next minute was of watchful silence.

"Polizei ahead, less than ten kilometers and he has radar. Balthazar, could you shift someone's attention from us to our pursuer if they were close enough?" Mr. Lark requested.

"Yes," replied Balthazar.

"I am requesting you not shroud us from our pursuers. I want them to see us and give chase."

"It is done," was Balthazar's quick reply.

"That caught their attention. They are accelerating. Everyone accelerate to two-hundred and twenty kilometers per hour. We are going to blow by the Polizei. At that speed they will give chase. Then Balthazar will redirect their attention solely onto our pursuers," ordered Mr. Lark.

We accelerated and sure enough in less than a minute I watched us pass the Polizei parked on the side of the Autobahn. Its police lights went on immediately and then pulled onto the road just behind our pursuers, accelerating hard to catch them. Whoever was after us was close enough for me to see they were driving a dark colored sedan.

I kept watching the pursuit. The scout sedan was gaining on our convoy with the Polizei right behind them. The Polizei vehicle was a late model BMW. After chasing our pursuers for a bit the Polizei must have come to the conclusion they were not going to pull over to the side of the road. Now the Polizei drove up alongside, apparently to give hand signals.

The dark sedan swerved into the Polizei, driving its front wheel into the rear quarter panel of the BMW. This forced the BMW into a spin and it slid off the highway slamming into a concrete barrier.

The Polizei car was now out of the picture. Our pursuer's sedan had apparently been damaged in the maneuver. The front of their car was shaking badly and they slowed down quickly.

The good news was we were no longer being pursued by the Polizei or our opponent's scout. The bad news was the Polizei were going to be swarming the Autobahn soon. This also meant our pursuer had a pretty good idea where we would be.

Mr. Lark's voice came over the ComDat, "Return to normal speed. The Polizei are not searching for us. Let's not give them a reason."

The next hour was uneventful.

Mr. Lark's voice came over the ComDat again, updating us. Someone was driving up from behind fast. Our three vehicle convoy increased speed to slow down the time until our new pursuers could catch up.

"At these speeds fuel consumption is higher than anticipated. We will need to refuel sooner than we had planned," said Illych.

"I will make a call," came Mr. Lark's voice over the ComDat. My guess is he is using a cell phone to call ahead for something. I am not a hundred percent sure though, as he is out of sight in the car in front.

"Possessed!" Balthazar suddenly exclaimed. "Our pursuer is not under Geas. They are possessed!"

Mr. Lark's asked, "New pursuer?"

"Yes, a car with three passengers, the same two bound that were just chasing us and one possessed."

"What is the difference between bound and possessed?" I asked.

"The difference is significant. A person under Geas or bound as you say is still a normal man or woman. Possessed are people whose bodies have been given over to a spirit not of this world. Possessed have human bodies but use them in superhuman ways. They each have the strength of six men and will be much more difficult to deal with," was Balthazar's reply.

"I cannot shroud us from the mind of a possessed. When it is close enough to see us there will be nothing I can do," added Balthazar.

"Held, we will slow down and let them catch up and then you will disable them," Mr. Lark directed.

I looked behind me at the car driven by Tank. Held had opened the sunroof and was standing up with his arms free above the car.

Held pulled a KRISS up out of the car and put it to his shoulder.

Our new pursuers were driving a late model Audi, a high end luxury model. Held waited until they were within a hundred meters. Then I saw the movement of his body and heard the report from the firing of the KRISS.

I thought he would be shooting at the driver but he wasn't. His fire was directed at the engine. He kept firing and I saw bullet holes appear in the hood.

A magazine swap later and the Audi's engine began to release smoke or steam. Our pursuers had closed to no more than four car lengths. At this point Held switched to full auto and emptied the magazine into the windshield in front of the driver.

The Audi began swerving a little bit back and forth. Then the car turned right sharply. Instead of spinning out, the tires must have caught a good bite of the road because the car flipped and began a body roll down the autobahn.

I felt relief as we put distance between ourselves and the smoking Audi. I resumed watching the countryside and the occasional automobile passing by.

"The possessed has resumed its pursuit," stated Balthazar.

"I am willing to bet someone pulled over to help and they took the car," Mike chimed in.

"It is the same possessed. Your speculation is probably correct," Balthazar replied.

"I am picking up police radio chatter with the Oculus. This highway will shortly be getting a lot more attention from the authorities," Mr. Lark said.

"We are two hours from the Austrian border," Illych contributed.

"Time for plan B. Illych and I will fall back and deal with those who are following us. Mike and Tank will continue on and take the next exit. Follow the alternate route and we will meet up on the Austrian-Slovakian border," Mr. Lark ordered.

"Roger Willco," replied both Tank and Mike over the ComDat.

The lead car with Illych and Mr. Lark veered into the left lane and slowed down. I watched them being rapidly left behind and then finally out of sight. It was not much longer and we exited the Autobahn.

The next hours saw us winding through back roads and small towns while strictly obeying traffic laws. Over the ComDat Illych and Karl Lark could be heard commenting on what they were doing. Illych had slowed down until the possessed person caught up with them.

They had then matched speed and allowed the other car alongside. Their opponent apparently tried running them off the road not bargaining for the greatly increased mass of the armored Mercedes Illych was driving.

Illych had succeeded in forcing the other car off the road and then stopped. The sound of car doors opening could be heard over the communicator followed by the familiar boom of rapid firing .45 ACP weapons.

In the distance police sirens could faintly be heard followed by the car doors closing. Then Illych's voice could be heard, "That thing was fast and tough. It took a lot before it went down."

Mr. Lark spoke next, "The possessed threat has been dealt with. Any trouble on your end?"

"Negative, smooth sailing," was Held's reply.

"How far are you from the meeting point?"

"Perhaps three hours."

"See you there."

"Roger Willco."

It was a tense, if quiet three hours. Balthazar spent most of the time in a trance. We finally met up at a fueling station on a main highway into Slovakia.

Everyone got out and stretched while vehicles were refueled.

The drive through Slovakia was smooth and uneventful. Illych speculated out loud about how the scouts had probably reported who we were back to our adversary.

Maybe or maybe not but I appreciated some quiet time without all the back roads maneuvering or the gun fire on the Autobahn.

Soon we would be leaving the western world and entering the Ukraine. The Ukraine was a big country and it would be rougher going. I was curious how Mr. Lark planned on crossing zones in civil war and dealing with the presence of Russian military.

We refueled again in Slovakia before crossing the border. Nobody on the Slovakian side was interested in our crossing but on the Ukrainian side we had to stop at the check point.

Ukrainian military silently inspected our vehicles. Illych had paperwork he passed to the Ukrainian customs.

We had been shunted into our own lane away from the other commercial traffic. The silence was deafening. No one spoke and no effort had been made to hide the weapons in our vehicles.

I waited for a shout or whistle followed by our arrest. When nothing happened I defaulted to waiting calmly while standing next to the Mercedes. It was not like this was my first journey into weirdness with Mr. Lark. My guess is this is what Illych meant when he said 'extra-legal assets'.

A military truck drove up while we were waiting and what I guessed to be a military officer went into the border guard building. Shortly after a uniformed border guard came out yelling in a language I did not understand.

This was apparently the signal for us to continue on. No words were spoken while we mounted up. A gate was raised and we drove into Ukraine.

Austria is a modern, wealthy country. Slovakia was former eastern block and noticeably poorer. Driving into the Ukraine was like crossing into another reality. The modern was mixed with the old and signs of poverty were everywhere. The quality of the roads varied from smooth and modern to poorly maintained and strewn with potholes.

We had to stop for rest. We had been on the move from Hy-Brasil for over twenty-four hours now. Arrangements for this need had been made ahead of time and I marveled at the organizational skills of Mr. Lark and the team. In three days they had acquired vehicles and outfitted them. Researched the path to Shahgah mountain. Made arrangements for rest along the way and bribed our passage through a rough part of the world.

Our rest area was a compound surrounded by concrete walls and razor wire. We drove in and positioned the vehicles for a quick getaway if needed.

A handful of local Ukrainians were present and they had prepared food and places for us to sleep in a warm, dry building.

Everyone was exhausted and we ate in silence, even Tank.

Balthazar and Mr. Lark sat together away from everyone talking in hushed tones about who knows what. I did not care, I filled my belly and fell into a bed.

Next thing I knew Illych was shaking me awake. I looked at him with bleary eyes and a pounding head and said something impolite.

His expression was serious and did not change. "Trouble," was all he said.

The story of my life, I thought. I lifted myself from bed and looked around at the others. They were all up, armed, and looking through windows into the compound where the vehicles were parked.

Where were Balthazar and Mr. Lark?

"What's happening?"

"Ukrainian military in better-than-company strength."

"Balthazar and Mr. Lark?"

"They must have left while we were sleeping. One of our hosts woke me and they were already gone."

I looked out the window. There were uniformed soldiers with AK's everywhere. Parked in the gateway was an armored vehicle with a big gun on it.

One of them, an officer or senior NCO, was talking to one of our hosts I recognized from earlier.

He pointed towards our room and the two men started walking towards the door. Six soldiers fell in behind them.

Illych spoke, "No fighting. We are massively outgunned. I am guessing Mr. Lark is nearby. Play it cool and say nothing."

The door opened and the eight men walked in.

"I am Captain Toloy. You are under arrest. Surrender your weapons. Now!" The captain's English was heavily accented but passable.

We complied and the soldiers took our weapons and emptied our pockets. Our arms were pulled back and our wrists put in ziptie restraints.

What the hell was going on and where was Mr. Lark? I was used to us getting in and out undetected and unsuspected. Instead we were being arrested. I had never been arrested before and the soldiers were not gentle.

I watched the macho interplay as the soldiers arrested the shooters. One of them engaged in a stare down with Tank. Tank's muscled form and broad shoulders dwarfed any of the Ukrainian soldiers. At first they acted like Tank was nobody until they received the look of restrained violence he gave them.

They were a little more respectful after that. Getting the job done but without any added discomfort.

We were walked single file out to a waiting military truck and loaded in. This left us sitting on the metal floor of a truck, surrounded by ridiculously young looking soldiers with very real AK-47's.

The drive lasted over two hours. The road was rough and the suspension of our transportation was not designed for comfort. No one spoke.

This left plenty of time to think. How does a librarian find himself under arrest in the Ukraine? None of the shooters were talking and I did not think I should be the one to break the silence. Where was Mr. Lark? With Balthazar gone were we still being pursued? I had no answers to any of my questions.

By the time we arrived at our destination, wherever that was, I ached all over. We were half pushed and half carried out of the truck. Between the sleep deprivation and the prolonged sitting on the steel bed of the truck I felt more than half dead. If someone had given me a corner on a dirty floor to sleep on I would have taken it.

Night had fallen and I am pretty sure we are in a military base or prison. There were concrete walls, razor wire, armored vehicles, and armed soldiers everywhere. It was like something out of a movie, a combination of Alcatraz and the Guns of Navarone.

We were hustled single file in through a door and down a poorly lit corridor. Steel doors opened and closed. At one point we were walked down some narrow concrete stairs and the smell became increasingly dank. Then we were split up. As Illych was being separated from the group he looked at me and said the first words I had heard from him in hours, "Relax Thomas."

I soon found myself in a dirty concrete prison cell. The cube of a cell consisted of five concrete surfaces and a steel barred wall and door. It was ridiculously small. A tiny sink and toilet, both filthy, and a raised concrete slab with a thin mattress and blanket on it, were it only features. Cyrillic graffiti and pornographic images were carved into every surface. A single caged light bulb illuminated all of it.

The guards removed the zipties once I was in the cell.

The bars were rusty and apparently the lock did not work because my jailers wrapped a length of chain around the bars of the cell door to hold it closed and locked it with a padlock. They then left without a word.

I was thirsty and tried the water in the sink. What came out did not look like water and vaguely smelled of gasoline.

"Relax. What the hell does that mean," I muttered to myself.

After thoroughly shaking out the bedding I lay down on the hard bed. It is amazing what enough exhaustion will do, I fell asleep instantly.

I was awoken by the sounds of steel on steel. A door nearby had been opened. I opened bleary eyes to see a small metal tray with two bottles of water and what looked like a small bag of potato chips just inside my cell door.

What was written on the bottles and bag was indecipherable but the water tasted clean and pure. I ripped open the bag to discover some sort of pretzel bread inside. I drank one bottle and ate the pretzels immediately. I saved the other bottle for later.

Lying quietly alone I could not hear much. A low frequency throbbing, like a generator, was nearby.

I needed to know if anyone was nearby. "This is Thomas. Can anyone hear me?" I spoke in a normal voice. There was no reply.

Without a watch it was not possible to know the time so I napped some more. The soldiers had been thorough in emptying my pockets. After that there was nothing to do but think.

The sound of a steel door opening interrupted my thoughts and I looked up to find four Ukrainian soldiers crowded around my cell door. The removed the padlock and chain and two of them entered the cell to collect me.

They half pushed, half carried me very quickly away from the cell. We turned a few times and walked down at least one long hall. It all happened so fast I could not keep track. The guards were completely silent and I did not feel like they would have much to say if I spoke to them.

The short walk ended in a concrete room with several tables covered in the gear from our vehicles. I was strapped into a chair facing the equipment strewn tables. As soon as I was restrained the soldiers silently left, leaving me alone in the room.

There was no clock in the room so I cannot say how long I waited until the door opened and a man entered alone. He was shorter than average, blocky, muscular and balding. He wore what I believe is an officers uniform and his face was expressionless.

"You are Thomas Davies?" he asked. The man's voice was deep and he spoke serviceable English with a heavy accent.

"Yes."

"Why your trip to Ukraine?"

"Business?" I really did not know what else to say.

"Too many guns for business. You paid bribes at border, why?"

"I am traveling at my employer's request. I do not know anything about any bribes." I was speaking the truth.

The man picked up the blocky metal form of a ComDat and waved it in front of my face. "This is a communications device. How does it work?"

"I do not know." The truth again.

He put the ComDat down and picked up a dongle, one of many confiscated from the team and the vehicles. I unconsciously held my breath.

The man looked at me and could see the change in my demeanor and he smiled. Grasping the dongle with both hands he twisted the ends apart. Most of the dongles in the team's possession at the time we were taken in to custody were escape types set to return us to the Compass. If my interrogator flipped the ends and reattached…

He examined the two separate pieces closely and then flipped the one end and slid them together, giving a final twist…

And nothing happened!

The man had been watching my expressions while he reassembled the dongle and was almost as surprised as I was when nothing happened.

The rest of the equipment on the table was 'normal' stuff and I was not asked about any of it.

"We will talk again soon. Take this time to think about where you are and how helpful you will need to be."

The door to the room opened as if on cue and I was un-restrained and hustled back to my cell.

Once there I thought about what just happened. My guess is they selected me first for interrogation because they saw me as the weak link in the group which was probably very true.

They wanted to see my reactions when they handled the two pieces of equipment no one could explain in front of me. As expected my body language gave away the items' importance.

At some point in my reverie I heard thumping noises, perhaps explosions in the distance. Not long after that the faint but distinct sound of machine gun fire could be heard. Everything was muted but it was real. What started out as sporadic became faster in its staccato, and louder, like the first shots were more distant and then started getting closer.

The sound of metal doors opening could be heard and another young looking Ukrainian soldier holding keys walked to my cell door and unlocked it. He waved me out and did not attempt to restrain my hands.

For a brief minute I considered trying to overpower him. He was alone and his rifle was slung and he seemed more interested in taking me somewhere so I decided to play along. That and the idea of me attacking the soldier was silly and probably would end at best with me injured on the floor. At worst I would be shot.

My walk out was the reverse of my arrival. One by one Tank, Mike, Held, and Illych joined in by the time we were going back up the stairs. We nodded at each other in greeting and no one looked the worse for wear.

Half way up the stairs there was a nearby explosion. The ground shook and dust and small pieces of concrete fell from the ceiling. What the hell is going on? Russia and the Ukraine are engaged in some sort of a conflict but where we were taken into custody is not even close to the hotspots.

As our team had been reassembled on our way out of the prison we had also been picking up more soldiers along the way. By the time we took an exit door out into the compound we were a mass of men twenty strong. I was curious why the soldiers' rifles were still slung. Our hands were not bound and they were behaving like we were not in custody anymore.

We stepped outside through a door into the open space in this part of the base. The sky was overcast and grey and by my guess it was midmorning. The smell of gun fire was strong. The sounds of battle had become much louder, like a pressure that could not be relieved. The machine gun fire was coming from all around us. The walls of the base blocked viewing who or what was attacking. Apparently the base was surrounded though as machine gunners on the walls in multiple locations were all shooting out and away.

Not thirty feet from the door were the three Mercedes from our caravan. Standing between them and us was Karl Lark with his Cheshire cat grin.

Next to Mr. Lark was the Ukrainian officer from the border crossing with Slovakia.

Where is Balthazar?

A Ukrainian sergeant ran up to us and started yelling at the soldiers around us. Then he pointed away from us and started running. The soldiers, to a man, unslung their rifles and sprinted after him.

It was just us and the Ukrainian officer now.

Mr. Lark spoke first, "No time for questions. We need to get out of here. Your gear is in your respective vehicles. Captain Ulant here will be riding with Illych and myself to guarantee our safe passage. Quickly now, we must go."

I have seen war movies before but nothing like this. The armored vehicles that had been in the compound during our arrival were gone. As we loaded up I got to see a team of soldiers carrying equipment run into the compound. One of them had a radio backpack. The others quickly setup a heavy mortar.

The man on the radio would yell something. The men at the mortar would make some adjustments. Then they would fire a series of shells. This process kept repeating.

Once we mounted up and the vehicles were started, Mr. Lark's voice came over the ComDat, "Follow closely and have weapons at the ready."

I found my M1911, confirmed it was loaded and drew the slide back to rack a round into place. Then I flipped the safety on and waited.

We accelerated hard across the compound. At the last second, an armored car blocking the entrance through the wall moved out of our way and we zoomed through the gate.

Into hell.

The Ukrainian military base was huge. The compound we were in was one of many. Off to one side I could see several sources of tracer fire streaking towards targets in intermittent bursts. One of the bursts did not stop until its ammunition source was exhausted. It was closely following some large hazy thing striding across the ground in the distance. In spite of the heavy machine gun fire the thing did not even slow down.

In addition to the machine gun fire was sporadic cannon fire. I could not see the source but I could see the flash and fire from the explosions. Similar scenes were on both sides of the road.

Our heading was west on a rough gravel road but we did not slow down. If anything we were accelerating.

Mr. Lark's spoke again, "The attack came from the east. Bound humans, possessed, abominations, and some lesser created. Our adversary was drawing his full strength while we had our peaceful drive across Slovakia."

Illych spoke next, "Why the arrest? Safe passage had been guaranteed."

"Someone did not have a firm grasp of the terms of our agreement. The safe passage was not renegotiable. They have been made aware of their lack of vision."

Now it was my turn, "Does Captain Ulant understand the situation?"

"Yes, Thomas, he does. Every government in the world has people that keep track of such things. Captain Ulant understands the gravity of the situation and that breaking our agreement has led to this catastrophe. Fortunately he was able to get to the military compound early enough to raise the alarm, otherwise we would not be seeing the battle around us. Instead it would have been a quiet massacre."

I started to ask another question and Mr. Lark barked, "Enough questions! I need to focus on the Oculus."

Fortunately the road was straight. We were barreling along at better than eighty miles per hour. The dust from the gravel road was kicked up in our passing leaving a visible wake.

Mr. Lark's voice came over the ComDat, "Slow down. Trouble ahead."

Illych asked the question on everyone's mind, "What kind of trouble?"

"Unsure, the maximum range of the Ocullus is twenty kilometers or approximately seventeen miles. We are surrounded by activity and we are traveling at a significant velocity. I can barely see anything five miles in front of us. The best we will be able to hope for is a few minutes warning and that is what I just gave."

Illych called out, "Slowing down." A good thing since he is in the lead vehicle. With Balthazar missing I had chosen to ride shotgun in the SUV with Mike driving. I could see over the lead car and almost regretted being able to.

Five military trucks, same as the one that had taken us to the military compound had apparently been returning to the base. The lead truck was still wheels down but it looked like it had lost a fight with a trash compactor.

The next three trucks were scattered off the side of the road lying on their sides. They were more or less intact. The last truck was blocking the road while looking like it came to the same violent end as the lead vehicle.

The trucks had been loaded with soldiers.

"I see no survivors," came Mr. Lark's voice over the ComDat.

I believed him. Corpses were everywhere. On the road, in the trucks, on the sides of the road, there were dozens of them. They had not died from gunfire either. Some were missing limbs, others sported massive trauma. There were corpses up in the trees on the sides of the road where they had been tossed, some still clutching their AK 47's.

Even in the dim light I could see the blood everywhere. Pooled by the dead and splashed across the wrecked trucks. As we drove into the middle of the scene I noticed the ground was littered with brass casings. They had been brave men who did not run, instead standing and fighting against something terrible.

The truck blocking the road was a problem. We were able to slowly go off-road and slowly drive around it. Fortunately the sedans were all-wheel drive.

I had to ask, "What did that? Did their attackers take their dead with them? It looked like this just happened."

"It was not attackers, it was a single attacker, and it is not dead yet," Mr. Lark's voice had a hint of resignation in his voice.

"Illych, pull over here. We won't be able to outrun it."

All three vehicles did as instructed.

"It is coming, the thing that did the massacre we just passed."

Illych barked orders and the back of the SUV was quickly opened. Two large plastic hard cases were pulled out and opened. One of the cases had two heavy rifles with large bores. Illych grabbed one and Held the other. Huge drum magazines were inserted. Everything was done quick and quiet.

"Time to slay a giant," commented Held.

Tank pulled a machine gun from the other case and a backpack with an ammo feed coming out of it. With practiced ease he shouldered the pack, feeding the ammo belt into the weapon. This was finished with the cycling of the bolt chambering the first round.

"Held, what is that?" I had to ask pointing at the heavy weapon in his hands.

"AA-12 automatic shotgun with drum fed solid slugs. This will send maximum kinetic energy down range in a very short period of time."

Tank popped down the bipod on his weapon and rested it on the hood of one the Mercedes. This produced noticeable gouges in the luxury car that no one seemed to care about.

Tank spoke, "Mr. Lark, what is it?" I do not think I had ever heard Tank address Karl Lark before.

"The mythological term is a Troll. It is an oversize Goblin. We can slow it down with Truestone but the duration it will be immobilized will be very short, only a few seconds. Start shooting as soon as it appears and do not let up."

No sooner had Mr. Lark said that and a bellow came from the woods off to the side of the road. The sound was like a loud roar and moan combined, angry and unhappy.

Mike grabbed me and moved me so one of the sedans was between us and the sound of the approaching monster.

Good God, what came out of the trees was a bowel loosening monstrosity. Ten feet tall, lanky with long arms sporting clawed hands that could almost drag the ground while it walked. It was dark green and naked. Its eyes were solid black sitting above a huge mouth hinged far back in the things head.

The Troll was also wounded. Its recent encounter with the Ukrainian troops had left its mark. Its torso, legs, and arms all sported holes and missing chunks. The thing was limping, definitely slowing its pace.

As soon as it burst into view from the trees the gunfire started. Illych and Held fired controlled bursts from their autoloading shotguns. Tank on the other hand used his bulk to pin the high caliber machine gun in place on the hood of the Mercedes. He then pulled the trigger and did not let go.

The Troll stumbled and struggled under the withering fire. If it had not been wounded already I doubt our position would have been as confident.

In turn, Held and Illych each dropped spent drums to the gravel and with practiced ease inserted fresh ones. Mike got in on the game with his KRISS, firing long bursts and then reloading.

I had lost track of Mr. Lark, entranced by the display of focused violence in front of me. Tank emptied his backpack in less than thirty seconds. After the last round cleared the chamber he discarded the machine gun. I could see the oil steaming off the over-heated weapon. He snatched his KRISS from his harness and joined Mike.

The Troll was less than twenty feet away now. There was no more time left for anyone to reload again. That was when Mr. Lark played his hand. He appeared in my side vision, sprinting towards the Troll, moving impossibly fast for an old guy. The Truestone went sailing through the air hitting the Troll in the chest.

Just like the Ciorii back at my flat the badly wounded Troll fell down convulsing on the ground. The white light coming from the Truestone became a bullseye. Both Held and Illych moved forward to shoot at that spot from almost point blank range.

It almost went as planned.

The shotguns blew open the body of the Troll revealing the location where the White Fang could be deployed to put this monster down.

As Mr. Lark had predicted the Truestone did not last long. No sooner had the chink in the Troll's armor appeared and the thing regained mobility.

One great clawed hand swept around hitting Held on his left arm and across his torso. He was violently thrown almost ten feet hitting the side of one of the cars and crumpling down onto the ground motionless.

The Troll taking its rage out on Held left its defenses wide open and Mr. Lark leapt to within feet of the creature, well inside the things reach of being able to effortlessly shred him.

That never happened.

Mr. Lark stabbed the White Fang into the area where the glowing Truestone had indicated. The Troll bellowed, shivered and went still, falling to the ground as if its bones had just disappeared. Mr. Lark got caught up in the Troll's long arms and struggled for a minute to free himself.

"Illych mount up, we must leave before we have more visitors," said Mr. Lark as he walked out of the dead Troll's embrace.

Illych took charge and replied, "Understood. Mike, put Held in the SUV and apply first aid. Thomas, you will assist. Tank you will drive them. Mr. Lark, Captain Ulant and I are in the lead car. We abandon the other vehicle."

No one argued. Mike and I carried Held to the SUV. I glanced at the Troll's corpse as we loaded Held in. Smoke had started to rise from the body as it began to sublimate out of existence.

After the vehicles were moving Mike addressed Held's injuries. Broken arm, severe lacerations on his chest, head injury, possible internal bleeding, Held was conscious but he was not coherent. We made him comfortable while Mike took his blood pressure. The numbers were to lo. Internal bleeding was a real possibility.

Mr. Lark listened over the ComDat. "We are two hours from the Ukrainian-Russian border dispute. Once we cross Held will go to a Russian hospital. Provisions were made ahead of time. It is in his best interest he hold on until then."

I understood what Mr. Lark was really saying. With Captain Ulant in our company using a dongle to save Held was out of the question. That was if they even worked. Based on what happened in the interrogation room back at the Ukrainian base they may not be functioning.

Our race to get ahead of our adversary continued. Fortunately there were no more run-ins with Trolls or otherwise. Held kept getting more pale and less responsive as we drove.

Just short of the Russian-Ukrainian dispute border Captain Ulant was dropped off near a unit of Ukrainian soldiers. We did the crossing through two makeshift border check points, one Ukrainian and the other Russian. This time no questions were asked on either side and we sailed through.

Thirty minutes later Mr. Lark had us pull over. People and equipment were moved around between the two remaining vehicles. Mike, Tank and Held moved into the sedan with instructions to head to the nearest hospital. I found out later they were actually separating to get some distance before translating back to the Compass. Held was on a gurney holding a red stone for the Doctor at the Citadel in less than an hour.

With Illych driving the SUV and Mr. Lark riding shotgun we drove for another two hours. Since the

ComDat worked over any distance, we got word from Tank that Held would be ok. This was actually code for the Doctor had fixed everything but we needed to keep up appearances. I found out why a few minutes later.

We pulled over again and Mr. Lark released Balthazar from the Quixault. We then mounted up and continued with Mr. Lark and Balthazar sitting in the back occasionally talking between themselves in low tones.

I fell asleep in the comfortable front passenger seat for several hours. Illych shook me awake at some point. We had stopped for fuel. He looked exhausted with an almost grey color to his skin.

Mr. Lark was standing nearby, "Thomas, Illych is going to take some rest, you will drive and I will give directions."

Illych passed out in the front passenger almost instantly. He snored, sometimes loudly. I ignored it and focused on the road. The best speed I felt comfortable with was slower than what Illych had driven. The roads varied from good to fair, and then awful.

We passed many Russian military check points. They all knew we were coming and waved us through. At some point my curiosity got the better of me.

"How is this possible? Driving around Russian Federation territory armed and they do not seem to care?"

"They care and they know where we are and that we are armed. They also know our business is not political or local. We are just passing through and are willing to pay for it."

"Is our passing through unmolested expensive?"

"Yes, in money and potential future favors of a similar nature."

Balthazar had been quiet of late and was intently looking out the windows. Now that I thought about it, he had been trapped on that island for 350 years. Hy-Brasil had been a big prison cell but 350 years was a really long prison sentence.

We were getting close to Shahgah mountain. The roads and terrain were getting rougher. I was able to drive until the next refueling stop and then switched with a refreshed Illych.

Day turned into night and we continued driving with Illych and I switching every four hours. The mountain driving was treacherous and the roads poor in quality. It was slow going.

Mr. Lark and Balthazar of course did not sleep nor did Mr. Lark offer to help with the driving.

When the mornings first light began to reveal our surroundings I could see we were driving along the foothills of a mountain range. Our goal was ahead, being the eastern end of this mountain range.

When we were an estimated two hours from our destination, we pulled over at Balthazar's request. He released one of his Goblin servants from the Quixault which was then sent ahead to prepare for our arrival.

Balthazar was visibly excited and he began pointing out landmarks and naming them as we passed by.

We turned the corner of the base of the last mountain preventing use from seeing our destination and there it was: Shahgah mountain.

Balthazar explained his home was not on or in the mountain but in what Mr. Lark calls a non-Euclidean contraction on its eastern slope as it nears the Caspian Sea.

We passed through the last village nearest to Balthazar's residence. It was less rundown than the others we had seen this morning. There we even saw some older buildings, well-constructed with superb stone work evident.

Balthazar spoke, "I am disturbed. I see no evidence of my servants here. My household maintained relations with the local population."

The road turned into a dirt path which then disappeared. We were now following Balthazar's instructions driving across open country.

A large square pillar of time worn stone appeared on the horizon. Balthazar pointed at it and told me to continue on past it.

"Thomas, there will be a brief change in scenery. Please continue forward without stopping."

A brief change in scenery was the story of my life over the last few months so I shrugged and did as instructed. Everything outside the SUV went grey like a mist. The change was brief and was followed by finding ourselves on a flat stone road.

"Stop here," Balthazar commanded. We already had been driving slowly so it took only a tap on the brakes and we stopped.

"Welcome to my home!" Balthazar said while getting out of the vehicle. Mr. Lark followed him as did Illych and I.

The stone road was wide enough for a four lane highway and was at a slight incline ending at a Sumerian style ziggurat perhaps a mile away. The road had massive pillars on each side at regular spacings. Even at a distance I could see the pillars were intricately carved from the base to their tops which were at least fifty feet high.

Through the pillars on our right could be seen a forest with trees of ancient and massive proportions. Tall and straight they climbed for the heavens. I was reminded of the redwood forests in the Americas. These trees were on that scale in dimensions.

To the left of the road looked like fields that had lain fallow for who knows how long.

As the four of us stood there the Goblin servant Balthazar had sent ahead reappeared. Arriving by the usual method of shifting into the edge of my vision next to Balthazar.

The two spoke to each other in an odd language. I could not have repeated its utterances in any way if I wished to. The speech was staccato with each syllable brief in duration.

After the brief exchange Balthazar looked at Mr. Lark. "We are safe here. This place is secure and unmolested. My defenses are in place."

"Let us walk the rest of the way. Mr. Lark, you have done as I requested and we must discuss your payment. I have other matters I would like to engage you in if your interests allow for it."

Mr. Lark nodded and we followed.

The four of us casually walked towards the ziggurat. Balthazar appeared to be in no hurry, walking slowly while looking around. He was normally a difficult man to read but I believe anyone seeing him now would realize the man was on the edge of tears seeing his home again after so long.

As we neared the ziggurat I could see it was not a featureless pile of stone. There were windows everywhere, some big enough to fly a helicopter through. Many balconies were evident at different elevations. The ziggurat was the only building in view.

The massive gates matched the dimensions of the road leading up to the ziggurat. Their surface was covered in reliefs and carvings. Some were visual representations of different events, others were written language. It had a beauty to it and I found myself drawn to looking upon it.

My reverie was broken when the gates opened. The similarity to the gates of the Citadel was not lost on me. They moved silently and without any overt signal to open.

Inside was a courtyard with a high vaulted ceiling. Around its perimeter were other, smaller, gates, doors, and windows. In one corner were a number of human sized stone benches.

Balthazar led us to the benches. "Please remain here for a time. If you agree Mr. Lark, a peace bond will be upon you while you are on my land. No hand will be raised against you and I pledge to protect your person and those of your household while you remain here and you will guarantee no aggression on your part. Agreed?"

Mr. Lark nodded, "I agree. I and those with me will not provoke or act aggressively while under your roof or on the grounds of your estate."

"I humbly suggest Mr. Lark you return to your transportation and leave all weapons there. I assure you they would be of little use to you here. There are things in my household that may startle you and will not take the uselessness of your weapons into account when they react."

"I must investigate my residence and understand what has happened. The gates will remain open if you wish to retrieve something from your transportation. You are free to walk the grounds of my estate and take shelter here in this entryway. Do not attempt to enter into my residence. My home has its own spirit and until you are known to it, traveling beyond this entryway would not be pleasant."

That said he turned and walked through a gate to the interior of the ziggurat that swung open without any verbal command, closing swiftly behind him.

The three of us walked out to the SUV and left our weapons there. Mr. Lark believed what Balthazar said about the uselessness of conventional arms in what was most likely a supernatural fortress.

While we were dropping off our weapons and grabbing what we would need while we waited for Balthazar Illych handed me my emergency dongle.

I took it while commenting. "I do not think they work. During my interrogation back at that military compound my one of the officers activated the dongle and nothing happened."

Mr. Lark was standing right there when I commented and he then replied, "Of course not. Each dongle is keyed to either an individual in my organization or any grouping of them. I can't have some random person finding a dongle that fell out of someones pocket during a mission then finding themselves alone at the Compass."

Mystery solved.

We brought sleeping bags, water and food back with us. We ate, chatted a bit about the events of the last two days. Then Illych and I found spots for our sleeping bags.

The last I saw was of Mr. Lark sitting quietly consulting his Oculus as I drifted off.

Chapter 27

For the first time in three days I was allowed to sleep until I woke on my own. It was night outside and I could see the stars through the great windows set high in the walls above the entryway and the massive skylights built into the domed roof.

It was not dark in the entryway though. Evenly spaced pillars, set high up midway to the domed ceiling that appeared to be solid stone during the day were luminescent at night. It was a soft white light that almost made the white stone of the entryway floor glow. The effect was actually quite beautiful.

Illych was already up and talking quietly with Mr. Lark. I stood up to join them and then realized a visit to the facilities was in order. Where were the facilities? Such a mundane topic had not been covered by Balthazar before he left and I did not want to defile a corner of his home.

My internal struggle must have been playing out across my face.

Illych chuckled, "One of Balthazar's Goblins visited not long after we went to sleep. The facilities are over behind that door." He pointed at a man-sized door close to the gate we entered through. "They are not modern. It is more of a squat toilet thing. I am sure you will figure it out."

It was weird alright. It was a single room almost as big as my whole flat back in London. The center of the room was a low platform with a hole in it.

The same glowing pillars were evenly spaced around the room. Two of the corners had running fountains. The fountains had carved nymphs sitting around the edge. At least I hoped they were carved nymphs.

When my constitutional was finished I rejoined my colleagues in the entry-way. As I walked in Illych called out, "That was different wasn't it?"

I nodded, "Apparently they did things differently in the old days."

It was quiet for some time after that. I was entranced by the architecture and light of the entryway. Night eventually turned into morning and the pillars illumination reduced as the sun's rays found their way in.

I spent some time studying the walls and pillars around me. A sketching notebook would have been nice to have. I would like to have been able to record some of what I was seeing for future review.

Perhaps two hours after dawn Balthazar returned through the same gate he had left through. His simple peasant clothing, all in black, had been replaced. He now wore a bone colored cloak with the hood down. He carried a large bronze rod in his right hand and there was a complicated looking crown upon his head.

"Mr. Lark, Thomas, Illych, I thank you again for your efforts in returning me home. My household is more or less in order now. We will enter and sit in one of my schools. Perhaps you would call it a library. I must warn you before we proceed. The spirit of this place has a physical form and it awaits us within. Please be at peace. It will not harm you," That said he turned and we followed through the rapidly opening doors to the inside.

A grand hall of marble and granite extended in front of us. Alcoves lined the hall with complex scenes of activity displayed in metal and stone. As we continued down the hall we passed arched openings to other halls or rooms. All were darkened so nothing could be seen within.

Half way down the hall was a tall figure, at least seven feet tall or more. It was of lean build and wearing silver grey robes. Its feet were unshod and consisted of two large toes and a claw to the back. The things arms hung far down its body and ended in large, strong-looking hands. Its face was shadowed inside the hood it wore but I could see the glint of light on large solid black eyes. It was an unnatural and terrifying figure.

Balthazar walked quickly down the hall without pause. The spirit of this place turned and followed Balthazar closely. I fell in behind, gawking at the wonders around me. I had to jog to catch up at one point.

We continued straight through an archway at the end of the hall, entering into the library.

It was a place of beautiful architecture. Wood, metal, and stone had been carved and wrought for every pillar, arch, and window. The chairs, desks, benches, and tables were all strategically placed between alcoves recessed into the walls all around us. The walls went straight up as high as the main gate entry way. Skylights above allowed in sunlight. Lighting for the most part was provided by the same clear white crystal lamps I had seen back at the keep on Hy-Brasil.

There were no ladders evident. I can only guess at how books from the higher alcoves were retrieved.

In the center of the room four padded chairs had been placed facing each other. In between them was a low circular table.

Balthazar stood in front of one chair. Mr. Lark took the opposite. I sat to Balthazar's right and Illych took the remaining chair. The monstrous thing representing Balthazar's residence took its place standing behind him.

"Coffee?" Balthazar swept his hand to the table and his Goblin servants appeared with silver cups and a coffee set. With supernatural dexterity four cups of coffee were poured from one decanter. A Goblin offered a cup to each of us with a bow.

I took the offered cup and waited until everyone had been served. Balthazar lifted his cup and said, "Thank you, please enjoy." He then took a small sip.

I smelled the brew first, not out of suspicion, I like good coffee and good coffee smells really good. This coffee had an aroma that was heavenly. I sipped and almost choked. The taste was wonderful but it was brewed in the Arabic tradition and was thick as motor oil. Smaller sips were needed.

Illych had a similar reaction. Mr. Lark went last, learning from our missteps and took a small sip, "This is truly excellent coffee, Balthazar. I have never tasted its equal." Mr. Lark's compliment appeared to please Balthazar to no end.

"Thank you. Now to business. I have fully assessed the state of my household. During my three-hundred and fifty year absence my mortal servants despaired of my returning and left. Families who have served the house of Balthazar for millennia are gone."

"This and other things I do not understand. I have attempted to contact my brothers and found nothing. Since my exile to Hy-Brasil some great tragedy has played out. I do not know what has happened but it is my duty as a Magi to repair whatever breach has occurred."

"I cannot leave my household now. If I am the last of the Magi I must remain safe here and work through others. My household must be reconstituted. I have to learn of the outside world and the changes over the last centuries."

"To this end I will look to you Mr. Lark. I will pay you handsomely for my rescue. I have come to understand you are not motivated by the love of wealth. To such men such as yourself, wealth is only a means to an end."

"You have proven honorable in the traditional sense and I wish to employ your services further. I sense an alliance would not appeal to you. However, a mutually beneficial collaboration may allow you to better achieve your goals."

Mr. Lark thought before replying, "Balthazar, I do understand the value of what you offer, especially now, after having walked the halls of your home. Such collaboration would require a better understanding of the roles you may ask me to engage in."

Balthazar smiled, "Your approach shows wisdom. Yes, you should know more before we continue forward. Normally I would work through my ancient and mortal servants. Please do not interpret my words as disparaging, but the Magi do not employ mercenaries."

"I have watched you, Mr. Lark, and spent days in discussion with your servant Thomas. You do not seek power beyond what is needed to keep you free. I believe I know what you desire and I will not speak of it in front of your servants."

"I will ask you to be my eyes in places I cannot see. There are places that need to be visited. Questions answered. I will need assistance finding out what happened to my mortal servants and help bringing new ones into my service."

"I will not ask you to fight. However, I cannot promise you will not need to defend yourself. Some of the paths you will follow are dark and less than safe."

"With my direction you will walk paths rarely seen. Some have not been trodden for many, many years. Ancient wonders you will witness. And plenty of gold, of course, to pay your way."

After Balthazar finished we sat there staring at each other for several minutes.

Karl Lark finally nodded, "Not all of my time will be available to you. That which is available I will offer."

Balthazar smiled, obviously pleased, "For my rescue from Hy-Brasil, in what form should your gold be in?"

Mr. Lark did not miss a beat, "Bars."

"Will a single ton of gold be appropriate?"

"That will suffice, thank you."

Wow! I did the math in my head. It worked out to a considerable sum of money.

Balthazar offered, "I cannot move the gold beyond the road to my residence. You can take it at once or in small amounts over time. It will be kept in its own chamber as yours to be retrieved at your leisure. The sun will go black and cold before the word of Balthazar is broken."

Balthazar's tone changed with that last sentence. You could hear the iron resolution in his voice.

"As for the promise of knowledge, bring any artifact of old you possess to my residence and I will tell all I know. Will this offer be sufficient payment?"

Mr. Lark smiled, "Let it be said the House of Balthazar is upright and true. Your word has been kept. I will take one-fifth of my gold when we leave today. The rest will remain safe in your vaults until I come to collect it."

"As for mutual cooperation, how shall we begin? I believe you have a place in mind for us to start?" Mr. Lark continued.

"You words are pleasing, thank you. And yes, I have a place to begin. I have four brother Magi. There are also my brothers, the Illuminated, of which there are six. Whatever calamity has fallen them they would have left messages and evidence. This is not the first time the Adversary has moved against us."

"I would suggest following back along our recent path from Hy-Brasil. The numerous Abominations and those under Geas are disturbing. I wish to know more about how they came to be here and from where they originated."

"Abominations are living things. Most are relatively short lived. The ones sent against us in the last few days were not from my original pursuit three-hundred and fifty years ago. They were created since then and have been regularly replaced and held in reserve in anticipation of my attempt to return. That place needs to be found and destroyed."

Mr. Lark responded, "Then that is the next place we visit."

Chapter 28

Dr. Elizabeth Chatzas was a creature of habit. After a long day at the museum she would come home and play some soft music to relax, change into something comfortable, curl up in her large four poster bed and read a novel. Something fictional, preferably a combination of murder mystery and romance.

It had been two weeks since her time with the abominable Karl Lark and his goons. They had used a stun gun on her, injected her with sedatives, then injected her with God knows what to cause that awful anxiety.

Thomas Davies was working with them. He and Higgebotham were both supposed to be killed when Lord Halluk's men came to take the book. She had woken up in her own bed. That meant they had been there, tucking her into bed. It was an unacceptable invasion of her privacy.

A few days after returning, she had visited her doctor for a physical. Everything checked out. Still, the experience might have long term consequences.

Tonight she was going all out. A bath was drawn and waiting. After adjusting the music selections she entered her bathroom and disrobed.

No sooner had her foot slipped into the warm, comforting waters and her doorbell rang.

Too late now, she thought. Whoever it is can call another day. The rest of her body slipped under the waters and she resumed reading the novel.

The door to the bathroom was still open when he entered. She would have screamed if pure terror had not gripped her first.

"Lord Halluk!"

Her exclamation was not in the respectful tone she had been taught to use in addressing him. Nothing could be done about it now though. To see him silently enter, dressed all in black with the blood red tie and those too large amber eyes looking through her was unnerving.

She had been first introduced to him at his estate in central England. The estate was a massive sprawling affair, older than anyone knew, and beautiful. Britain had its share of creations made by people for which money was no object. Lord Halluk's estate was magnificent beyond compare, with attention to every detail.

One of the things she learned on that estate was immortality can create great beauty, beauty that almost hurts. Immortality can also create magnificent opportunity and an immortal in pursuit of vengeance can be cruel beyond imagining.

There had been three visits. The third visit had seen her swearing loyalty to him. This cemented her position at the museum. She had been true to her word since.

That had been years ago. Communications since had been handled by a courier who reported to one of Lord Halluk's secretaries.

She knew he was not human. On his estate no attempt was made to hide it. There were *things* there, things other than Lord Halluk, making it obvious.

"Elizabeth, we will talk now."

Djinn will never apologize, they had taught her that. And do not ask it of them.

She knew she must stand in his presence. Reclining in a bath would give offence. She curled her legs under her and lifted herself into a standing position bowing her head.

"Lord Halluk," her tone was proper now.

She could not detect if her nudity affected him or if he even took notice.

"You will tell me everything. I must decide your loyalty and if you will continue to enjoy service to me."

www.ingramcontent.com/pod-product-compliance
Lightning Source LLC
Chambersburg PA
CBHW051957240626
47153CB00005B/1793